GO, IVY, GO!

Book #5, The Ivy Malone Mysteries

By

Lorena McCourtney

Go, Ivy, Go!

CHAPTER 1

I like garlic. Garlic toast. A hint of garlic in meatloaf and spaghetti. A sprinkle of garlic salt on baked potatoes. Delightful!

But after a week of eating everything from garlic scrambled eggs to garlic enchiladas, roast garlic, pickled garlic, garlic won-tons and garlic tea, the drift of that familiar scent as I passed Mac's motorhome curled my toes. Surely he wasn't trying that recipe for garlic cheesecake he'd mentioned yesterday, was he?

The motorhome door swung open. "Hey, are you hungry? I'm making Parmesan chicken. It'll be ready in fifteen minutes," Mac called.

"*Garlic* Parmesan chicken?"

"A hundred and forty-nine people on the internet say it's fantastic! With cheese-garlic biscuits."

Oh, joy.

Mac himself, usually odorless except for a nice whiff of some evergreen-y soap he uses, has now taken on a garlic aura of his own. Me too. My breath came close to annihilating a couple of patrons at the local library where I work part-time, and an innocent aloe plant went into cardiac arrest when I breathed on it. Although I have to admit Mac's scent of eau-de-garlic doesn't keep him from being the most attractive silver fox in the RV park where we're staying. As evidenced by the number of women using various sneaky techniques to try to lure him into their clutches. I'm sure that redhead in the travel trailer across the street deliberately sabotaged her own hood vent fan so she could ask him for help yesterday.

"I'm going to run home and take a look at my mail." I waved the oversized envelope that I'd picked up at the RV park's mail center. "Can I bring anything? Dessert?"

"No, we're all set. I'm trying a recipe for garlic fudge too."

Be still, my racing heart.

It isn't as if Mac has plunged into some eccentric garlic-geezerhood, I reminded myself. This was legitimate research for a magazine article. That's what Mac does. Travels around the country and writes about interesting places and events. He'd gone to a big garlic festival for three days, spent every day for the last week at a nearby garlic farm, and was taste-testing all these recipes so he could select a few to accompany the article.

"I'll be right back," I called to Mac, hopefully squelching any ideas the redhead, now sneaking surreptitious glances at Mac while she watered the geraniums around her travel trailer, might have about pouncing on the Parmesan chicken—and Mac—herself.

Garlic is good for your health, I reminded myself as the scent trailed behind me like an invisible fog. It's also supposed to keep vampires away. Actually, I've never been troubled by vampires, but if any are lurking around the RV park, I should be safe.

In my own motorhome, four spaces down from Mac's, I sliced the big envelope open eagerly. I don't get mail often. It goes first to a forwarding outfit in Missouri, where it's bundled for sending on to another forwarding location in Arkansas and then on to Oklahoma. When I finally call Oklahoma and give them a temporary address, it's sent on to me. All this to thwart any vengeful Braxtons still on my trail, of course. Although there isn't much to forward these days. I've been gone from Madison Street back in Missouri, where I first encountered the Braxtons, for almost three years now. My monthly Social Security payment goes to a bank account in Iowa, and I don't have any credit card bills. I never use a credit card that the resourceful Braxtons might be able to track.

Now I read a letter from an acquaintance in Arkansas, and I was pleased to hear from her. Less pleased with a past-due bill for a couple months of water and sewage fees on the house on Madison Street. How could that be? The house has been empty since the property management company evicted the last non-paying renter a year ago, at which time I'd given up on renting, and all the utilities had been shut off. Also a bill from the electric company. What was going on? I'd have to call and try to straighten things out.

The next letter had the unfamiliar return address of something called Radison Properties with an address in Springfield, Illinois. Trying to sell me something? Lots of

3

luck, guys. Buying a roll of "forever" stamps before the price goes up again is a big investment for me.

I read the letter with surprise and elation. Radison Properties wasn't selling. They were buying! It was also quite a generous offer on the house, especially considering the current state of the real estate market. Only ten percent immediate cash, but the balance would be paid in nine months, and they'd pay all costs of the transaction. There it was, a solution to the ongoing expenses of property taxes, insurance bills and worries about vandalism of an empty house! I'd jump on this like my cat Koop—now draped over the passenger's seat of the motorhome like an elongated orange cushion—on a dish of tuna.

But the enthusiasm fizzled with my next thought. *Sell* the house Harley and I had shared for years, the house I'd lived in for more years after Harley passed on? The house where my son Colin grew up? I thought of my roomy kitchen, with all that counter and cabinet space. My upstairs bedroom, where the morning sun poured through the big east window. My bathroom, where I could stretch out in the old-fashioned, claw-footed tub. Unlike bathing in the bathroom of my 24-foot motorhome, which is much like curling up in a plastic teacup.

A rush of homesickness unexpectedly whooshed over me, an almost fierce desire to go *home*. I'd always figured on going back to Madison Street someday, after the threat from the murderous Braxtons faded away . . .

Several months had passed since I'd had any indication I was still on a Braxton hit list. No bombs planted

---

under my motorhome. No ominous powder in an envelope. No skulking strangers. No unexplained fires. No murderous threats.

Maybe I *could* go home now!

An almost overwhelming desire to instantly jump behind the wheel and make a headlong dash for Missouri hit me. I wanted to see the big maple out in front of the house and stick my hands in the garden dirt out back. Okay, I'm not much of a gardener. My tomatoes tend to resemble some mad scientist's experiment gone awry. But that tree by the garage, cheerfully immune to what my neighbor Magnolia called my "black thumb of death," always produced a bountiful supply of pie cherries. And those glorious lilacs in the spring . . .

I could be back in Missouri in three days from here in central California. Maybe less if I really put the pedal to the metal.

My enthusiasm dropped a notch when I considered Mac's probable reaction to this. He'd undoubtedly rain on my homeward parade. Tell me that the only reason the Braxtons weren't planting bombs under my motorhome or ambushing me in an alley was because they hadn't been able to find me lately. That showing up on Madison Street would be like waving a yoo-hoo flag at them. He'd advise I sell to this Radison Properties outfit fast, before they came to their senses and withdrew the offer.

A sobering thought: he could be right.

But I really needed to go back before making a decision on the house, didn't I? Maybe the place was worth

5

a lot more than Radison Properties was offering. Maybe the Madison Street area had suddenly become retro-fashionable, *the* place to buy.

And maybe, once I got there, I'd decide to stay. The possibility shimmered like some hidden treasure suddenly exposed to light. Home!

CHAPTER 2

Maybe I'd just not show the letter to Mac right now. No point in starting his downpour. He was headed for Montana in a few days to do a magazine piece on an old mining town, complete with ghost prospectors, and also to visit his son and family. I'd planned to stay on here in California until funding for my job in the Historical Collection room at the library ran out. We'd talked about meeting later on the Oregon coast. I could call him from somewhere on the road and tell him I'd decided to detour to Missouri first.

That was how my relationship with Mac MacPherson worked. We kept in cell-phone touch regularly, and sometimes we moved our motorhomes in unison. But sometimes we went in different directions. We'd danced around the subject of marriage a few times, but we'd never managed the giant leap into it.

But I couldn't *not* tell him what I was thinking about doing, I realized with a heavy sigh. Not telling him wouldn't exactly be *lying,* but it came under a truth-avoidance classification that snagged like a dead fish on my conscience.

I clomped on over to Mac's motorhome, letter stuffed in the pocket of my blue shorts, feeling a little grumpy with my conscience.

I had to admit both the Parmesan chicken and the garlic-cheese biscuits were great. Even the garlic fudge was passable. Actually, all Mac's recipes were good individually; it was the garlic *en masse* that was getting to me. I waited until after we'd eaten, when we were drinking iced tea, blessedly garlic-free, under the motorhome awning, with the sun blazing a red-gold-purple sunset off in the west, to show him the letter.

"Sounds like a good offer, although immediate cash would be preferable to waiting nine months for the payoff," he commented in a neutral tone that gave no clue to what he was thinking. He set the letter on the metal table between our chairs. "Are you going to take it?"

"I'm thinking I should go back before I make a decision."

The neutral tone vanished. "You can't be serious!"

He planted his glass of iced tea next to the letter on the little table and peered at me as if looking for my lost marbles. Plenty of clues now about how he felt.

"I guess I'm a little homesick."

"You aren't thinking anything more than a temporary visit, are you? A day or two?"

"Sometimes I get tired of roaming the country."

"Ivy, you know what a . . . propensity you have for getting involved with murder. That young woman right there on Madison Street. The woman you worked for in Arkansas. That survivalist couple in Oklahoma. The man who plunged from a window in Colorado."

Well, odd as it may seem for a little old lady, that "propensity" was true. My life does seem to involve dead bodies and murder more often than the average LOL. Although I'd arrived in Colorado well after that man plunged out the window and I never even saw the body, so he didn't really count, did he? I made a noncommittal murmur to Mac.

"Murdered bodies followed by killers out to get *you*," he added.

"I haven't been involved in a murder for, oh, months now," I protested.

"But, if you go back to Madison Street, you may very well find yourself involved in one. *Yours.* You will be the dead body. You do remember the Braxtons, don't you?"

It was a facetious question. Of course I remembered the Braxtons. They were the reason I'd been on the run all this time. I'd helped capture and convict one of their own for murdering a sweet young neighbor back on Madison Street, and the vengeful Braxton clan had been making a unified effort to eliminate me from the planet ever since.

"I think they've forgotten about me. They haven't tried anything for months."

"That doesn't mean they won't do something as soon as they realize you're back in town." A stormy stalk to the end of the awning before he returned to scowl down at me. "When are you thinking about doing this?"

I had to be practical. The library job was paying rather well, and the extra money came in handy. "Maybe when my job at the library ends next month."

Mac is generally calm and congenial, not a ranter or

9

arm waver, but he ranted for several minutes about what a bad idea my going back to Madison Street was. Somewhere in the middle of the rant, I made up my mind. Yes, I was going to do it. I was going back to Madison Street. Maybe temporarily. Maybe permanently. After that I tuned him out and studied the blue motorcycle tattoo on his waving arm. He's always been . . . well, not *secretive* about the tattoo, but definitely not forthcoming. It isn't gross, as tattoos go. It just seems so puzzling. Mac isn't really a tattoo kind of guy, and he's never shown any particular interest in motorcycles. I asked him once if he'd had some fascination with motorcycles when he was younger, and he'd said no. So why a blue motorcycle tattoo? And why so reticent about it?

He'd just gotten to the point of reminding me that the Braxtons had once set fire to my house back on Madison Street, with me in it, when a new thought occurred to me.

"Hey, you can come along!" I threw in an appeal to his nobler side. "Be my protector."

He considered that for about two seconds before he said, "I have a better idea."

"Which is?"

"Let's get married." Real urgency filled his voice. "Now. Right away. No need to go back to the house. Just sell it. We can trade in both our motorhomes on a newer, larger one. We'd have only one RV park rental fee. One motorhome to license and insure. One gas tank to fill. Or maybe we'd get one of those diesel-pusher kind."

On a practicality ranking, that proposal probably rated a "10." However—

As if suddenly realizing what he'd said sounded more like a pitch from a used-RV salesman than a proposal, Mac dropped to one knee by my webbed lawn chair. "I'm sorry. I didn't phrase that very well. I know I'm not the most romantic guy in the world, but you know how I feel about you, Ivy. We should have gotten married a long time ago. Will you do it now? Marry me?"

Mac MacPherson isn't terribly romantic, true, but he does okay in the romance department when the occasion arises. He's great at moonlight walks on a beach and kisses under mistletoe. On Valentine's Day he gave me a card that said, "You light up my life," surrounded by illustrated fireworks, and he took me out for lobster too. For my birthday, thankfully back in pre-garlic days, he'd made a tower of cake layers, with a single heart-shaped candle on top.

And he *was* down on his knee right now.

"I don't know how long it takes to get a marriage license here, but surely not more than a few days. We'll take a honeymoon before going up to Montana. I saw this great place in Baja on the internet the other day. Beach right outside the door. Palms and bougainvillea. Hot tub. Restaurant. We'll specify no garlic."

Tempting.

"We might even think about settling down somewhere if you're really tired of traveling."

"The house on Madison Street is available," I reminded him.

"Not Madison Street."

"But that's *home*."

He turned it into a home-on-the-range song. "Oh, give me a home, where the Braxtons don't roam . . ."

I glowered at him. I can do a pretty good glower if I try.

He stood up. Mac's bones don't creak even if he qualifies for a few more candles on his birthday cake than I do. A bit stiffly, he said, "I apologize for my outburst. It's just that I get a little worked up when I think about you walking right into danger."

"I appreciate that."

But I could tell he was a little miffed when he muttered, "Well, think about it, okay?"

"About getting married or about going back to Madison Street?"

"Whatever."

***

I thought about it. I talked to the Lord too, as I always do about any important decision. Was Mac also doing that? Mac was a skeptic when we first met, but he talks to the Lord himself now. I don't know if Mac heard any words of wisdom from the Lord, but I wasn't getting anything. Nothing about marrying Mac, nothing about going home. Mac would probably say, as he had before, that when God is silent it may be because he's expecting us to use a little good sense of our own. Mac's interpretation of "good sense," of course, meaning my staying away from Madison Street and the Braxtons. I kept hoping for something more specific direct from the Lord.

Two days later, Mrs. Hernandez came into the Historical Collection room where I was going through an estate of books, some treasures, some trash, that had been donated to the library. The elderly woman making the donation had apparently liked everything from books on California history to raising insect-eating plants to steamy scenes in 18th century boudoirs.

"You do such incredible work, Ivy." Mrs. Hernandez touched her fingertips together. "And you're so knowledgeable. We've been so fortunate to have you."

The words were flattering, but I heard a subtle past-tense in them. I warily stood up from where I'd been crouched over a box of books. "I enjoy working here."

"But I'm afraid I have some bad news. We just found out we won't have funding for your position beyond this week. I feel bad, springing this on you so suddenly, but we had to use some of the grant money to repair the air conditioner and it cost so much more than we expected . . ."

Oh no! I'd counted on a few more weeks of the extra income.

My moment of disappointment evaporated as I suddenly realized what this was. Not calamity. Opportunity! The message from the Lord that I'd been waiting for. "That's okay. Actually, something has come up that I need to take care of, so this will work out fine."

***

I told Mac about the end of my job and what I'd decided. I could tell he wasn't convinced this was a definitive sign from the Lord, but he seemed more resigned than surprised by my decision. He didn't rant and rave. Neither did he get down on his knees and beg me to change my mind. On my final morning at the RV park, he helped roll up the awning and disconnect the water, sewer, and electric lines on the motorhome. He even whirled me around for a good-bye kiss. A great kiss even if he didn't break his stolid silence and his expression had all the warmth of a polar vortex.

"You could still change your mind and come with me," I said.

"You could still change your mind and not go."

I put a foot on the retractable step of the motorhome. "I'll keep in touch."

"Not if the Braxtons get you first."

And a cheery good-bye to you too.

I could see him in the rearview mirror as I drove to the RV park exit onto the highway. I stuck out my hand and waved. He didn't wave back.

I tried not to feel uneasy. We'd parted before. He probably hadn't returned my wave only because he missed seeing it.

But this parting felt different than those other times. This had a finality to it that had never been there before.

***

Although I was impressed, as always, with the Lord's imagination and creativity in the beauties of mountains and desert as I drove across the country, this trip was not a shining advertisement for the joys of life on the road. In Arizona the motorhome engine overheated and I had to stop to have it checked out. In New Mexico I had not one but *two* flat tires. In Oklahoma some creepy guy wandering around the rest area where I was parked tried the motorhome door. That unsettled me enough that I got up, jumped into the driver's seat in my pajamas, and roared outa there.

But in my haste I took a wrong turn somewhere and wound up on a desolate road with neither a head- or tail-light in sight. A sign beside a gas station that looked as if it hadn't pumped gas since the '60s read *Skeleton Valley, Pop. 14.* I pulled over and, keeping a nervous eye out for wandering skeletons, tried to figure out from a map where I was. But Skeleton Valley was nowhere to be found. Except maybe in the Twilight Zone, and I didn't have a map for there.

The thought niggled that the Lord might be putting these roadblocks in my way to warn me that I'd misinterpreted the "sign" of the end of my job. Or maybe, I rationalized, it was a reverse message reminding me of the drawbacks of motorhome life and telling me that it *was* time to plant myself on Madison Street and stay there.

By morning I'd gotten back on a highway that looked as if it belonged in this dimension. At least the familiar golden arches of a McDonald's loomed in the distance. I kept thinking Mac would call, but he didn't. Stubbornly I didn't click his number on my cell phone, either.

And, late on the fourth day, with a gentle summer dusk settling like a blessing around me, I arrived on Madison Street. Home!

I drove slowly, savoring the familiar sights. Big maples lined the street, just as I remembered, the old sidewalk beneath them humped by roots. The houses, which I knew might look old and a bit shabby in full daylight, were familiar friends in the warm dusk. Most were dark, occupants probably sitting out back enjoying the cool evening after the heat of the summer day. So quiet and peaceful. A marvelous absence of traffic. An older woman with stooped shoulders, her elbow braced by a muscular young man, shuffled along the sidewalk. I didn't recognize them, but this was how I remembered Madison Street, the kind of place a caring grandson would take his grandmother out for an evening stroll.

My old friend Thea's house looked dark and bleak, which gave me a pang. Thea had passed on even before I left, and her old house reminded me I wouldn't see her again until we hugged on the streets of heaven.

Did anyone I knew still live on Madison Street? My across-the-street neighbors, Magnolia and Geoff Margolin, of course. They'd sold their house quite a while back and bought a place near Phoenix, but they'd turned out not to like hot Arizona summers, so when they had a chance to get the old place back again, they'd grabbed it. But they spent most of their time traveling in their motorhome, same as I did, although for a different reason. They'd spent a week here last fall and said then that many of the houses were rentals now. Was that what Radison Properties planned for my place? I wondered if Magnolia and Geoff had also received an offer on their house.

Magnolia and Geoff were in the cool Northwest this summer, Magnolia busy chasing down some distant relative.

Most people use the internet for genealogical research these days, but Magnolia prefers a hunt-'em-down-in-person approach. She likes to put photographs and personal information with her genealogical charts.

With darkness settling in, their big yard light suddenly blazed to light. Their place looked as well kept as ever. A yard maintenance company kept everything in top shape. Grass green, shrubs trimmed, magnolia leaves glossy. Oh, and I could still see that profile of Nixon's face in the outline of one of the trees. Growth had altered it a bit since I'd been gone, but that nose was unmistakable.

Some of the light spilled across the street onto my place. A different world there. I couldn't afford yard maintenance fees. Weedy stalks rose out of dry, unmowed grass. Rose and lilac bushes straggled under the windows. Alarmingly vicious looking weeds dominated the garden area. A screen sagged at one window, and another hung by a corner. Wind had blown last fall's leaves into ragged hills against the garage door. The cherry tree I'd pictured as strong and fruitful was a tangle of dead branches, like something out of a zombie movie.

I felt a shiver inconsistent with the warm evening dusk. Maybe I should just grab that Radison Properties offer and run . . .

No. I briskly turned the motorhome into the driveway. I could rake and mow and water. Wash windows and fix screens too. I'd make friends with whoever lived in the area now, people like that older woman and her grandson. Maybe Magnolia and Geoff would give up RVing and come home too, and Madison Street would be almost like it used to be. Though, without Thea, never quite what it once was.

"You'll love it," I told my furry co-pilot as he stood up and stretched. "You can dig in the dirt while I'm working in the garden."

I'd never had much luck gardening, but as of right now I vowed to change that. I'd read gardening books. Take a class. I'd grow tomato-shaped tomatoes, not ones with odd resemblances to dead presidents. I'd have the yard in tip-top shape in no time.

Did that mean I figured on staying here?

Could be!

I parked in the driveway, fished my long-unused keys out of a drawer, and stepped out. Koop jumped down from the passenger's seat, ready to follow. "You wait here. I'll get the house unlocked and come back for you."

I went to the back door of the house, the door we'd always used most. Tattered leaves had drifted against it too. And hey, what happened to the screen door that used to be here? But the long-unused key turned easily. I felt almost as if I were opening a Christmas present from the past. Home!

Inside, an odd disorientation unexpectedly hit me. The curtains were pulled shut, turning the kitchen into a shadowy cave. And the air? Way past its expiration date.

No, more than that. A definite *smell*. I turned, trying to get my equilibrium back, and clunked into something. There'd never been anything in the middle of the kitchen before. I peered closer. Oh, the kitchen table, usually under the window, was over here now.

I straightened a fallen chair beside the table, stirring the stagnant air. A stuffy smell? Well, not surprising. The place had been closed up for over a year, since that last renter was evicted. But something more in the scent. Musty? Rancid? Moldy? Spoiled? A definite *yuk* factor to it.

I automatically tried to turn on a light before remembering even as I clicked the switch that it wouldn't work. The utilities were turned off. I'd get everything turned on tomorrow. And straighten out those odd bills at the same time. Right now, what the place needed was a good airing out.

I felt my way around the table and stumbled to the window. I yanked the curtains open, letting in some light from Magnolia's yard light. A cabinet door hung by one hinge. The open door of another cabinet revealed a few cans of food and a carton of Ritz crackers. Dirty dishes filled the sink. Cigarettes spilled out of a half-full pack on the counter. I opened the refrigerator door. No light of course, but the smell in there— Eeewww. All I could make out were blobs on the shelves and mold climbing the walls. Maybe this was where that smell was coming from. I slammed the door shut.

Hadn't the property management company had the place cleaned after those last tenants were evicted? Certainly didn't look like it.

I tried the water faucet. Nothing happening there, either, of course.

In the living room I had to pull the drapes open before I could see anything. I'd rented the house furnished, but now everything was gone except the old sofa and a recliner. The sofa was missing a cushion and that favorite old recliner appeared to have developed leprosy of the upholstery. But, oddly, there was an addition that hadn't been there before. A window air conditioner that some renter had apparently left behind. Well, lose some, win some.

The smell grabbed me in the living room too. I'd have to go out to the motorhome for a can of deodorizer and a flashlight before I looked in the bathroom or upstairs. I headed for the door, then hesitated.

The house felt odd. There wasn't the welcoming sense of home I'd expected. Instead the house felt strange and unfamiliar, even . . . hostile. As if strangers lurked in shadows and dangers hid in corners.

I scoffed at that. My own home *hostile*?

I'd planned to sleep in my old bed here in the house tonight, but now I decided I'd have to postpone that. Only because of the lack of lights and water, plus the scents of disuse and stuffiness, of course, not because of any *hostility*. I opened every window and propped the back door open too. Halfway back to the motorhome, I realized I was *scurrying*. I deliberately made myself slow to normal pace.

"We'll stay out here just for tonight," I told Koop when I opened the motorhome door.

He yawned and blinked his one good eye at me. Koop is a very laid-back cat.

I fixed a ham and cheese sandwich for supper, fed Koop some of his favorite Fancy Feast, the kind with gravy, and went to bed early. Big day tomorrow. Get the utilities turned on and those bills straightened out. Air out the upstairs too. Start cleaning.

***

I didn't sleep great, even though there was no noise from street or neighbors. Koop usually curls up on my bed, but this night he padded restlessly. And I couldn't seem to get that unpleasant smell out of my head. It clung like a bad dream.

But in the early morning, when I stepped outside and sniffed, all I smelled was the familiar and wonderful freshness before a hot summer day in Missouri. I impulsively decided to take a quick tour around the old neighborhood, maybe see someone I knew. The Daggitts, Ed and Marie, were always up early working in the big garden in their side yard.

Not this morning, however. Their house had that shades-pulled, empty-eyed look of vacancy, and the yard was as weedy as my own. In fact, most of the houses that I'd last night assumed were dark because the occupants were outside enjoying the evening were actually vacant. One had boarded up windows. A tire-less car on concrete blocks decorated the yard of another. Only slightly less dilapidated cars sat in the driveways of a couple of places that appeared to be occupied. A basketball hoop on a stand had fallen into the street. The figure of a rearing horse made of welded slabs of metal, with mane and tail of copper wire, stood in one yard. Not exactly fine art, but attractive in a funky way. Better than the garbage strewn in the yard next to it.

Getting back to my own place, I saw the missing

screen door, frame broken and screen torn, now leaning against the side of the garage.

I determinedly made myself think of happy days here, days when the kitchen smelled of baking bread and children's shouts and laughter sounded in the yards. Harley building birdhouses in his woodworking shop in the garage. Me tying fishing flies for him. Colin building a treehouse in the maple tree and tangling in the branches when he tried to parachute out of it with an inflatable mattress. Giggling with Thea as we colored our hair together, hers coming out a soft beige, mine a strange burned-beet color. Magnolia and Geoff barbecuing in their back yard. Meeting Mac for the first time at one of those barbecues . . .

That last goodbye with Mac poked a hole in my determinedly upbeat thoughts. The happy memories leaked out and others barged in. Colin, disappearing in a ferry accident during a peacetime assignment in Korea, his body never found. Harley's passing. Thea's too.

But it was a beautiful morning here on Madison Street today, and God never intended for us to dwell on the sadness of the past when he had much more waiting in this life and beyond. I briskly fixed oatmeal with sliced bananas for breakfast, then marched to the open back door of the house.

I took Koop with me. He arched his back and hissed the instant I set him on the kitchen floor. "Lighten up," I scolded. "This is home."

Another hiss. His stubby tail jerked like a disapproving wag of finger.

Maybe it was the open pack of cigarettes on the counter. Koop is fanatically anti-tobacco.

In daylight, I could see everything more clearly. Not an improvement. I tentatively lifted the lid on a garbage can by the door. Empty cardboard cartons of macaroni and cheese topped by three empty wine bottles. But no smell emanating from it. The kitchen table looked as if it had been used for table-top dancing. With logger-style boots. Two chipped flower pots held dried and dead remnants of some unidentifiable plants. The cans of chili, chicken noodle soup, and tuna in the cupboard bore dents, as if they'd been picked out of some bargain bin at the store.

I couldn't disparage that, of course. Sometimes I pick a can out of the dented bin too.

In the bathroom, the medicine cabinet still held generic aspirin and Pepto Bismol, and powder from an overturned can of foot-fungus remedy trailed across the counter.

After an overnight airing-out, the smell wasn't as heavy as it had been last night. Plenty of scent upstairs, however, when I went up there to open windows. Maybe a mouse – or a whole herd of them - had crawled between the walls and died.

Ugh.

Koop echoed my opinion with another hiss.

A battered sleeping bag lay on my bed, a flattened pillow sticking out of it. Cigarette butts half-filled a jar-lid ashtray on the night stand. A dark stain blotched the carpet. Spilled wine from one of those bottles in the garbage can?

Cobwebs draped the corners of the room. Purple pants and several faded sweatshirts hung in the closet, a pair of old brown shoes on the floor beneath them. Certainly not mine, but they looked as if they'd fit a woman about my size. A hairbrush entangled with hair as possum-gray as my own sat on my old dresser. That spooky feeling returned, and I had to fight an urge to run headlong back down the stairs.

I opened the bedroom windows, then went down the hall to the closed door of the upstairs bathroom. I briskly shoved the door open. And got blasted by a scent strong enough to make me a little dizzy. Koop, warily following me around the house, skidded claws on the hallway floor as he made a fast getaway. I put a hand over my nose and peered further into the bathroom. I didn't see anything to cause such a scent.

A well-used bar of Ivory lay in a soap dish. A single toothbrush hung in the holder, under it a flattened tube of toothpaste. A threadbare towel draped the rod by the sink. Long ago, Harley had installed a hand-held showerhead over the tub. An unfamiliar plastic shower curtain concealed the tub now. I yanked it open, shower curtain rings rattling on the rod.

A lumpy pile of ragged blankets covered the bottom of the tub, and I realized this was definitely the source of the scent. What was under those blankets? Rotting garbage? I felt a big rush of indignation. I was almost certain I'd paid that property management company for a cleanup.

Right now what I wanted was to get this smelly mess *out* of here. Along with that ratty old sleeping bag in the bedroom.

I reached into the pile, intending to gather up everything and haul it outside. But my hands bumped into something, something both squishy and lumpy. And then I looked at the end of the tub where the blankets had pulled up when I grabbed them.

Toes.

CHAPTER 3

Bare toes. Blackened, shriveled bare toes.

Dead toes.

The blankets fell out of my hands. The air in the bathroom closed in on me. Heavy. Suffocating. My scalp prickled and my own toes numbed. Queasiness clumped in my stomach. I grabbed the shower curtain for support. It ripped and tangled around me like a plastic shroud. I fought it away from my head and shoulders and looked at those awful toes again. Something – *someone* - was under those blankets. Someone had crawled into the tub and *died* there.

Mac's warnings about dead bodies rose up to choke the back of my throat. Because here was one. Right in my own bathtub. Nausea billowed deep inside me, followed by a dizziness that spun the room around me. Flying sinks and bathtubs and toilet stools zipping around like some mad poltergeist on a rampage.

Not fair! This isn't what I came home for. I want bubble bath in my tub, not a dead body!

I took a deep breath. Mistake. Do not take a deep breath in the presence of a dead body in your bathtub. But I also chastised myself for my self-centered grumble about bubble bath. A person had *died* in this tub.

26

Lorena McCourtney

Maybe not, I momentarily rationalized. Maybe I'd made a mistake. I risked another peek.

No mistake. Definitely dead toes. The dizziness and nausea billowed again, but I forced them down. No time for that now. Right now I had to *do* something. I steadied myself against the door frame and clawed my way out of the shower curtain, then tore down the stairs and out to the motorhome. Koop was hiding under it. He dashed inside when I opened the door. I grabbed my cell phone. The first number that came to mind was Mac's. But no point in calling him, much as I unexpectedly wanted to. I tried to punch in 911.

Nothing. I hadn't been able to plug in the phone for several days while I was on the road. Now I might as well be trying to make a call on a rotten potato.

I ran down the street toward the yard with the welded horse. I shoved through the gate and hammered on the door. A long-legged young woman in skimpy cut-off jeans opened it.

"I need to use your phone! I have to call 911!" I held up my own dead-potato phone.

I could see me through her eyes. Wild-eyed, wild-haired, panicky little old lady. But she didn't hesitate. Without asking questions, she grabbed a cell phone from the coffee table and handed it to me. "Okay, sure! Come on in."

I punched in the numbers and gave the woman who answered a frantic description of what I'd found. She wanted to know a lot of things, but I just gave her my name and the address and told her no medical help would be necessary. This body was *dead.* I handed the cell phone back to the

27

young woman.

"There's a dead person in your bathtub?" she asked as if not certain she'd heard correctly even though she'd been listening.

"I think she's been in there quite a while. At least I think she's a she." The clothes in the closet had been for a woman, but I couldn't know for certain if the owner of those clothes was also the occupant of my bathtub. Although that conclusion seemed likely.

"Who are you?" the woman asked, her tone doubtful. She had long blond hair scrambled atop her head with a couple of blue clips, nice skin, no makeup.

"I'm Ivy Malone. I live down the street. I mean I used to live here. I haven't been here for a long time. I just drove in last night in my motorhome. And then this morning—"

"What's going on?" A bare-chested guy in raggedy jeans came into the room rubbing a towel over shaggy blond hair. His muscles rippled. He looked as if he'd just stepped off the cover of a Bodies-R-Us magazine. His bare feet left wet tracks on the wood floor. Even his toes looked muscular.

The woman motioned toward me. "This is Ivy Malone. She lives down the street. There's a dead body in her bathtub. She called 911 about it."

They exchanged one of those married-people glances that says something without words.

"Well, I think I'd call 911 too, if we found a dead body in our bathtub." He lifted a muscle-sculpted arm and dried a hairy armpit. "Is it anyone you know?" he asked me, not unkindly.

28

I recognized him as the guy who'd been taking the elderly woman for a stroll last night. Knowing that about him made me feel kindly toward him even though he seemed to have a rather casual attitude toward dead bodies in bathtubs. Oh, wait. Now I understood the look that passed between them. Woman saying, *I think she's off her rocker about a dead body in her tub, but she doesn't look dangerous. Humor her.* Muscle-Man silently saying, *Gotcha.*

I looked around the small living room. The glass top of the end table by the sofa rested on the back of an elephant made of pieces of pipe and old pan lids artfully welded together. The upraised trunk of the elephant held a circle of glass, on it a miniature elephant made from a tin can and a teapot spout. On that stood a tiny circle of glass and an even tinier elephant. Elephants to infinity? The glass-topped coffee table in front of the sofa had angled nuts and bolts for legs. Tin-can lids framed a picture on the wall. A chandelier made of some kind of wheel, maybe something off an old-fashioned buggy, hung from the ceiling by chains. Bulbs covered by copper shades dangled on more chains from the wheel. The Early Junkyard School of Interior Decorating?

"These are . . . interesting," I said.

"I'm a junk sculptor," the guy said. "I have a shop set up out in the garage. I'm working on a cow with motorcycle-handlebar horns and taillight eyes now. Would you like to see it?"

"Umm, maybe later."

"Eric is very artistic," the woman offered.

Okay, I could go along with that. Art is in the eye of

the beholder. Although bicycle-handle horns might be stretching it. And I wouldn't want to be under that chandelier in an earthquake.

The guy laughed, as if he made no claim to artistic talent himself. "You'd be surprised how well this stuff sells at flea markets. I call them Ockunzzi Originals. By the way, I'm Eric Ockunnzi, and this is my wife, Tam— "

"Tasha," the woman broke in. "Tasha Tremaine."

We all shook hands. I thought it a little odd that Eric got his wife's name wrong, and her last name wasn't even the same as his. But that's okay. Their generation does things differently than mine. I appreciated that Eric was careful not to crush my hand with his muscular fingers in the handshake.

"Does your grandmother live here too?" I asked. "I saw you taking her for a walk last evening when I drove in." I turned to Tam/Tasha. "Or maybe she's your grandma?"

The two exchanged glances. "Grandma comes and goes," she said. "She isn't here right now."

"Maybe I can meet her sometime?"

"We might be able to arrange that," Tam/Tasha said.

"I remember some people named Caulkins used to live here. I guess they moved away?"

"We don't know any Caulkins, do we?" Tam/Tasha asked the Man-of-Muscle.

"We rent through an agency, so we don't have any contact with the actual owners. We asked if the owners wanted to sell, but apparently it's some big company that's buying up everything in the neighborhood. Look, why don't you sit down for a minute?" The guy motioned me toward

30

the sofa. "You look a little pale. Finding a dead body in your bathtub must be traumatic."

"Would you like something to drink?" the woman asked. "Green tea? Coffee?"

A tranquilizer, perhaps? To help rid you of bizarre delusions about bodies in bathtubs?

"Thank you, no. I'll just go back to the house so I'll be there when someone comes. The body is in the upstairs bathroom."

"How about if I come with you?" the guy suggested. "Just in case you need help or something."

Help? "I wasn't planning to move her. And it's a little late for CPR."

Admittedly, that was a little snarky, because I knew they didn't believe me, but he didn't seem to notice.

"I'll come along anyway," he said. "Just in case." This time he left the *in case* open-ended. In case my mind slipped even further, and I forgot where I was going? In case I had some bizarre delusion about outer space aliens hiding in trees?

Eric disappeared down the hallway and came back pulling a T-shirt over his head, flip-flops on his feet. I was fascinated by the size of both the footwear and T-shirt. Was there a place called Muscles-R-Us where guys like him shopped?

"Have you seen anyone at my place in the last few months?" I asked.

"You were living there when we moved here in February," Tam/Tasha said. "Remember? We met once when you were carrying a grocery sack home. I asked if you needed help, but you said you could manage. Then a funny looking vegetable fell out of the sack and I asked what it was, and you said it was a parsnip. But you usually avoided me."

"I wasn't here in February. And I never buy parsnips." The Lord no doubt created parsnips for a purpose, but I've not yet found what it is.

Tam/Tasha peered at me more closely. I wasn't sure if she thought my memory was fading like some old photograph, or if she was confused because of something I'd encountered before. *You little old ladies all look alike. I can't tell you apart.* Whoever named these the Golden Years must have mislaid his glasses. How about the Invisible Years? Not that elder- invisibility is all bad. I've found that it can come in rather handy at times.

Eric tucked my hand under his arm, and we headed for the door. "You want to come with us?" he called back over his shoulder to Tam/Tasha.

"Sure. I don't have to leave for work yet."

So we tromped back down the street to my house, short, dumpy me between these tall, blond specimens of youthful magnificence. At the back door I said, "Thanks for walking me home. I'll be fine now. I'll just wait outside for the police to arrive."

"We can wait with you," Eric said.

"You really think someone will come?" Tam/Tasha asked Eric over my head.

"I think they have to check out everything," Eric answered, also over my head.

"No matter how implausible it sounds?" I tossed in.

Guilty expressions flooded both their faces, and finally Tam/Tasha said gently, "You have to admit finding a body in your bathtub does sound unlikely. Maybe what you saw was just, oh, you know, rags and stuff someone dumped in there."

For a moment her comments made me doubt myself. *Had* I made a mistake and seen dead toes that were really only . . . what? What else looks like blackened, shriveled, dead toes? What else smells like *death*?

No, I wasn't mistaken. Dead toes. Attached to a dead body. But I felt a little defensive. "I've found dead bodies before."

Eric and Tam/Tasha exchanged glances over my head again, and she patted my shoulder. "Don't you just hate days like that?"

They didn't believe me, but I resisted an impulse to march them upstairs and prove there really was a dead body in the bathtub. If it was a crime scene, strangers shouldn't be wandering through.

Hey, not a crime scene just because there was a dead person in the bathtub, I instantly reminded myself. Perfectly normal deaths probably occurred in bathtubs all the time. No doubt there were government statistics on that somewhere.

"Would you like to come out to the motorhome and sit down while we wait for the police?" I suggested politely.

"I'm just going to run upstairs and take a look around, okay?" Eric said. "Maybe we'll discover this is all a misunderstanding and we can call 911 again and cancel—"

I tried to interrupt with my concerns about contaminating the scene, but before I could finish the sentence, Eric had already disappeared into the house, his flip-flops flapping. Tam/Tasha sat on the back steps.

She patted the worn step beside her. "We can sit here. I'll stay with you."

I sat down in the approved spot. "Okay. Thanks." I decided this would be as good a time as any to nose around for information. "Quite a few houses here on Madison Street appear to be vacant. And a lot more rentals than there were when I was living here."

"Yeah, it's kind of going downhill, isn't it? But we still like it. We've saved up some money, and we asked about buying the place we're renting. But some out-of-state company owns it, and, like I said, they seem to be buying up everything they can get hold of. We'll probably have to move again once they get everything bought."

"What does this company intend to do with the houses?"

"We've heard all kinds of rumors. One is they intend to build a new shopping mall. Or maybe a high-end condo complex or retirement home. Or the buyer is a survivalist billionaire who's going to build a mansion-fortress where he'll be safe from nuclear or zombie attack, whichever comes first."

Any of which involved destruction of my old house. I squirmed around to look back at it. I loved this old place. Even with sagging window screens and a dead body in the bathtub, I loved it. I changed the subject.

34

"I'm sorry, but I'm not sure about your name. Is it Tam or Tasha?"

"Well, uh, both. I mean my real name is Tammy Ockunzzi but my professional name is Tasha Tremaine."

Before I could speculate about what kind of profession, she added, "I'm an actress. Tammy sounds so, oh, you know, cheerleader-ish, and Ockunzzi— I mean, Eric is a sweet and wonderful guy, and I love him very much. But the name Ockunzzi. . ." She gave me a help-me-out glance.

"Ockunzzi sounds fine to me. Very sturdy."

"Okay, I know not wanting to use Ockunzzi probably sounds snobbish or pretentious or something, but an agent I talked to a few weeks ago said it didn't project a professional image. It's hard to spell too, and she said it could really hold me back." She squinted into space as if trying to picture Ockunzzi on a marquee somewhere. I gave it a squint too. Okay, Ockunzzi wasn't exactly charismatic, but it was a good, honest name.

"Maybe you need a new agent," I suggested.

Tam/Tasha ummed.

"Does Eric mind?" I added.

"No, but he keeps forgetting. So I have to remind him. I'm trying to use Tasha all the time now so we'll both get used to it."

"Missouri doesn't seem like a hotbed of opportunity for an acting career."

"We've thought about using the money we've saved to move out to California, but I'm taking acting and singing lessons here, and I do get an acting opportunity now and then. If I have to do something else for the money, I just pretend it's an acting job. Like last week I had a three-day job walking dogs for this dog-walker woman who was sick. So I did it as if I were in a movie, where I was playing the part of a private investigator using the dog-walking as an undercover disguise."

"An interesting approach."

"Right now I'm about to start this new acting job. Except it's very hush-hush and I can't talk about it." She touched a finger to her lips. "But it'll be terrific experience."

I was mildly intrigued by a hush-hush acting job, but before I could ask anything, a thud from somewhere in the house interrupted. Tasha turned and peered uneasily through the open door behind us. "What was that?"

"There's nothing up there but the dead body. And Eric looks as if he can take care of himself anyway."

"Oh, he can! He won the Muscle Man of Missouri title last year." Tasha paused and gave me a sideways glance. "You really do think there's a dead body in that bathtub?"

"I'm sure of it. I *saw* it."

"I'll just run upstairs and make sure everything's okay, then. Sometimes Eric—"

She didn't say what sometimes happened when Eric encountered dead bodies in bathtubs, but she hastily stood up and rushed inside. After a moment's hesitation, I followed. Hopefully, fingerprints and footprints in the bathroom wouldn't matter. It wasn't, after all, a *crime* scene. The woman just happened to die there. I carefully avoided any contradictions to that thought. Like, can a dead woman pull blankets up over her own head?

Tasha was already at the bathroom door when I reached the top of the stairs. She screamed. Like a psycho sitting on a pin. It didn't sound like acting.

CHAPTER 4

I ran down the hallway. Tasha was kneeling beside something on the floor of the bathroom. I looked over her shoulder.

Eric. Crumpled like a dishrag. A muscular dishrag, of course.

"What happened?" I gasped. I don't believe in zombie uprisings, but something had apparently zapped Eric .

The blankets that had covered the body in the tub lay in a tangled heap on the floor. Eric must have yanked them off. I started to look in the bathtub but instead turned my head away. I didn't need to see any more of the body. Tasha peered over the rim of the tub. She turned greenish and made a muffled urpy sound. She hurriedly put one hand over her mouth and the other on Eric's forehead.

"I think he ... lost consciousness," she said.

I interpreted that. "He *fainted*?"

"Eric has a very sensitive nature." She sounded defensive. "I guess we didn't really believe there was a dead body in the tub. But there is. It's . . . uh . . . deteriorated. There's a big hole in it. And the teeth are all strange."

A body that had been in a closed-up house in Missouri for – how long? *Deteriorated* was probably a

38

euphemistic way to put it. *Strange teeth* was a puzzler, and *a big hole* had ominous implications. Making this a picture of an older woman climbing into the tub for a peaceful passing into eternity was getting harder to do.

I didn't say *I told you so* about the dead body to Tasha, but I was thinking it. Along with, *The next time a little old lady tells you there's a body in the tub, you'll believe her, won't you?* What I said was, "Does he need a doctor?"

"No, it's happened before. Gruesome things really get to him. Remember that old G*odfather* movie*?* He went out like a light when he saw the dead horse's head. He'll be okay in a few minutes. But I think we should get him out of here so he won't look in the bathtub again when he comes to."

"Good idea."

She got one arm and I, carefully avoiding looking in the tub myself, grabbed the other. The arms were limp and floppy, but moving Muscle-Man was one of those easier-said-than-done activities.

"How much does he weigh?" I muttered. Dragging the motorhome might be easier. At least it had wheels.

"Two-forty-five. Only eight percent body fat. But he's very sensitive," Tasha repeated.

High sensitivity and low percentage of body fat didn't make him any easier to drag out of the bathroom. After considerable grunting and tugging, we finally got most of him out in the hallway. His flip-flops had come off in the process. His toes, though still muscular, looked oddly vulnerable now, and he still hadn't regained consciousness.

"I'm sorry we didn't believe you," Tasha said.

"It was nice of you both to come help anyway. You might make use of that scream if you ever need one for an acting part. It was a real goose-bumper."

"Really?" Her blue eyes brightened. "I'll remember that. Thank you."

Hopefully she wouldn't decide to practice it here on Madison Street. There hadn't been any sirens – or maybe it was just that the scream had numbed my ears to siren sounds - but now I heard a vehicle outside.

"I'd better go down and talk to the police," I said. "Don't touch anything." Rather tardy advice, of course, considering that we'd more or less mopped the floor with Eric.

Going down the stairs, I wished my friend Matt Dixon, who was a detective on the police force the first time I got involved in a murder, was still here. But he was now a Special Agent with the FBI, and he and his wife Haley lived down in Arkansas.

I went out the back door expecting to see a police car and officers, but what I saw was another motorhome in the driveway behind mine. A familiar motorhome. And getting out of it – Mac!

I was so glad to see him. I wanted to run and throw my arms around him. But his stiff shoulders as he strode toward me instead had me saying, "What're you doing here? I thought you were off to Montana to look for ghost prospectors."

"I decided to stop in here along the way."

He spoke as if it were like a pit stop for a burger and fries, but a straight line from central California to western Montana does not run through Missouri. He'd taken a detour of something like fifteen hundred miles or more to get here.

A police car started to turn in behind Mac, but the driveway was already full of motorhomes, plus the little Toyota pickup Mac pulls behind the motorhome when he's traveling. The officer at the wheel parked the police car at an angle on the dry grass. One middle-aged male officer and one sturdy woman officer, both in dark sunglasses, got out. He was bald; she had red hair sculpted into a bun tight enough to do a face lift. Except she was much too young to need one.

"A report came in that there's a dead body in the house at this address," the man said.

"The body is in the bathtub upstairs." I waved in that general direction. "There are a couple of people up there, but they don't have anything to do with the body. They were just looking." I realized right after I said it that that sounded peculiar, as if I'd been selling tickets for self-guided tours. "One of them may be unconscious."

That was enough to send the officers storming into the house without asking more questions, although the woman paused long enough to yell back, "Nobody leaves! We have questions to ask you."

"But I just got here," Mac protested. "I don't know anything. But that's okay," he added hastily in response to her stern look. "I wasn't going anywhere anyway."

"Good." The woman officer transferred the stern

41

look to me. "Don't let anyone else come inside."

Right. No more tour tickets.

That left Mac and me looking at each other, Mac with silver-gray eyebrows raised in a questioning arc. He looked good. Khaki shorts, light green polo shirt, and that disreputable old straw hat that somehow manages to look rakish instead of bag-lady-boyfriend on him. Even that blue tattoo and his knobby knees looked good.

Mac crossed his arms over his chest. "A dead body in your bathtub?" he inquired.

"Okay, go ahead and say it," I muttered. Just because he looked good, and I was glad to see him, didn't mean he wasn't going to go snarky on me. "You warned me. You told me so."

"I admit an I-told-you-so is tempting," Mac agreed. "Although I hadn't figured even you would come up with a dead body this soon. My apologies for underestimating you." He gave me a complimentary bow of head.

"Maybe you'd prefer the dead body was *me*. Although then you wouldn't have anyone to say 'I told you so' to."

"Has anyone ever mentioned that sometimes you sound as if you should be riding on a broomstick instead of driving a motorhome?" he grumbled.

We glared at each other for a long minute.

Okay, I'd started this by being a tad snappish. "I'm glad you're here," I finally said.

He was still scowling, but he grabbed me in a big Mac-hug. I was still a little unhappy with his grumpy attitude

about my coming home to Madison Street, but I was too glad
to see him not to hug back.

"I came because I missed you," he said. "I tried to
call but I couldn't get through."

"My phone was dead." Still was.

"I was worried about you. Apparently with good
reason." He held me off at arm's length and inspected me.
"Are you okay?"

"A little shook up," I admitted. Yes, as I'd told Eric
and Tasha, I'd found dead bodies before. But it isn't as if this
is something you want to incorporate into your daily routine.

"You want to tell me what this is all about?" Mac
said with a wave at the police car.

Someone had put a couple of rickety old benches
under the maple tree, so we moved over there into the shade
and sat down. He kept hold of my hands while I told him.
Arrival yesterday. Smelly house. Staying in the motorhome
last night. Finding a sleeping bag and a woman's clothes in
my bedroom this morning, followed by wrinkled, blackened
toes under blankets in the bathtub. Running to the neighbor's
house. Calling 911.

"I didn't deliberately *try* to get involved with a dead
body. I wasn't sticking my nose in where it didn't belong." I
needed to emphasize that point. Because, what my friend
Special Agent Dix called my "mutant curiosity gene," has
gotten me in trouble before. "It just . . . happened."

"You're thinking this is a natural death? This woman
just crawled in your tub and died?" He sounded skeptical.

"Tasha said there's a big hole in the body," I

answered uneasily. "And the blankets were pulled up over her face. But that doesn't necessarily mean she was *murdered*."

"No?" He lifted his eyebrows and crossed his arms over his chest again.

"The police haven't said anything about murder."

"What would you expect? An officer rushing out and screaming 'Murder! Murder!' like some guy on a TV infomercial yelling to get your attention?"

Okay, probably not. But I still didn't want to think of the woman as *murdered*. In my tub.

"You don't know who the body is?" Mac asked.

"No. Except I figure it must be the woman who was wearing the clothes and using the sleeping bag." And drinking the wine out of those bottles in the garbage can. Could she have been drinking, stumbled in the bathroom, and taken the blanket with her when she fell in the tub?

"The police will probably find something to identify her. Maybe it's a renter, someone the rental agency can identify?" Mac suggested.

"I quit renting the house after that last eviction. But there was food in the kitchen and a few things in the medicine cabinet. I've heard about people just moving into a vacant house and living there." This, I realized, could explain those utility bills I'd received. Somehow the woman had managed to get the utilities turned on, but when she wound up in the bathtub, the bills had gone unpaid. Eventually the utility people had looked up the property owner, me, and sent the bills to me through my complicated forwarding system.

"How about the unconscious man? Who's he?"

I explained about Eric and Tasha coming back to the house with me after I called 911 from their place. "He's a big, muscular guy. But very sensitive," I added, repeating Tasha's words. "They were trying to be helpful."

Eric and Tasha came out the back door. Although Eric was conscious now, and the flip-flops were back on his feet, he still looked disoriented. He wobbled as Tasha led him over to the maple tree and nudged him onto the other bench. With his 245 pounds, the bench creaked and groaned and the legs sank deeper into the ground.

"Are you okay?" I asked him.

"I don't understand why that happens. Makes me feel like a big wimp," he muttered. He jiggled his shoulders and slapped his thigh as if to check it for feeling. "Once back in high school I passed out when a guy I tackled in a football game broke his nose and bled all over me."

I patted his shoulder. "It's okay to be sensitive."

"Does anyone know what time it is?" Tasha asked. "I have to get to work."

Although it seemed much later, when Mac looked at his watch he said, "Nine-fifteen."

"Actress work?" I asked Tasha

"I'm working at the Heartland Grocery today. I do food demonstrations and hand out samples." She beamed and pretended to hand me a sample. "Would you like to try our wonderful new tofu sausage? It's terrific for breakfast or snacks. Anytime! Delicious and healthy too!"

Tofu sausage? Making that sound irresistible indeed took some acting talent. But Tasha was succeeding, because Mac said, "Hey, I wouldn't mind trying a sample."

"I'd better run back to the house and call to tell them I'll be late. I didn't bring my cell phone. You'll be okay?" she said to her husband.

He nodded. She kissed him on the forehead and started a long-legged lope toward the sidewalk.

The woman officer came out of the house. She was on a phone, no doubt calling for backup. This was more than a two-officer job. The Medical Examiner's office would have to be called in. There would undoubtedly be an autopsy. But when the officer saw Tasha heading down the sidewalk, she waved an arm and yelled at her. "Hey, you can't leave until you answer some questions!"

Tasha reluctantly returned. "I don't know anything."

"But you may have talked to the dead woman," I pointed out. "The woman with the parsnip."

"But that was *you*."

"No, it wasn't. I haven't been here for almost three years."

"No discussing the case," the woman officer said. Up close she still looked sturdy, but even younger, about junior-high age. Like most doctors these days.

She separated us so we couldn't talk to each other. Good police procedure, although her flustered attitude suggested doing it was like trying to herd grasshoppers. Somehow I doubted she'd been a police officer for long. She sent me to stand by my motorhome, Mac to wait by his. Eric clung to the bench he was sitting on. Tasha rebelled and clamped an I'm-not-moving hand on his shoulder.

"We won't talk to each other about the dead woman," she said.

Policewoman frowned, but she accepted that compromise.

More police people arrived. Radios crackled. A fire truck and an ambulance showed up. It wasn't chaos, but it wasn't exactly the finest example of authority in action when the fire truck and a police car backed into each other.

We were questioned separately. Mac's session with a sharp looking Hispanic officer was brief, Eric and Tasha's with a different officer a little longer. Lucky me, I got Ms. Junior High. She looked at her hand a couple of times, introduced herself as Officer DeLora and asked my name.

"Ivy Malone."

"But the dead woman is Ivy Malone," she objected.

"She can't be Ivy Malone," I objected. "*I*'m Ivy Malone. What makes you think she is?"

"Identification."

"What kind of identification?"

"A library card. It was in a purse in the bedroom. Along with mail addressed to Ivy Malone." She frowned as if realizing that was information she probably shouldn't be sharing with me.

"Anyone can fake a name to get a library card," I pointed out. Although it seemed a lot of bother for such a minor thing.

"Why would she fake it?" Officer DeLora scoffed.

"Maybe *you're* faking your identity."

"Why would *I* fake it? Look, just let me go in the motorhome and I can prove who I am. I have a driver's license."

She wasn't about to let me go in the motorhome alone, although I didn't know what she thought I could do in there. Escape by doing a high-tech morph of motorhome into flying machine? Or maybe she thought I had an AK-47 stashed in my closet. She followed me inside. Koop met us at the door. He didn't hiss at her, but he backed away when she started to pet him.

"Cats usually like me." She sounded unexpectedly dismayed by Koop's rejection.

"Are you a smoker? Koop has a real hangup about smokers."

"No! I quit."

I lifted my eyebrows at her hasty claim. Koop is better than police profiling when targeting a smoker.

"My mother thinks I've quit." She shot a guilty glance back over her shoulder as if afraid Mother might be standing there listening. "And I'm really trying."

Koop, stickler that he is, doesn't give points for trying. He flicked his stubby tail and headed for the bedroom. I handed her my driver's license and the registration on the motorhome. Both were from Colorado, where I'd spent some time and where my good friend Abilene now lives with her veterinarian husband. It was her address I'd used for the license and registration. Another of my tactics for hiding from the Braxtons, who seemed to have tentacles everywhere.

"That's an older address," I explained. "I'll be living here in my own home now."

"You're saying you own this place?"

"For more years than you are old."

The officer took down all the information from both license and registration, though she didn't seem convinced of my identity even yet. The other woman was *in* the house, also with identification, and there's that old saying about possession being nine-tenths of the law. Did that nine-tenths apply even if you were dead?

Someone from the Medical Examiner's office arrived while Officer DeLora was grilling me. Crime scene people showed up along with a couple of guys in plain clothes that I thought were probably police force detectives. People collected on the sidewalk to watch. Tasha had left after being questioned but she was back now, one hand protectively resting on her husband's shoulder again.

Officer DeLora finally finished with me, although she warned there might be more questions later. I couldn't think what else they might ask, unless they wanted to know what brand of undies I wore. She'd already asked about everything else, including whether I had false teeth. Fortunately she didn't try to check for herself, because by then I might have given her a demonstration of LOL tooth power.

Finally we both went outside again, which is when I realized the small but curious crowd was on the far side of a newly-erected barrier of yellow crime scene tape. Mac was already on the other side of the barrier, and Officer DeLora took me over there too. I tried to ask her about the *crime scene* aspect of this, but she headed back to the house without telling me anything. A little later she returned and asked permission of both Mac and me to search our motorhomes. It was a politely phrased request, but I knew the clout behind it. If we didn't agree, they'd just get an official search warrant. Mac shrugged and said okay, and I did too.

A little later, two men came out of the house carrying a stretcher with a dark body bag on it. I'd never known the dead woman, and I didn't know how she'd died, but this was such a bleak ending to anyone's life that I had to blink back tears. Who was she? Did she have family to mourn her? Would anyone come to claim her body? The stretcher disappeared into the back of a van.

Now what? Both Mac's and my motorhomes were included within that barrier of yellow tape, officers now going through them. I couldn't think there was anything to find, but who knew what innocent item they might target as incriminating evidence? This was obviously going to complicate my plans to move into the house. I suddenly doubted that even after I could move in that I'd ever be able to use that upstairs bathroom again, no matter how much bubble bath I dumped in the tub.

Mac and I drifted together to watch what was going on. An officer came out of the house with a video camera and panned the outside area, including us in the cluster of people standing around. Were they thinking a killer might return to the scene of the crime?

I rejected that question. *No killer. No crime.* Just a dead woman who happened to expire and tumble into my tub. That's my story and I'm sticking to it.

"Did you find out anything while you were being questioned?" Mac asked.

"No, it was all questions, no answers. Although Officer DeLora did let slip that the dead woman had a library card and some mail with the name Ivy Malone on them. And I already know that someone ran up some utility bills when there wasn't supposed to be anyone living here."

"She was passing herself off as you?"

"It looks that way."

Mac gave that some thought while an officer came out of the house carrying an armload of items individually packed in plastic evidence bags and placed them in a police car. Mac nodded thoughtfully.

"At least now you know why the Braxtons haven't been trying to kill you for the last few months," he said.

"Why's that?"

"Because they thought you were dead, of course. They thought they'd already killed you. And dumped you in the bathtub."

CHAPTER 5

"You don't know that!" I objected. Too vehemently. Because what Mac said made all too much sense. Tasha had said the dead body had a "big hole" in it. There was that stain in the bedroom, which I now realized was more likely blood than wine. The ominous circling of crime-scene tape was a plain indication of how the police viewed this. And the Braxtons hadn't made any threatening moves on me in the last few months.

The Braxtons had discovered someone living in the house, someone identifying herself as Ivy Malone, and then they'd done what Braxtons did when they encountered an Ivy Malone. They finished her off. Why did they put her in the tub? Maybe something about taking longer for the body to be discovered or to contain the odor? Or maybe just some morbid Braxton whimsy?

Guilt hit me like an avalanche. This unknown woman had wound up dead in a tub and then a body bag because of *me*.

I tried to squirm out from under that weight of guilt and responsibility. Passing herself off as me had been the woman's choice; it had nothing to do with anything I'd done. Maybe the Braxtons hadn't killed her. Maybe someone had tried to burglarize the place and killed her in the process.

Maybe the zombie uprising had started here.

Yeah, all kinds of possibilities. But the biggest possibility by far was that the Braxtons, thinking I'd probably come back to Madison Street sometime, had kept an eye on the place. They didn't do an intensive investigation when someone using my name started living in the house; they just killed her. Did she look like me? There may have been some resemblance. Tasha had thought we were the same person. But being generically older and gray haired was probably close enough to get her murdered.

A follow-up jolt: if I'd been here that could have been me in the bathtub.

None of which lessened the guilt I felt for the death of the woman who'd fatally entangled herself in my identity. It was dangerous to be Ivy Malone.

"Did you tell them about the Braxtons?" Mac asked.

"No." I'd been so shocked by discovery of the body, Eric's swoon, and my misguided determination to keep this out of the murder category, that I was still a little numb. "I guess I'd better do that."

"And then you can pick up and leave town before the Braxtons realize they made a mistake and come after the real you."

I managed to catch Officer DeLora's eye when she came out of the motorhome. I motioned her over and told her I'd thought of something that might be helpful. She kept me on the far side of the tape, but we moved away from the curious crowd. I told her about the Braxtons, how I'd helped catch and convict one of the clan in a murder case, and how the others had vowed to make roadkill out of me. How they'd first tried to do it with a fire right here at the house and then a bomb under my old Thunderbird down in Arkansas, how I'd been running ever since. She surreptitiously flexed her left hand a couple of times while we were talking. I wondered if she'd recently injured it in line of duty.

"So what you're saying is—?"

"I think the Braxtons killed this woman thinking she was me."

"That's a very serious accusation."

"She was murdered, wasn't she?"

In spite of the conspicuous crime scene tape, Officer DeLora refused to confirm or deny that. Instead she asked, "And this person you say you helped convict was—?"

"Beaumont Zollinger, usually known as Bo."

She pounced on that. "But you said *Braxtons* were out to get you."

"It's a big family. The man who threatened me after the trial was Drake Braxton. Bo Zollinger is his half-brother. I don't know what the aunts and uncles and cousins and in-laws may be named. But they're united in an effort to get me. A family project."

"You're saying the whole family is in on some big conspiracy to kill you?" Officer DeLora was as skeptical as Koop is when I'm creeping up on him with a tuna tidbit in one hand and a worm pill hidden in the other.

"Yes, that's what I'm saying. My grand-niece down in Arkansas calls them a mini-Mafia. They seem to have tentacles everywhere. I think they got my original forwarding address because one of them worked for the postal service. Another time they managed to track me through credit card purchases, which probably means they have a spy in the banking system. Which is why I never use a credit card anymore."

"Using information obtained as a postal or bank employee for personal purposes would be illegal and have serious consequences." She sounded very righteous about that.

"Bank robbery isn't legal. Neither is hijacking cars, shoplifting Cheerios, or stealing an identity. All can have serious consequences. But it's *done*." And, like all crimes, no consequences if you aren't caught

Her frown and tap of pen on notebook acknowledged the possibility of some person in a responsible position using that position to accomplish a nefarious goal. Which still didn't mean she thought the Braxtons had done it to me or the woman in the tub.

"You think I'm paranoid, don't you?" I grumbled. "Or cruising in the senile lane."

Officer DeLora didn't comment on my mental condition, but her sideways glance suggested she was giving these possibilities serious consideration.

"At the very least, eccentric," I added.

"We're all a little eccentric in our own way."

Which implied an eccentricity of her own? What was it? On impulse I tossed out a question. "Why do you keep looking at your hand?"

"I don't!" She fisted the hand, then rested her fingers

on the gun at her hip and gave me The Look.

I got the message. No questions. Which had never stopped me before, of course. I tossed out one on a different subject. "Why did you want to know if my teeth are real or false?"

That question apparently caught her while she was still off-balance from the hand question, and she answered this one. "The body has false teeth."

Which connected with what Tasha said about the teeth being "all strange." As the body deteriorated, the false teeth had loosened and gone awry. I started to tell Officer DeLora that she could check with Dr. Sorenson, who could tell her the real Ivy Malone had her real teeth. But then I remembered Dr. Sorenson had retired and moved to Florida even before I left Madison Street. The world keeps changing.

"Look, whether or not I'm paranoid, senile, or eccentric, there's something you can check out. The records from the trial. They won't tell you about the Braxtons threatening me, but they will tell you what Bo Zollinger did and how I helped convict him."

"I'll do that." This time the pen moved up to tap her jaw. "The Braxton name sounds familiar. I know I've seen or heard it somewhere. . ."

"On an FBI Most Wanted List?" I suggested.

She didn't realize the question was at least semi-facetious. "No, something local. But I just can't remember. . ."

"You don't have any idea yet who the dead woman really is?" I asked.

"At this point she's Ivy Malone."

Would I see an obituary for Ivy Malone in the newspaper? A startling thought. But hey, maybe not a bad idea! Then the Braxtons really would think they'd finished me off. Maybe I shouldn't be trying so hard to prove my identity. Let the dead woman be Ivy Malone. I could change my name to something more interesting. The name India had always appealed to me. I instantly added a glamorous sounding last name. India Cristobal!

"If you are the real Ivy Malone, and you're convinced this 'mini-Mafia' is out to get you, why did you come back?" Officer DeLora challenged.

A good time to tell her I was mistaken. That I wasn't really Ivy Malone. That my saying I was had simply been a temporary identity crisis, one of those senior moment things. Give her my "real" India name. But, as usual, the truth is what comes out of me. Besides, I'd need a whole new wardrobe of filmy, swirly things, maybe even castanets, to be India Cristobal.

"Because this is home," I said simply. "I wanted to come home."

She considered this for a moment and then nodded. "I can understand that." A far-off look in her eyes unexpectedly said that *home* meant something to her too.

"You're not from around here?" I asked.

"No, I moved up from Texas a few—" She broke off and grabbed back her usual stern demeanor. *No questions.*

Only then did I realize Mac had followed us and was hiding more or less discreetly behind a dead bush in the yard.

He came out when Officer DeLora snapped her little notebook shut.

"I'll include all this in my report," she said "But don't leave town. We may need to talk to you again."

"I'm sure you know that isn't an enforceable order," Mac said affably. He clasped an arm around my shoulders. "If someone isn't under arrest, she can come and go as she pleases. We're both headed for Montana."

I blinked. *Both* headed for Montana? Since when? Officer DeLora gave a frustrated huff. Because the other point Mac had said was true. I'd had enough experience with law enforcement in recent years to know that even though people are often told they can't leave an area, that wasn't enforceable if they weren't under arrest.

Officer DeLora didn't admit Mac was correct, but neither did she argue with him. Unfortunately, at least from her viewpoint, she didn't have enough reason to arrest me to keep me here. Unless maybe she could make a case out of my impersonating Ivy Malone?

She apparently decided to appeal to our nobler natures now. "I'm sure you're both as eager as we are to find out who killed this woman." To me, "Your presence could be very helpful."

What hit me in that statement was the bottom-line fact about this dead body. I'd been doing mental gymnastics trying to detour this ever since I'd first seen those toes in the tub, but there was no getting around it now. Officer DeLora had made it fact. This wasn't just a dead body. This was a *murdered* dead body. In my bathtub.

Sometimes it seems as if there's an inexorable link between murder and me. Like macaroni and cheese. Salt and pepper. Jekyll and Hyde. Ivy and murder.

Mac and Officer DeLora were still discussing the situation. She was emphasizing how helpful my sticking around would be. Mac was saying my life might be in danger if I did.

I held up a hand. "I'd be more inclined to stay if I could be in my own motorhome, but it's inside the crime scene tape. So is Mac's. If I could occupy mine and Mac could leave in his—? They have already been searched."

"You intend to leave the area?" Officer DeLora asked Mac.

Mac gave me a glance that put Officer DeLora's stern look in the amateur category, a glance that said *We both need to leave. Now.* I started to deny that. Just Mac would be leaving. Although I had to admit zipping out of town right behind him might be the smartest and safest thing to do. I could follow him up to Montana or head for the Oregon coast. Leave the Braxtons behind again.

Mac gave a noncommittal shrug, and Officer DeLora said, "I'll see what I can do about getting the motorhomes released. Until then both of you stay outside the tape." Officer DeLora gave Mac The Look. "And that *is* enforceable."

***

Processing of the crime scene went on. Officers came and went. A few lookie-loos remained, but most of the small crowd drifted away. Somewhere along the way Tasha and

Eric also got away. An officer came out and rearranged the yellow tape so that the motorhomes were outside it.

"You'll be leaving now?" I asked Mac.

"You'll come with me?"

I dodged a decision by saying, "I'd like to visit the cemetery while I'm here." I hadn't been to Harley's grave since I left Madison Street.

"I can hang around for a day or two. I'll pull the motorhome out on the street so you can get in and out of the driveway."

I started to say something about the city not allowing RVs on the street but realized that might not be true now. It used to be, to park an RV here, it had to be in a garage or out of sight behind a house. But the city also used to get nasty about overgrown weeds, and a car up on blocks in a yard would earn an immediate citation, so apparently they weren't paying much attention to enforcement on Madison Street these days. Maybe a shortage of personnel because of budget problems? Or maybe Madison Street had just been written off by city authorities.

The crime scene people still weren't done by the time Mac and I shared a salad for dinner in my motorhome. It was too hot to cook anything. Afterward we took a stroll over to the shopping center where I'd always gone for groceries when I lived here. I picked up a local newspaper to see what they were reporting about the bathtub body, but it was only a small item on the third page. Much bigger news was a convenience store robbery in which both a clerk and a bystander had been killed.

Mac suggested ice cream at a new place in the shopping center, and we sat at an outside table with our cones, mine butter pecan, his blueberry cheesecake. It seemed like a time to glorify the good ol'days, when Madison Street had friendly neighbors and a nonexistent crime rate, when the flavors of ice cream were a simple choice between vanilla, chocolate and strawberry. I, same as almost everyone in my age group, sometimes lamented that the "good ol' days" were gone, but I liked some changes. Wasn't it great to have all these wonderful flavors of ice cream now? I'd try coconut-macadamia next time.

Maybe I'd make another change and sell the house too.

But then guilt and responsibility for that woman's death kicked in again.

By the time we got back to the motorhomes, the crime scene people had closed up the house. I hoped that meant they were done. Lack of electricity for lights was a hindrance for me, but they surely had their own light system and could have continued. But, arguing against the hopeful possibility they were done, was the crime scene tape still fluttering in an evening breeze.

We used the battery power in Mac's motorhome to watch a DVD but I excused myself by 10:00 to go back to my place. All the windows were open, but humid heat still filled the bedroom. I could run the generator so I could use the air conditioner, but that might be noisy enough to rouse the ire of the few neighbors remaining in the area. I hadn't recognized anyone among the watching group this morning, and no one had given me a *Hey, Ivy, welcome home!* Madison Street was different now, no doubt about it.

And my thoughts kept circling back to the woman dead in the tub and the unpleasant reason she was there. Because of *me*.

Finally I got up to sit on the sofa and stare out at the house.

I'd come here so eagerly, sure that the ending of my job in California was a favorable sign from the Lord telling me to go *home*. But maybe the Lord hadn't been in the sign business after all, and I'd read something into the end of my job because that was what I wanted to see. Maybe all I was really doing here was setting myself up for Death by Braxtons.

CHAPTER 6

The crime scene people were back the next morning, along with a detective who put us through another round of questioning, but they removed the yellow tape before they left about noon. I immediately headed for the house. Mac followed. Koop chose to prowl in the garden weeds.

The crime scene people had done a thorough job of checking for fingerprints, as evidenced by the fine, grayish-black fingerprint powder covering every available surface. It looked like the collapse of a vast dust-bunny civilization. I'd known cleaning the house would be a big job even before this, and now, with the leftovers of a crime scene investigation everywhere, the task loomed as almost overwhelming.

"Does the police department pay for clean-up or send someone out to do it?" Mac asked.

"I don't think so."

"Insurance?"

"The premium was going to be so high with the house vacant that I dropped everything but basic fire insurance."

"You could just accept that company's offer to buy and let them take care of the cleanup. From what I hear, they won't care what shape it's in because they'll be bulldozing everything down anyway."

"Where'd you hear that?" I asked.

"Oh, you know. People."

Right. Mac is an outgoing, gregarious guy. People talk to him. He can go for a stroll in a new town and come back with information on everything from directions to local RV parks and churches to the tumble some old lady took chasing teenagers away from her stash of homemade wine. The small crowd outside the yellow tape had no doubt been full of information. As proved when Mac added, "Stay away from the people in that yellow house on the other side of the street."

I felt mildly alarmed. "They're dangerous?"

"Very. You go anywhere near them, and they'll inundate you with cucumbers. They're new gardeners who wanted to make a few pickles and didn't know eighteen plants would produce enough cucumbers to start their own pickle factory."

I'd never overproduced cucumbers, but I'd had zucchini that grew so big and so numerous so fast that I began to think they had world domination in mind. "Did anyone know the dead woman?"

"A couple of people had talked to her, but she mostly kept to herself. No one could remember what name she used, but she let them think she was renting the place."

She'd apparently done a careful balancing act. Passing herself off as owner Ivy Malone to the utilities and library people but making neighborhood people think she was legitimately renting the house. Unfortunately for her, the

Braxtons had latched onto the Ivy persona.

"Did anyone say what the company would do with the area after they bought and demolished the houses?" I asked.

Mac had heard the same rumors I had, including the billionaire survivalist, but the most prevalent belief was that the company was planning to put in an artificial lake and build luxury condos around it.

I felt a wave of indignation. My house was old and ordinary, but I didn't want it sacrificed on the altar of marble countertops, upscale bathrooms, and a pond full of designer fish. I remembered hearing about an elderly woman in the Atlantic City area who'd refused to sell out, and there her old house stood surrounded by glitzy casinos. Maybe I'd be the Madison Street version, stubbornly raising tomatoes shaped like Nixon or Reagan in the midst of condo owners frustrated with the eccentric holdout next door. This was, after all, my *home,* so why shouldn't I stay?

Dumb question. One answer, and it was spelled B-r-a-x-t-o-n-s.

"I think I'll clean it up anyway. Just . . . in case." In case what? I was suddenly free of Braxtons because the entire clan was kidnapped by UFO aliens?

Mac didn't argue. "Then we'd better see about getting the utilities turned on," he said briskly. "Cleanup is going to take water and electricity."

"I don't expect you to help."

"I know. But I'm offering."

Mac planted his feet and crossed his arms, practically

daring me to argue. The wary side of me suspected he was plotting more time to convince me to put Madison Street in my rear-view mirror permanently, but I also knew that was unfair. Mac's a good guy. He helps other people too, not just me. Like back at that California RV park, where he spent several days helping an elderly guy build a doghouse. For a mutt the size of a Brontosaurus. In any case, I'm not one to do the old cut-off-the-nose-to-spite-the-face thing by stubbornly turning him down. I could use the help.

So I just smiled brightly and said, "Great! I appreciate that."

***

We took Mac's pickup to go to the power company office first. I tried to convince the woman at the front desk that the unpaid bills weren't my responsibility. She semi-wavered, but finally said she'd have to consult a supervisor first. The supervisor took me into her private office. She was fifty-ish but looked more like a cheerleader than a supervisor. Petite size, curly blond hair, short skirt, and fuzzy kitten earrings. In spite of the cheerleader look, however, she was also immovable as Mt. Rushmore. Their records showed that Ivy Malone was the person who'd had the electricity turned on last December, and owner Ivy Malone would have to pay the past-due bill before it would be turned on again. So Ivy Malone—the frustrated one standing here—paid.

I did glean one interesting fact from the first woman at the front desk. This faux-Ivy hadn't used Madison Street as a billing address. The bills were sent to an address with a street name unfamiliar to me. So the woman had definitely given this some thought and figured out that if she used Madison Street as a mailing address, the bills would be forwarded on to the real Ivy Malone, *me,* who would then know an unauthorized person was living in the house. So she'd had the bills sent elsewhere and probably paid with one of those money orders you can buy anywhere, same as I'd been doing. Until her unexpected demise, and then, when the bills went unpaid, the power company had looked in the property records at the assessor's office and billed me at the Madison Street address, where they joined the maze of my forwarding system. I jotted down the mailing address the woman had used. Someone there must know who she really was. I also made arrangements to have the electricity turned on as soon as possible.

Same situation, same address, with the water department, so I also had that past-due bill to pay before water would be turned on. I thought there might be some way to fight this double-identity thing, but I didn't have time for a long squabble with bureaucracies that undoubtedly had more money and clout than I had. I needed the utilities now. I wasn't *un*perturbed with the woman about all this, but, dead in the bathtub, she'd already gotten the worst of the deal.

We stopped at a store, and I picked up some heavy-duty cleaning supplies, though I had to wonder what I'd do with that big bloodstain on the bedroom carpet.

We couldn't do anything with the house until the utility people came, so this seemed a good time to visit the cemetery. I planned to take my motorhome, but Mac offered to go in his pickup. I expected he'd wait in it when we reached Parkdale Heights Cemetery, but he came along. At Harley's grave, and then Thea's, he didn't say anything, but he comforted me with a squeeze of arm around my shoulders. I'd never had a headstone put in for Colin. There had been no body to bury, and I'd always held off doing a headstone because that made it too final, an admittance that my son really was never coming back.

"Maybe it's time to get a headstone for Colin," I said in a small voice.

"Can I help?"

"I'll see."

He turned me to him and held me for several long minutes while I grieved once more.

On the way home, Mac, with guidance from his smart phone, located the address the faux-Ivy used for utility bills. But what had seemed a great clue instead fizzled like a bad recipe. The address wasn't a residence, just one of those private mailbox places with which I was already familiar. I went inside, but they couldn't or wouldn't tell me anything. Faux-Ivy had apparently covered all the bases.

Except the one that put her dead in the bathtub.

Back home, we discovered, much to my surprise at the speedy action, that everything had been turned on. A flick of switch brought a light! The refrigerator hummed. A turn of faucet brought blasts of water and air from long-unused pipes, and then a steady stream. The first thing I did was run out to the motorhome for my cell phone and plug it in to revive it. I still used the el cheapo flip kind, "disposables" some people called them, though I'd had this one for months. I'd heard they were untraceable and hoped that was true, in case the Braxtons had infiltrated the cell phone world too.

We changed clothes and pitched into the cleanup. Koop still refused to have anything to do with the interior of the house and I, after a couple hours of scrubbing the grayish-black fingerprint powder, made the unhappy discovery that it tended to turn into smears of abstract art rather than washing away. I didn't see any dead presidents in the designs, but I did spot a tornado carrying a 7-legged cow into space. I also discovered that, up close, a scent of death permeates *everything*. Furniture. Drapes. Carpet. We dragged the sofa and recliner out to the back yard, and I tossed the drapes over them. I couldn't throw out the living room carpet, but I inundated it with several cans of spray deodorizer.

I didn't find anything personal about the faux-Ivy who had occupied my home, but I did run into bits and pieces of her life. An old grocery store coupon for pork and beans, two cans for a dollar. A recipe for caviar and smoked salmon canapés. A packet of radish seeds. A list of the gluten content of various foods. A booklet on growing marijuana for fun and profit. A woman of diversified tastes and interests, it appeared.

We were both too tired to cook that evening, so we tried to find a restaurant Thea and I used to like. It was gone now, but we located a new Chinese place and had great Szechwan shrimp, chicken chow mein and fried rice. Mac's fortune cookie cheerfully said he would be taking a profitable journey soon, which seemed appropriate. Mine was a puzzling, "Beware the purple cow."

I knew I had Braxtons to beware of, but unless one of them was using a purple-cow disguise, I had to doubt the cookie's accuracy. I crumpled the scrap of paper and left it on the table.

Next morning when we moved upstairs to start cleaning, we made a discovery about that bloodstain on the bedroom carpet. It wasn't there. No, the crime scene people hadn't generously used some for-official-use-only cleaning fluid on it. The entire section of rug was gone. They'd cut a big oblong out of it. I was appalled. I couldn't afford new carpet.

Mac, bless him, didn't mutter something about this being one more reason to abandon the house. He suggested a simple, man-type solution. Move the bed so it covered the cut-out area.

That worked fine. The smelly mattress was a lost cause, however, and it joined the sofa and chair in the back yard. Which meant I wouldn't be sleeping in the house for a while.

Mac, more blessings on him, took care of the upstairs bathroom cleanup. He also repaired and re-installed the screen door. I'd wondered about the garage, padlocked with a lock to which I had no key, but Mac peered through a crack and said the building appeared to be empty. Good. I didn't need another unpleasant surprise, like finding a garage full of marijuana plants the woman had been growing for fun and/or profit. Though I now had to wonder about the identity of those dead plants in pots I'd found in the kitchen.

That afternoon, while I scrubbed away the ominous civilization clinging to the interior of the refrigerator, Mac rented a mower and tackled the yard and garden area. He found several items discarded among the garden weeds. Another empty wine bottle. A plastic frame holding a photo, in surprisingly good shape, of Elvis. And a mannequin's head, bald. We set them aside to show the authorities. They didn't look like clues to me, but you never know.

That same evening, Officer DeLora unexpectedly showed up. Mac had gone to the store to pick up some half-and-half for morning oatmeal, so I was sitting alone, in a lawn chair under the maple tree, reading my "Our Daily Bread" devotional. She was in uniform but driving an older Toyota Corolla rather than a police car. This late in the day, her stiff bun drooped and several red strands straggled out of it, but her expression was still stern enough to wilt weeds.

CHAPTER 7

I didn't expect Officer DeLora to accept my offer of iced tea, but she did. When I came out of the motorhome with ice clinking in plastic glasses, she was sitting in the other lawn chair. She dropped a hand to where Koop was circling the chair. He sniffed her fingers delicately and she started to stroke his head, but he backed away with a warning twitch of stubby tail.

"That isn't fair," Officer DeLora objected as if she'd just received the social snub of the year. Her stern expression wilted as limp as her hair. "I really have almost quit smoking. I had only one cigarette today. Actually only *half* a cigarette."

"It isn't like an official reprimand for dereliction of duty," I said kindly.

She didn't comment, just jiggled her shoulders as if trying to shake off Koop's disapproval.

"Is this an official visit?" I asked. "We found a few things in the yard that we thought we should show you."

I led her to the discarded sofa, where Mac had piled the photo of Elvis, the mannequin head, and the wine bottle. She examined and thanked us for conscientiously saving them, but dismissed them as meaningless to the case. My opinion also, although I'd been hoping she'd want to take them to a police lab. Now they were something more I'd have to dispose of myself. We went back to the chairs and our tea.

"I came because I have some information I thought might interest you," Officer DeLora said when she sat down again. "Some of it is official and some isn't."

"Okay."

"I finally remembered why the Braxton name sounded familiar. Our Deputy Chief of Police got married a while back. To a woman whose last name was Braxton. Sylvia Braxton. So her name isn't Braxton now, of course. It's Haldebrand."

For a moment, the Haldebrand name bounced around in my head as if looking for a place to land. It sounded vaguely familiar. Had I heard it somewhere in connection with the Braxtons back at the trial?

Then the more important part of what Officer DeLora said hit me like a blast of that smelly stuff in the refrigerator. The Braxtons had slyly placed a family member right there in the home of a top officer of the police force, in his *bedroom,* a setting notoriously favored by *femme fatales* for extracting secrets. Now, through her, the Braxtons would have access to all kinds of information, with databases available only to law enforcement. They'd have a nationwide network of police departments at their disposal. New and improved ways to run me down. I couldn't escape their tentacles anywhere!

Then I took a deep breath and put the brakes on my runaway panic. Surely not even a Braxton would go so far as to *marry* someone as a way of hunting me down. That was surely inflating my importance in the Braxton world. They must have bigger and better grudges and conspiracies to occupy their time. Besides, the Braxtons thought they'd already disposed of Ivy Malone. Although. . .

"How long ago were they married?"

"Last fall, I think. It was before I joined the force. I know about it only because the woman who had my desk at the station before me did a lousy job of cleaning out the desk, and the clipping about the wedding was in there. Along with some old coupons from Suzanne's Donut Shop." She rolled her eyes at the cliché of cops and donuts.

So the wedding would have been before the Braxtons killed the woman they thought was me, and back then they *were* still looking for me.

"How old is this Sylvia Braxton Haldebrand?" I finally asked.

"I have no idea. I'm just telling you what I saw in the clipping." Officer DeLora impatiently shoved a wayward strand of red hair back in the bun and stabbed a pin in it. "What difference does it make how old she is?"

"If she's young, she's probably a Braxton by birth. Taking me down is practically in her genes. If she's older, maybe she was a Braxton by previous marriage." In which case I could hope she'd signed off on the Braxton conspiracy, and her marriage link with a high-up member of the local police force was pure love. A comforting thought, though not one I could grab onto with much assurance. The Braxtons had a no-holds-barred mentality and a pit-bull

74

tenacity that might even include a spy planted in a bedroom. "Do you know anything about her background?"

"I didn't do an in-depth investigation, no." Full exasperation now, as if Officer DeLora wished she'd kept memory of where she'd heard the Braxton name to herself. She crunched down on a chunk of ice as if trying to reduce it to molecular level. "I think you're making way too much of this. I can't believe our Deputy Chief of Police would marry into a mini-Mafia of crooks, as you called them. He's been with the Department a long time. Impeccable reputation."

Yeah, maybe I was going overboard. But the faux-Ivy was *dead,* and I doubt she'd think I was making too much of anything. "So if you don't think the Braxtons are involved, who *do* you think killed the woman in the tub?"

"It looks as if she was trying to hide out here, so it was probably someone she knew and was afraid of. Someone who had it in for her because of some past grudge or conflict."

Which meant that at this point the Braxtons weren't even a blip on the radar of law enforcement investigation of this case. But that didn't mean I could escape the *Braxtons'* radar.

Okay, Mac was right. Time to pick up and make tracks out of town before the mini-Mafia figured out that even though it was bothersome to have to kill me twice, I was readily available for the second time around. Could they already know I was here? I wavered over that one but finally decided, probably not. The case of an older woman dead in a bathtub probably wasn't enough to warrant the immediate attention of a Deputy Chief of Police, especially with the much bigger news of convenience store killings. I should have a few days of anonymity before the spy in his bedroom, and then the entire Braxton clan, found out that a surplus Ivy Malone had turned up here.

Maybe someday it would be safe to come home to Madison Street, but today wasn't the day. Okay, time to hit the road.

But that logical decision again snagged on guilt and responsibility. Could I just drive off and forget about a woman who had died because of a connection with me?

"That was the unofficial item I was going to tell you," Officer DeLora continued. "The other information is official. The dead woman definitely isn't Ivy Malone."

Good to hear. There are mornings when I tend to give myself a good poke to make sure I'm still alive and kicking. But just to be sure, I asked, "How do you know?

"In some conditions, an undisturbed body may dry out and mummify, making fingerprints fairly easy to get, but this one didn't." She wrinkled her nose as if remembering the scent that still loomed way too large in my own scent-memory. "So it was difficult getting fingerprints off the body, but we finally got a partial. Using that, along with all the other fingerprints in the house, the body has been identified as Lillian Hunnicutt, age 64. At least that was the name under which she was fingerprinted. She'd been arrested various times, mostly for minor shoplifting. Toothpaste and soap and socks. And Ritz crackers.

Apparently she had a real taste for Ritz crackers because that came up several times."

Which reminded me I'd found an unopened carton of Ritz crackers in the cupboard. Somehow that struck me as sad. The woman had gone to the trouble of acquiring the crackers, likely by sleight of hand, but she'd never even had a chance to open them.

"She's been married at least twice," Officer DeLora added. "Which meant name changes, and she's also used various aliases. We do know she's been incarcerated a couple of times, and she spent an occasional night at a local homeless shelter. She was also institutionalized briefly with a mental problem."

I reflected on the details of the woman's sad life and death. Homeless. Incarcerated. Institutionalized. Murdered. But in spite of a life that sounded rough and lonely and full of mistakes, Lillian had a certain amount of smarts. She'd figured out how to hijack a place to live and then solved the problem of utilities too. She'd managed to keep the bills paid and buy, or shoplift, the occasional parsnip and Ritz cracker. Maybe, in my house, she'd even been trying to start over. Eat radishes she raised herself, and work her way up to caviar canapés. Except that she'd made the fatal mistake of passing herself off as me.

"Has her family been notified?"

"So far, we haven't located any family."

Sadder still. No family. All alone in the world. Dead in a bathtub. Carried off in a body bag. The Braxton killers walking free. Maybe they'd held a gleeful We-Got-Ivy celebration, with beer and barbecue and balloons for the kids.

"Will you keep looking for a next of kin?" I asked.

She shuffled her feet on the dry grass and looked mildly uncomfortable. "I'm using 'we' in the . . . departmental sense. I didn't personally identify her from fingerprints. And I'm not personally trying to find her next of kin. But I'm sure someone will keep at it because it might help find her killer."

"Or killers?"

"I don't think it's been determined yet if more than one person might be involved."

"The Braxtons are big on teamwork." Though apparently they hadn't yet gone in for matching Team Braxton T-shirts.

Officer DeLora chose to ignore my teamwork comment, which I did not find encouraging. Law enforcement was totally ignoring the Braxton connection. Why? Easy answer: because no one believed an LOL's wild story of a Braxton conspiracy to kill her and killing Lillian Hunnicutt by mistake.

"Although not finding family may be because Lillian Hunnicutt isn't her real name, of course," Officer DeLora continued. "Her identity hasn't been released to the media yet, because family hasn't been notified, but I'm telling you because I thought the name might mean something to you. Perhaps a relative or acquaintance?"

Lillian Hunnicutt. I thought hard about the name, but I couldn't dredge up anything. I found a certain sadness even in her name. Lillian. It gave me an image of a grandmotherly type woman, sweet and old-fashioned, generous with hugs and cookies. And yet she'd wound up alone and dead in a body bag. I finally shook my head. "Doesn't ring any bells."

"Well, let us know if you happen to think of anything." She stood up to leave.

"Is your hand okay now?"

"There's nothing wrong with my hand!" She hastily shoved the hand behind her back.

"Oh. When you were here before, you kept looking at it. I thought maybe you'd injured it."

She gave an odd bark of laughter and brought the hand out to study it. Short, no-nonsense fingernails, unpolished. No wrinkles or veins marring the smooth skin. Did I once have hands like that? I stuck both my LOL hands around behind my back.

"No, I didn't hurt it. Actually—" She broke off as if she'd started to say something but was reluctant to go on.

"Actually?" I prodded.

She opened and closed the hand. "Have you ever heard of Miranda rights and the Miranda warning?"

"You have the right to remain silent. Anything you say or do can and will be used against you in a court of law," I quoted. "You have the right to an attorney. If you cannot afford an attorney, one will be provided for you."

Officer DeLora blinked at me in amazement. "You know the whole thing?"

"There are a couple more lines, about whether the person understands the rights and if he or she is still willing to talk to you. But an officer can ask questions without giving that warning, if the person hasn't been arrested, just like Mac and I and everyone else was questioned."

"How come you know this stuff?" She gave me an even closer peer as if comparing my face with wanted posters. "You've been arrested?"

No. Although I've come close a few times. But back when I was hiding out at a friend's apartment waiting to testify at Bo Zollinger's trial, I'd filled the days learning about computers and the internet. I was afraid a Braxton lawyer might somehow manage to have me arrested, so I looked up and memorized the Miranda warning. So if authorities came after me, I'd know if they were doing it according to the letter of the law. I'd also run across the words to that silly old Mairzy Doats song, and sometimes they still invade my head at odd times. *Mairzy doats and dozey doats—* I kicked them out now before they grabbed hold of vulnerable brain cells.

Instead of answering Officer DeLora's question now, however, I had one of my own. "What's the Miranda warning got to do with your hand?"

She opened the hand and looked at her palm once more. I could see some black marks on it.

"A few weeks ago, I had to question a guy we had under arrest. I needed to do the Miranda rights warning, but I got nervous and told this guy he was entitled to an—" She broke off and groaned. Her shoulders sagged. "To an alligator. And if he couldn't afford an alligator, one would be provided for him."

"An *alligator*?"

She nodded. "I couldn't sleep the night before. I'd been watching some TV show about swamps and alligators and . . . I don't know . . . it just came out."

The guy must have wondered what kind of justice system they were running, although I didn't say that.

"Anyway, after I messed up that time, I wanted to make certain it didn't happen again." She shoved her hand over where I could see it. There, written with one of those permanent markers that doesn't wash off, was a single word, the word that should have been in her recitation about Miranda rights. *Attorney.*

A cop with a crib note on her hand.

"I put it there so I wouldn't make another mistake and tell someone else we'd provide him with an alligator. Or who knows what might pop out of my mouth?" she added gloomily. "Asparagus. Accordion. Alfalfa."

I nodded. Other unfortunate possibilities came to mind. Albatross. Anteater. Aardvark. I didn't mention them. No point in putting words into her head that might pop out at some inopportune moment.

"Some officers carry a little card where it's all written down, and then they just pull that out and read the warning to the person when they need it," I suggested.

"Good idea." Her mouth drooped. "But with my luck I'd make a mistake and pull out a recipe card and find myself telling him to take a cup of chopped green peppers and add a half cup of chopped onion."

"That could be a problem."

"My older sister Shannon is a police detective down in Texas. She almost single-handedly solved a murder case involving a wife killing her husband, and she made a spectacular jump off a burning building in the process."

"Impressive."

"This after being valedictorian and prom queen of her high-school class and getting a full college scholarship to study criminology. We used to play cops and robbers when we were kids. I always had to be the robber, and she always caught me and snapped her play handcuffs on me. I've been handcuffed so many times I can't even stand to wear a bracelet," she added with more gloom.

"You haven't been on the police force long?"

"Is it that obvious?" she asked with a morose rattle of ice cubes in her glass. She answered her own question. "Of course it is. Shannon would *never* make that dumb alligator mistake like I did. Our folks are so proud of her."

I realized now why she had the stern hairdo and cultivated the even more stern expression. She was going to catch up with her sister, whatever it took. Probably up to and including jumping off a burning building, perhaps with much more disastrous results than sister Shannon had.

"What's your name? I mean, besides Officer DeLora."

"Maggie. No, *Margaret*," she corrected firmly. "I was always Maggie back home, but now I'm Margaret."

"So you came up here from Texas to be a police officer and get out from under your sister's shadow?" I asked.

"It's a big shadow down there."

"I'll call you Officer DeLora," I offered, thinking maybe that would help her professional image of herself.

"Margaret is fine when I'm not on duty." She hesitated, shrugged. "Maggie's okay too. Sometimes I forget to answer to Margaret."

Margaret/Maggie and Tasha/Tammy, both struggling with names. I'm glad I've always been fine with my Ivy.

"Did you always want to be a police officer like your sister?"

"I wanted to be a chef. A vegan chef. I like creating new recipes." Her face brightened perceptibly. "A new gazpacho I made last week turned out great." The light dimmed. "But a new recipe for gazpacho is so . . . insignificant compared to bringing justice in the world like Shannon does."

"Is your family vegetarian?"

"Are you kidding? If a meal doesn't include a slab of meat the size of a barn door, it isn't a real meal."

"I'm sure the Lord appreciates a good vegan chef as well as a good police officer. Not everyone is meant to be a cop. Maybe you should think about doing what you'd really like to do. Live up to your own dreams, not your sister's."

"I've thought about quitting the force," she admitted. Then her voice turned fierce. "But I won't do it without accomplishing something worthwhile and meaningful. So far all I've accomplished is the alligator mistake that created a new by-word for the force. If anyone does anything really dumb now, he's 'pulled a DeLora.'"

"And you're determined to change that."

"I don't want to go out a loser, which is what I am right now. I want to catch Lillian Hunnicutt's killer." She looked at her palm again, then squeezed her eyes shut, and I could see her repeating the word to herself. *Attorney, attorney, attorney.* "I *will* catch Lillian Hunnicutt's killer."

She jumped up with an alacrity that suggested a blast into immediate action.

"You're going to go catch the killer right this minute?"

"Well, no. A homicide detective is leading the investigation, not me. I haven't made Detective yet."

"You mean you won't be working the case officially?" I felt a guilty flicker of relief. Lillian Hunnicutt's murder needed more than a cop with a crib note on her hand. But a second flicker was regret. Whatever Officer DeLora lacked in expertise or experience, I was sure she made up for in determination.

"I've requested assignment to work with Detective Sergeant Atkinson on the case, but I don't know if I'll get it."

"Don't forget the Braxtons. They're involved."

"Right now I'm going home and get this stuff off my hand."

"And after the hand scrubbing, you're going to eat a slab of meat the size of a barn door?"

"Why would I do that? I'm a vegan." Then Officer DeLora narrowed her eyes at me. "Oh, I get it. You're making a point, aren't you? That I don't need to be a cop like Shannon any more than I need to eat like my family."

Okay, I'd made my point. Not subtly, but Officer DeLora got it. Subtlety is way over-rated anyway. "I suppose this is off the subject, but Tasha, the woman who was upstairs with the body when you first got here, was giving out tofu sausage samples at Heartland Grocery the other day."

"Really? I've never tried tofu sausage. Hey, maybe I'll stop over there and pick up some. It might be just what my new lasagna recipe needs."

"Happy eating."

***

Mac got back from the store right after Officer DeLora left. I passed along to him what she'd told me, that the dead woman was, at least for the moment, Lillian Hunnicutt, and the Deputy Chief of Police had a Braxton in his bedroom.

Mac's response wasn't unexpected. "Time to get out of Dodge, right?"

"No rush. I'm thinking the news that the real Ivy is back in town won't instantly work its way up to the Deputy Chief of Police, especially with the convenience store killings to solve. So the Braxton wife shouldn't hear anything through him about me for a while. And the Braxtons surely aren't watching the house now since they think they already killed Ivy Malone."

"Let's see about the headstone for Colin first thing tomorrow then," Mac said, apparently assuming that was what was holding me here now.

That was part of it, of course. But with the house clean and yard spruced up, this was beginning to feel more like home. Except for the hillbilly ambiance of the pile of smelly furniture in the back yard, and the slightly morbid touch added by the mannequin's head. "I'd like to get all that stuff hauled off too."

"Sure. We can do that with the pickup."

We watched another DVD that evening, then took a hand-holding stroll around the neighborhood. Afterward, we made separate trips into the house for showers in the downstairs bathroom, I guess because neither of us wanted to use that upstairs bathroom even if it was all cleaned and disinfected now. The hot water felt great, but I kept my shower short. Even in the downstairs bathroom, the shower scene in that old *Psycho* movie kept cranking around in my head. I didn't want to star in a Madison Street version of it.

And then I couldn't sleep.

I got up and listened to the radio. What I wanted was some soothing golden-oldies music, but what I got was call-in talk shows with callers spouting off about everything from crop circles to Bigfoot to conspiracies among toilet-paper manufacturers to make their paper ever thinner.

So I turned off the radio and just stared out the window at the house. Koop draped himself around the back of my neck, and I absentmindedly stroked both ends of him. His soothing purr rumbled through my body. I thought about my old home and Lillian Hunnicutt living in it, about the sadness of her life and the murderous Braxtons, about

86

Maggie DeLora's mixed-up ambitions, about Mac and me.

He hadn't said anything more about getting married. Maybe the proposal had a *delete by* date that had already passed. Did I want to be married? Sometimes it sounded like the happy-ever-after ending to a romance novel; sometimes it felt like a wrong turn down a one-way street. Maybe I'd just sell my motorhome and settle down to life by myself here on Madison Street.

A big pang instantly hit me. I'd miss Mac. Miss him a *lot*. The thought of Mac not being in my life felt like a big hole, not one that could be covered by moving a piece of furniture. And if I stayed here, the Braxtons would, sooner or later, come after me.

Could I outwit them, like that kid in the Home Alone movies? Rig up booby traps. Ensnare their feet in glue. Fix a net to fall on them. Dump cans of paint on them.

More likely, since the Braxtons weren't into slapstick, I'd wind up dead in the bathtub. Or dumped in a country creek. Or blown to unidentifiable itsy-bitsy pieces. Maybe I'd just disappear, and no one would ever know what became of me. Magnolia and Geoff would mourn me, and so would my niece and family down in Arkansas. Good friend Abilene out in Colorado, and Mac too. For a while. But eventually I'd just fade away, forgotten by all.

Would you like chips with that pity party?

I made a decision.

CHAPTER 8

I invited Mac over for breakfast, and we had waffles made on the microwave thingy I picked up at a yard sale. It was a great 50-cent investment. The waffles are crispy on the outside, fluffy on the inside, and I fixed bacon and scrambled eggs and fresh-cut cantaloupe to accompany them. Afterward, we took our coffee out to the lawn chairs under the maple tree.

From down the street, I could hear Eric Ockunzzi pounding in his shop. Birds twittered in the tree above us. A boy coasted by on a bicycle, feet on the handlebars. Across the street, the automatic sprinkler system was spreading a summertime fragrance of growing green things in Magnolia and Geoff's yard. A box overflowing with cucumbers sat in front of the yellow house down the street. A big sign said FREE! RECIPES INCLUDED! Koop perched on a branch high in the maple tree, Cat-King of the world, first time I'd ever known him to do something like that.

It was one of those moments that said, *You're home, and all's right with the world.* Yes, I'd made the right decision.

"Great breakfast," Mac said.

"I'm glad you enjoyed it. I was thinking shrimp salad for lunch." One of Mac's favorites.

He sat in silence for another minute before he said, "You're buttering me up, aren't you?"

I made an innocent gesture of hand to throat. Who, *moi?*

"Because you have something to tell me, and you figure I don't want to hear it."

"I've had a few thoughts after talking to Officer DeLora yesterday," I said cautiously.

"Such as?"

"Officer DeLora is a dedicated police officer, and she's determined to find Lillian Hunnicutt's killer. But she's so sure the impeccable Deputy Chief of Police wouldn't get mixed up with a family of unscrupulous criminals that she's downgrading my suspicions about the Braxtons."

"Downgrading as in pooh-poohing?"

Probably not a technical police term, but it worked for me. I nodded. "They think the killer was someone Lillian already knew and had trouble with in the past. Someone she was afraid of, which was why she was hiding out here."

"And your theory of Braxton involvement is just the rambling of a paranoid LOL."

I nodded again. Officer DeLora was more polite than that, and she might not even be consciously aware of the attitude, but it surely lurked down there in her subconscious. "I also keep thinking about the sad story of Lillian Hunnicutt herself. If they can't find any family, she may be in the morgue for who knows how long? With no one who cares about her. And it isn't right that her killers are just running around loose."

"I can agree with that, sure. But—"

"And the bottom line is, she's dead because of me." I held up a hand when Mac started to protest. "I know. I can try to squirm around that line of thinking. But it's true. I don't think any killer came out of the past to murder Lillian. The Braxtons did it. If it weren't for their vendetta against me, Lillian would still be alive."

"So you feel responsible for her death."

"Yes." The thought also occurred to me that maybe the Lord had been working on a different agenda all along. Maybe my coming back to Madison Street had more to do with the dead woman than with me. Had the Lord called me back because of her? First to find her there in the tub, and then to help bring her killers to justice? "I can't just run off and abandon her, as if her death were insignificant and trivial."

Mac drummed his fingers on his thigh. Finally he said, "You do realize the Braxtons aren't going to shrug and ignore you if you're right here under their noses, don't you?"

"I intend to convince Officer DeLora that the Braxtons are where the investigation should be focused."

"And jump right in to do it yourself if she doesn't go after them. Or even if she does," he added, still in gloom and doom mode.

I wasn't exactly planning to *jump* in. Though I might kind of *peek* in to see if I could help bring the Braxtons down. And I had an advantage Mac was forgetting, an advantage that even your average caped and masked superhero doesn't have. *Invisibility*. It was some time ago that I made the disconcerting discovery that I've aged into this state. People just don't *see* me anymore. That troubled me at first, but I'd quickly decided invisibility can be a handy asset. As it could be now.

"Ivy Malone, senior sleuth," Mac muttered. "Championing the cause of right over wrong. Bringing the evil to justice. You'd better get that cape patched up, and make sure it's in flying shape. And maybe practice some bullet-dodging."

"Missed taking our anti-snarky pill this morning, did we?"

Mac gave a long sigh. "You're a good, caring woman, Ivy Malone. A woman of character. True-blue. Trustworthy. Responsible. You care about people. You're willing to take risks for them."

I looked at Mac sharply. He was laying it on a little thick, but I could see from his eyebrow-scrunched expression that he wasn't into snarkiness or sarcasm now. He really thought all those complimentary things about me. I was flattered. Although I suspected that in this situation he also thought I was being a true-blue, trustworthy, caring, responsible *nincompoop*. That any woman with good sense would jump in her motorhome and run.

"You're also stubborn," he stated. "You are one stubborn, hard-headed woman. Which can be dangerous."

"Stubbornness can also be a useful, even admirable quality," I suggested. Stubbornly.

"If you say so." Then, as if he'd come to some decision, he slapped his thigh with a palm and stood up briskly.

"You're taking off already?" I asked, suddenly dismayed. I knew he'd be leaving before long, but I hadn't figured it would be this soon.

And this, I realized, might be a final parting. He'd made this big detour to see me, and I was stubbornly planting myself right here. I blinked, suddenly afraid I was going to go all girly with a flood of tears. I hid my emotions . . . stubbornly . . . behind a snappy question.

"Will you tell me one thing before you go?"

"What?"

"Why do you have a blue motorcycle tattooed on your arm? All the time I've known you I've wondered about that tattoo. You don't even have any interest in motorcycles. You told me that."

He lifted his arm and looked at the tattoo. It was very intricate, with lots of fine-line detail.

He let the arm drop. "No."

"No?"

"No, I'm not going to tell you. It's a secret."

"Now who's being stubborn?" I countered.

"It's an admirable quality, remember?"

Is there anything more frustrating than having your own words quoted back to you?

A wife would have a right to know. But you don't marry a man just to get the story on his tattoo. Besides, as far as I could tell, that hasty California proposal of marriage had been deleted, and marriage wasn't an option now.

I stood up too. I'd manage an unemotional goodbye

even if I had to blink my eyes sixty-seven times a minute to keep from getting all teary.

But what Mac said was, "I'm going to go find the closest RV park. I can't camp out in your driveway indefinitely."

"You aren't leaving?"

"Doesn't every sleuth need a sidekick?"

I thought I detected a hint of facetiousness in that question, but I was relieved. No, much more than relieved. Happy. Mac wasn't leaving!

But then he added, "I can't leave while the Braxtons are still after you," and my momentary joy morphed into indignation.

"I don't need a babysitter!"

Mac gave me an unexpectedly appraising look. "Ivy, when I look at you, I do not think of babysitting."

He had an equally unexpected gleam in his eye. Which gave me an unexpected thought.

"Should I be blushing?"

He winked. "Might be a good idea."

***

I thought Mac intended to drive around looking for an RV park, but he's more efficient than that. He let his fingers do the walking on his phone. While he did that I decided, with my cell phone now charged up, to make a few calls. First, my niece DeeAnn down in Arkansas to let her know I was back on Madison Street.

DeeAnn was doubtful about the wisdom of my being here, especially after I told her about the body in the bathtub, and she said to call her immediately if I needed a hideout or if they could help in any way. She said everything was fine with the family, and that grand-niece Sandy was now writing a teen news column for the local newspaper. She also said Sandy had a little gift for me. She wouldn't tell me what it was, just that she'd mail it up to me. I thanked her, but I felt a bit apprehensive. Sandy has a good heart but a sometimes rather startling teenage sensibility, and she keeps trying to prod me into the 21st century. Her previous get-with-it gifts have included thongs and toe rings. What now?

Then I called my young friend Abilene in Colorado and got some great news. She and her veterinarian husband were expecting their first baby next spring. They hadn't yet decided whether to find out ahead of time if it was a boy or girl. They were working on names for both.

I next tried to call my friend Matt Dixon, now stationed down in Arkansas with the FBI, but I couldn't reach him and left a message for him to call. "Just to chat," I added, so he wouldn't think I was in trouble. Again.

After that, I called the mail forwarding outfits through which my mail has been routed, and used my code to get everything changed to the Madison Street address.

Lastly, I called Magnolia and got a report on her latest genealogical adventure. Unlike meetings with most of the distant relatives she'd located, this encounter had not gone well. The woman she'd found was quite wealthy, with inherited money from a silver mine in Idaho, and she'd accused Magnolia of contacting her with a scheme for making some genealogical claim to part of the fortune. Of which, the woman had assured her, she wasn't going to get a penny.

"That's too bad," I sympathized. "I know you never had any thought of that."

"Of course not. And this coming right after I found the grandson of a third cousin's half-aunt, and he said I was ridiculous to think we were in any way related. That we probably didn't share more than six genes altogether."

"I think God gave us more shared genes than that, just because we're human."

Magnolia gave a big sigh. Magnolia is a hefty woman. She can give a really big sigh. "At the moment, I'm rather disheartened about my family."

Family used in the most all-encompassing way, of course. Because for Magnolia there's no relative too distant not to be embraced to her generous bosom as family. She doesn't so much have a family tree as a family jungle.

At the last minute I asked her if they'd received an offer on their place, as I had. She said no, but their mail hadn't caught up with them for almost a month.

"But I can't imagine selling out. Can you? I mean, Madison Street is our *home.*"

We talked a few minutes more, but she was so distressed about the unpleasant turn her genealogical investigations had taken that I never did tell her about the dead body in my bathtub.

By the time I finished the phone calls, Mac had located an RV park only a couple of miles away. He drove the motorhome and I followed with his pickup. The park looked new and probably hadn't even existed when I left Madison Street. He got a shady spot near the central grassy area with picnic tables and a horseshoe pit. He leveled the motorhome with the attached jacks, hooked up water, sewer and electricity, and unrolled the awning. Then we went out for the shrimp salad I'd suggested earlier. Afterward he dropped me off at the house, and I invited him back for dinner.

That afternoon, for the first time in much too long, I cooked in the kitchen of my old home. It felt, as grand-niece Sandy would say, awesome. Not that my motorhome's tiny kitchen is dreadful, but the house kitchen is so airy, the stove so large and roomy, countertops so generous I could tap-dance the length of them. Not that I'm quite up to tap-dancing in high places, but I did do a happy twirl beside the kitchen sink. The house filled with wonderful scents of pot roast and homemade bread and peach cobbler. Koop even deigned to come inside and settle on the kitchen window sill. The air-conditioner in the living room window sometimes sounded as if it were preparing to zoom off to outer space, but it cooled both living room and kitchen nicely.

I heard Mac's pickup pull into the driveway, and an old saying suddenly did a tap-dance of its own through my head. *The way to a man's heart is through his stomach.*

No way, I scoffed vigorously. I'd never resort to some cheap subterfuge like that . . . would I? Although I had to admit that sometimes my subconscious has an agenda of its own.

I was just getting the pot roast out of the oven when

a totally unrelated thought occurred to me. Nothing to connect it with what I was doing, no reason for the thought to pop into my head at this moment. But there it was. Actually doing more than *popping* into my head. The realization whammed into it like the whack of a baseball bat.

I just stood there with the hot pan of roast between my potholdered hands. I'd thought I was safely anonymous for a few days but—

Mac stuck his head through the door and sniffed appreciatively. He started to say something, but I cut him off.

"The Braxtons already know I'm here."

CHAPTER 9

"What do you mean?" Mac asked. "Have they been here and threatened you or done something?" He glanced around, fists clenched, ready to do battle with any lurking Braxtons. My hero! Although he'd be horrified if I called him that, of course.

"No, but— Remember I told you Officer DeLora said the Deputy Chief of Police had married a Braxton, so now her name was Haldebrand?"

"So?"

"At the time Haldebrand sounded vaguely familiar, but it didn't register with me why. Now it just came to me. That supervisor I talked to at the power company? Her name was Haldebrand." I plopped the pot roast pan on a hotpad on the counter. "So she doesn't have to extract from her police boss husband the information that I'm back in town to pass onto the Braxton clan. I waltzed right in and announced it to her. This might be where the Braxtons got the information that an Ivy Malone was living here before. The whole family has no doubt been wearing blisters on their fingers texting and facebooking and twittering the news to each other."

"The woman at the power company and the police guy's wife aren't necessarily the same person even if they're both named Haldebrand," Mac pointed out with what seemed to me unnecessary logic. "There may be lots of Haldebrands around."

"So you think I'm being paranoid?"

"I'm just pointing out a possibility. I don't suppose you know any first names?"

"Officer DeLora said the Braxton the Deputy Chief of Police married was . . . Susan. Or Simone. Or something like that. I didn't get the first name of the woman at the power company."

Mac got out his cell phone and started doing something with it that would totally baffle my non-smart phone.

"What are you doing?"

"Checking on Haldebrands in the area." He did thumb things for a minute. "There are several here, but none is identified as the Deputy Chief of Police. I see an Andrew and Clarissa Haldebrand—"

"No. I'm sure Officer DeLora didn't say Clarissa."

"There's an A.F. Haldebrand, and here's a Eugene and S. A. Haldebrand—"

"S.A.? That could be it."

"Also a Sylvester Haldebrand, a T. D. Haldebrand, and a Ted Haldebrand with a wife named Laura."

"So the Haldebrand woman at the power company may not be married to the Deputy Chief of Police Haldebrand." Which is exactly what Mac had said, of course. "Which means the Braxtons don't necessarily know I'm here." I tried to feel relief, but my bones had an unexpectedly achy feeling. Some people get an ache that says a change in the weather is coming. My bones aren't interested in weather predictions, and I'd never felt this particular ache before, but it definitely felt like a prediction. A *Braxtons-are-gonna-get-you* ache.

Mac started to clip his phone back on his belt but changed his mind and tapped something more into it. When someone answered the call he said, "I'm trying to locate a Mrs. Haldebrand who I understand works for the power company. I hope I'm not calling at an inopportune moment? I'm working on some genealogical connections, and I'm wondering if the Mrs. Haldebrand I'd like to talk to could be you."

Working on genealogical connections. Not an actual untruth. Mac has never done any genealogical research, but he has mentioned a couple of times that he was *thinking* about looking into his family background. They carried on several minutes of friendly conversation. Mac can talk to anybody about anything, and this woman was apparently happy to dive into genealogy. Now Mac tossed out various names – MacDonald, MacDermott, MacHenry – without ever actually including his own MacPherson, and they got deep into Scottish and Irish ancestry, how to do genealogical research while vacationing in Mexico, and, somehow, hobbies involving stuffed animals. During that time I put the roast back in the oven to keep it warm.

"So?" I said when he finally put the phone away.

"Her name is Sylvia, and she works for the power company. Her name before she married Gene Haldebrand was Braxton, courtesy of former husband Dwayne Braxton, with whom she has two daughters, Celeste and Beth. Her maiden name was McDougal. She's never been to Scotland or Ireland to check into McDougal ancestry, but she's hoping to persuade Gene to go next summer. She wondered about trying haggis. I advised her to start with a small bite, not a big mouthful. Scottish haggis is definitely an acquired taste."

An impressive amount of information for a few minutes of conversation. A little more time and he'd no doubt have known her date and place of birth, where she and Deputy Chief of Police Haldebrand honeymooned, and whether her belly button was an innie or an outie.

"I wonder if she still has close ties with the Braxtons?"

"She may have. She said one of her daughters lived with her grandmother, and they were having a big Braxton family get-together for the grandmother's birthday this weekend. She seemed like a nice, friendly person. She collects teddy bears."

"She didn't seem all that nice and friendly when she was telling me I had to pay that back bill on the electricity."

But Mac does have a talent for bringing out the nicer side of people. Now he added, "She names each of the teddy bears. Her latest is J. Edgar. Named after J. Edgar Hoover, whom her husband greatly admires."

I guessed there was as much logic to that as to my naming Koop after a former U.S. Surgeon General who was vigorously opposed to smoking.

I dished up pot roast and vegetables, sliced the

freshly baked bread, and added the salad I'd fixed earlier. We sat down to eat.

Mac was silent for several minutes while he ate double helpings of roast and asked for another slice of bread. Finally he said, "Does knowing it was a former Braxton you talked to at the power company change your mind about staying here for a while? We could be on the road within minutes."

Yeah, that was the great thing about motorhome life. If you didn't like your location at the moment, you picked up and moved, and took your whole life with you. For a few moments I was ready to do it.

But my reasons for staying kicked in again. My responsibility in Lillian Hunnicutt's death, which translated into a responsibility not to let the Braxtons get away with what they'd done to her. And this was *home.* The more I thought about it, the less willing I was to let the Braxtons run me out of it again.

Mac grunted as if he knew my response without my ever saying anything, and we continued the meal without words. I figured he was silently fuming about my stubbornness and what it would take to make me change my mind about staying. But when he finally spoke, after a big dish of peach cobbler, it wasn't about picking up and leaving.

"I don't think we should just sit here biting our fingernails and getting nervous ulcers while we wait for the Braxtons to mount an attack or an ambush or whatever they decide to do," he said.

"You never bite your fingernails or get a nervous stomach," I pointed out. Mac's stomach can take anything from a tsunami of garlic to chili hot enough to set a glacier on fire. His fingernails are unremarkable but also unbitten.

"I may start having trouble with both, worrying about you and Braxtons," Mac grumbled.

"Worrying is not a productive endeavor. The Lord advises against it."

"I know. It's like watering fake flowers. Keeps you busy but doesn't accomplish anything."

Not exactly Biblical words on the subject of worry, but maybe they were lost in translation somewhere.

"Whether or not I'm worrying is getting off the subject here," Mac added. "What we need to do is go after the Braxtons instead of waiting for them to come to us. Find out where they live, what they're involved in, what kind of relationships they have with each other. Where they're vulnerable. Check into family squabbles. Use the old divide-and-conquer technique to get something incriminating on them."

"I've had the impression that even if there are family differences, their desire to turn me into roadkill unites them."

"But no family is totally united. There are conflicts and internal feuds. We need to look for them."

"Okay. How?"

"The internet knows all. But first I need another dish of peach cobbler."

CHAPTER 10

After dinner, we drove back over to Mac's motorhome at the RV park. I had a computer for a while, but it crashed in a blue funk of death, and I haven't replaced it. Mac's laptop works on something called Wi-fi, which the RV park provided. I have an uneasy suspicion this is connected with a mysterious cyberspace cult with secret handshakes (or talon or tentacle shakes, whatever the case may be) and a language utilizing only two-letter words. Mac assures me, however, that it's a technology "everybody" uses these days. I suppose he's right. His laptop fired right up. Every time I seem on the verge of catching up with technology, it leaps right over me. Leaving me in a dust of pixels and bytes, ports and scripts, with enough acronym letters (DDR, BIOS, CPU, ISP) to make alphabet soup for an army.

Mac concentrated on the laptop, with me looking over his shoulder. He collected a list of a half-dozen or so Braxtons, with residential phone numbers and addresses. Also some Braxton businesses: Braxton Construction, Braxton Furniture, and an all-purpose Braxton Enterprises. No address for that one. Ever suspicious, the lack of address made me wonder if they were doing nefarious business from under a rock somewhere.

We also looked for the Zollinger name, possible relatives of the Beaumont Zollinger I'd helped convict. Braxtons and Zollingers are entwined because Bo Zollinger and Drake Braxton and a couple of others are half-brothers. Several residential addresses for Zollingers showed up. Also a Dr. Deena Zollinger, podiatrist, which rather surprised me since I'd never connected feet with a mini-Mafia. Maybe she had a concrete-shoe sideline? There was a Zollinger Brothers Computers & Communications business, and, rather ominously, it seemed to me, an Elton Zollinger, Attorney-at-Law. No doubt standing ready to find legal loopholes for any and all Braxton/Zollinger illicit activities.

Altogether, the Braxton/Zollinger spiderweb covered a wide territory and made a dangerous net of people who might have me on a hit list. I couldn't help a nervous glance out the motorhome window. Were they stalking me even now?

Unprompted by me, Mac made another quick search, this time on Radison Properties, the company that had made the offer on my house. A phone number and an address over in Illinois, the same information that was on their letterhead, was all that came up.

"Don't you think that's odd?" I asked. "Doesn't practically every business in the country have some kind of internet presence by now?"

"Did you ever try to call them?"

"No. Not yet." I'd put off calling until I stopped flip-flopping and settled on a definite plan for the future.

Although I was reminded of that old saying: *We plan – God laughs*. Not a malicious laughter, of course. But our plans may wander away from his, and he's the one in control.

"It almost looks like a front," Mac mused thoughtfully.

"Meaning—?"

"Maybe a company set up for the specific purpose of acquiring property without revealing who's actually behind the acquisition or what kind of company it is."

"Why would they do that?"

"Good question."

"Isn't it possible to dig deeper and find out who owns a company?" I asked.

"Probably. For a computer expert. Which I'm not."

Mac is so much better on a computer than I am that I think of him as an expert. "You're always doing research on the internet for your magazine articles."

"But I'm not usually looking for information someone may be purposely trying to hide."

Hide? "You think there may be something not quite legitimate about the offer on my house? Like it's a scam or something?"

I didn't really *want* to sell. I'd almost made up my mind I was here to stay. Yet the offer lingered in the back of my mind as an escape hatch if I needed it, and I didn't like the idea that it might be more trap than safety net.

"Not necessarily. Being secretive about company plans or new products to protect from piracy is a fairly common corporate technique."

But neither was it necessarily an admirable or legitimate technique if used to deceive the public in some way. The public, of course, including *me*.

Mac got into the tax assessor's records, which were public information, and found Radison Properties was indeed listed as owner of a number of properties in the Madison Street area, as well as a large piece a couple blocks over that had never been developed because it is so swampy. It had been for sale for years. The address for Radison Properties in the assessor's office was the same Springfield, Illinois, address as that on the letterhead to me. They were also behind on most of the property taxes.

Which also didn't necessarily mean anything, Mac said. Some companies simply did business that way, preferring to pay interest on the accumulated tax debt in order to use the money for current purposes. Although I tended to think that upright citizens and companies kept their property taxes paid up.

***

We went to an early Sunday service together the following morning, to the church I'd attended briefly before leaving Madison Street. A few people remembered and welcomed me, which was nice, but I answered questions about the intervening time with the vague explanation that I'd been "traveling." The pastor delivered an intriguing message linking Biblical prophecy with current Middle East events in the news. Biblical bad news: dangerous times are coming. Good news: so is Jesus. Afterward, we drove around checking out the Braxton and Zollinger addresses.

Drake Braxton, the man who'd threatened me at the end of the trial, had a gated residence of southern plantation style, with a tree-lined circular driveway. Money trees, from the looks of the place. He was apparently better off financially than I'd realized back then, or had done very well for himself in the intervening time. He appeared to be in the process of putting a huge new addition on to the house. Indoor swimming pool? It looked big enough. The other residences of both Braxtons and Zollingers were not as extravagant but definitely upscale. Deputy Chief of Police Haldebrand and his wife Sylvia lived in a big condo complex, nice but not champagne-and-caviar luxurious. No vehicles or people were in view at any of the residences.

We stopped for lunch at a Taco Bell and then went on to where Bo Zollinger's Thrif-Tee Wrecking was once located, and where I'd had a memorable encounter with a junkyard hound. A business manufacturing metal-fence materials operated on the site now, no indication whether it was owned by Braxtons and/or Zollingers. Bottom-Buck Barney's used-car lot, which Bo had also owned, was now a lawn-and-garden store.

Zollinger Brothers Computers & Communications, located in a strip mall, was doing a brisk business. I didn't go in, but Mac did and reported that in addition to computers and communications equipment, the store also carried safes and locks and home security equipment. He talked to a clerk and learned that, although the name wasn't changed, one Zollinger brother had bought out the other. She said the podiatrist-Zollinger was a relative, very knowledgeable and caring, opinion gained from the salesclerk's personal experience with ingrown toenails. Which didn't keep me from wondering about a possible concrete-shoe sideline. Also wondering if Ms. Zollinger was even now ordering extra concrete for a potential Ivy Malone fitting.

I didn't question how Mac had acquired those unlikely bits of information unrelated to computers from the clerk. I sometimes suspect Mac could get information out of a monk who'd taken a vow of silence.

The last place we went to see was the country address of an I.G. Braxton, a good eight or ten miles out of town. It was in an area of lush rolling hills, some wooded, some farmland, quite pastoral looking. The house was rambling ranch style, not as impressive as Drake Braxton's place, but it had the addition of a barn and stable, and white-fenced pastures enclosed black cattle and aristocratic looking horses. A sign arched over the driveway said "Braxton," with no indication whether it was a farm or ranch, or, given my sometimes morbid imagination, a covert setting for disposing of Braxton victims. An impressive array of oversized SUVs, chrome-heavy pickups, BMWs, and a Lexus filled a parking area. Identity of vehicles courtesy of Mac, because my capabilities there are limited to differentiating between pickups and cars. Except for old Thunderbirds, of course, because I have fond memories of the one I once owned.

It was no wonder we hadn't seen vehicles or people at the other homes; they were all congregated here. A *get-Ivy* brainstorming session?

A covered patio and large fenced yard screened by trees extended from one end of the house. We caught glimpses of kids chasing balloons in a playground of swings and slides, plus a couple of chubby pinto ponies lined up for rides. Rowdy country music blared from an unseen source, and an older woman danced with a toddler balanced on her feet. Smoke drifted from a barbecue manned by a guy in a cowboy hat, and a come-n-get it gong clanged.

I had to admit that it didn't look like a gathering of murderous conspirators. Was this the grandmother's birthday celebration Sylvia Haldebrand had mentioned to Mac? I reminded myself that looks could be deceptive. Even crooks and killers no doubt enjoyed the occasional birthday cake and pony ride.

I also had to consider the possibility there was no connection between the Braxtons and Lillian Hunnicutt's death. Or me. Maybe I'd spent the recent years hiding from people who'd forgotten all about me. Maybe some vindictive person truly had come out of Lillian's past to kill her.

I also reminded myself that just because the Braxtons and Zollingers didn't operate a business conveniently labeled Braxton/Zollinger Murder, Inc. didn't mean they *weren't* crooks and murderers.

The conflicting possibilities made my head feel as snarled and tangled as an unfortunate ball of yarn that had once fallen into Koop's clutches.

***

Back at the house, we had a supper of yesterday's cold roast beef, and then Mac went back to his motorhome to catch up on his e-mails.

I decided to enjoy a leisurely bath. I started to drag a chair from the kitchen to the bathroom to prop under the doorknob for protection, but at the last minute I scolded myself that it was time to stop acting as if a Braxton lurked in every dark corner. Although I did lock the back door. That wasn't paranoia, right? Just prudent.

I dumped enough bubble bath in the tub to suds up a small ocean, stretched out in the big tub, and relaxed till my fingertips went wrinkly in the hot water. I wished I could slip directly into bed, but I had to run over to the far side of the yard in my bathrobe to get to the bed in the motorhome. I hadn't taken my cell phone to the house bathroom with me, and it was tinkling when I stepped in the door. The caller was my FBI friend Dix, I saw from the information on the screen when I finally found the phone under Koop's belly on the arm of the sofa. For some unknown reason, he seems to consider the cell phone a personal buddy.

"Hey, Ivy, glad you called!" Dix said. "I didn't get back to you earlier because we were running down a bank robber. This guy thought he'd fool us by wearing a long red wig, big dangly earrings and fake fingernails, so we'd be looking for a woman."

"So did you look for a woman?"

"Crooks may be clever but then slip up on the basics. Rule Number One: if you're trying to look like a woman, be sure to shave. We nailed him."

"Good work."

"Thanks. Is everything okay with you, Ivy? We

haven't heard from you for a while. Are you still hiding out in the boondocks somewhere?"

"Actually I'm back on Madison Street." I filled him in on the offer on the house and the dead woman in my tub. "I've been suspicious that the Braxtons killed her, thinking she was me. But the police seem to think she was here hiding from some personal enemy, and I guess that's possible. She had kind of a shady past."

"Don't let your guard down, Ivy," Dix warned. "Even if the Braxtons didn't kill the woman in your tub, that doesn't mean they aren't out to get *you*. And don't let that mutant curiosity gene of yours get you in trouble."

Leave it to Dix to remember that I'm sometimes a little too curious for my own good.

"This doesn't have anything to do with that," he added, "but I was planning to call you even before you called us. Good news, I think. Though I suppose it's insensitive to call any death good news."

"Whose death?" I asked.

"Beaumont Zollinger. It happened back in June, but I just found out about it a couple days ago. He got in a fight with another inmate and was stabbed with a weapon made from paper clips the other guy had managed to collect while he was working in the prison library."

A paper-clip weapon. I suppose you could admire the creativity if not the deadly results.

"Anyway, now you don't have to wonder if Zollinger might escape or be released from prison and come after you himself."

I didn't go into a giddy whirl of celebration, but I couldn't squash a whoosh of relief. I'd sometimes wondered if Bo Zollinger's insistence on revenge was what fueled the Braxtons persistent search for me, and now that he was dead maybe their vendetta against me would languish. The family hadn't looked as if they were in mourning for him today. The gathering had appeared quite festive.

We talked a few minutes more, about the fixer-upper house he and Haley had just bought, and her job at a women's shelter. He, like niece DeeAnn, said if I needed help or a place to hide out to come to them right away.

Afterward I got a glass of iced tea from the fridge, but it was so hot in the motorhome that I went outside to sit in the shadows under the maple tree to drink it and consider the implications of Bo Zollinger's death. It didn't necessarily mean I was any safer than before . . . but maybe it did.

I talked a while with the Lord and this time made two decisions.

CHAPTER 11

I acted on one decision first thing next morning. I called Radison Properties to tell them I'd decided not to sell the house on Madison Street. I punched the numbers in fast before I could change my mind.

I didn't expect an instant pitch from some company bigwig trying to change my mind about not selling, but I did expect, if not an immediate secretary or receptionist, at least one of those menu things that might eventually result in contact with a live person. What I got was a canned male voice telling me to leave my name, number and why I was calling, and someone would get back to me.

Voice mail isn't a surprise when you're dealing with a one- or two-person business, but wasn't this rather odd for a company that must be involved in millions of dollars' worth of property transactions? I had the impression of a lone machine sitting in an empty room behind a locked door. I was so startled that I ended the call without saying anything. I told Mac about the call when he came over a few minutes later. I expected a comment on the peculiarity of this company's way of doing business, but he instantly jumped on a different aspect of the call.

"What did you call to tell them?"

"That I've decided to turn down their offer."

"Why do that if you'll be leaving when Lillian

Hunnicutt's killers are nailed?" He tilted his head and eyed me thoughtfully. "Except you're really not planning to leave, are you?"

Well . . . "I'm keeping my options about the future open."

"Maybe the fact that you didn't get hold of anyone is a sign that what you planned to tell them was a mistake. God's delaying tactic to give you time to make the right decision."

A sign was how I'd labeled the end of my library job in California, but I was reluctant to assign *sign* status to this uncompleted phone call. Although maybe Mac was right, and it *was* a sign that the decision to stay here was all wrong.

Ivy Malone, you're going all wishy-washy. Make up your mind and stick to it!

It isn't wishy-washy to change your mind if you've made a bad decision, I argued with myself. But I kept getting tangled up in which decision, to stay or to leave, was the bad one here.

"Are you going to call them again?" Mac asked.

"I think maybe I'll talk to someone who's already dealt with them first."

"Good idea." He didn't ask how I intended to do that. Good, because I didn't know. "So, are we going Braxton hunting again today?"

"I have some shopping I'd like to catch up on."

"Want some help?

"I can manage." Did he realize I was avoiding telling him what I was shopping for?

"Would you like to use the pickup? It would be easier than chasing around town in your motorhome."

I figured Mac would disapprove of what I intended to buy, so I didn't feel comfortable borrowing his pickup to do it. "Thanks, no. The motorhome will be fine."

He said he'd probably spend the day on internet research for a new article he was thinking about doing.

I didn't set out to do any full-scale snooping—really I didn't— but it occurred to me that I could slip into Braxton Furniture and maybe pick up some helpful information about Braxtons even if I didn't intend to buy there. I figured the store would be the furniture equivalent of Bottom Buck Barney's bottom-of-the-line used car sales, with immediate fumigation of any item purchased there required, but I was wrong. I didn't have to look at price tags to know the minute I stepped into the store that this was high-end stuff, way above my price range. A fact emphasized by the way the clerk with her heels and elegant angled blond bob sailed right past me to offer a welcoming, "May I help you?" to a fortyish couple in matching walking shorts.

I was momentarily miffed, then did a one-eighty reversal to pleased. Invisibility in full working mode! So what did I want to do with it? Prowling through office files might be a little iffy even for an invisible LOL, but I tried out several expensive beds and loftily gave them the Goldilocks *too hard* or *too soft* rating.

I strolled around and tried out sofas with prices that suggested the framework must be made of exotic wood grown on some exclusive tropical island, and the fabric woven from fairy hair by industrious elves with an excellent union providing top wages and elf benefits.

Then I spotted a sign, "Economy Smart Shop," with a sign pointing to a basement stairs. Braxton Furniture's snooty way of saying *bargain basement*? Curious about what this store considered "economy," I headed that way.

I checked the price of an overstuffed chair. Overstuffed with what? Hundred-dollar bills? At that price it should be. Not my idea of *economy*. I moved on and immediately stumbled over a pair of feet in the aisle. I managed to pick myself up before I hit the floor but not before giving the feet a good whack. I started to apologize but then realized that wouldn't be necessary. The feet were attached to long legs, and the legs attached to a flexible-bodied young man slumped on a beige sofa. For a moment, I thought—*oh, no, another dead body*. But then I realized that the young man was merely asleep, making vulnerable, snort-whistle snoring noises with his head thrown back. Some neighbors used to have a beagle that sounded just like that.

I started to tiptoe away, but his eyes popped open and he jumped to his feet.

"Can I help you?" Apparently I wasn't invisible to him, but he blinked several times as if I was out of focus. His dark slacks were rumpled and his white shirt scrunched sideways. A red tie flopped over a shoulder. He also had one of those little dabs of whiskers under his lower lip, the ones that look like the wearer should use a napkin to wipe away a hairy dribble.

"You work here?" I asked, surprised. He looked more like a customer trying out a sofa and accidentally drifting off to sleep. Or maybe a non-customer who'd just sneaked in for a nap in the kind of furniture he couldn't afford.

"Yeah. Sure. I work here. I was just, uh, resting." He fumbled with the red tie. "Can I help you?" he repeated.

"No, I don't think so. Thanks anyway. I'm looking for a new mattress, but the prices here are a little steep for me."

"Maybe you oughta shop somewhere else, then," he grumbled. Feeling guilty because he'd been caught napping? Or maybe he resented having that nap interrupted. Not a guy who was ever going to earn a Salesman of the Year award.

"Maybe you 'oughta' sleep somewhere else," I snapped back. "In fact, maybe I 'oughta' clue your employers in on your 'work' here."

"Hey, don't do that," he said, awake and alarmed now. He ran a hand around the back of his neck and wiggled his jaw as if it were still asleep. "They're already unhappy because I've been late a few times, and my dad'll kill me if I get fired."

"Why don't you get to work on time?"

"I never wanted to work here anyway."

The term *non sequitur* isn't in my everyday vocabulary, but the words fit here. I gave him a closer appraisal as he un-scrunched the shirt around his body.

"Summer job between college years?" I guessed. "You had in mind lounging by a pool and hanging out with your friends all summer, but your dad said you had to get a job?"

He shrugged, but the evasion of his eyes told me I'd nailed it.

"You should appreciate Braxton Furniture's generosity in giving you a job."

"They only did it because my dad made some deal with them."

Deal? Interesting. "I used to know some Braxtons," I ventured cautiously. "Drake Braxton, I think it was. He was in construction."

"That's Dirk's father. Dirk and Emily own the store."

Alarm twitched the muscles along my spine. I doubted if most of the Braxtons could pick me out of a lineup of LOLs, but my image was probably branded on Drake Braxton's vengeful mind. In spite of the twitch, I risked another question.

"Does he ever come in the store?" I glanced around uneasily, half afraid I'd find his beady eyes peering through an oversized arrangement of phony greenery nearby.

"I've seen him in here a couple times."

Okay, time for me to get out before Drake Braxton chose today to be another of those times, and I found myself in the river wearing concrete shoes. I took a moment more to ask, "Is Emily the elegant looking blond woman upstairs?"

"That's her. Dirk's the guy with the diamond ring big enough to put your eye out if he flashes it at you."

The answer, at least semi-snarky, suggested he may

Go, Ivy, Go!

have some issues with his employers.

"It was a rather close-knit family back then, but I heard . . .?" I let the question drift off, giving him a chance to fill in with information that might be useful. It was unlikely a sleep-on-the-job employee would know anything, but sometimes the most unlikely people *do* know something.

"Yeah, everyone's gung-ho on family stuff. Though—" I thought he was going to toss out something really juicy, but he broke off and eyed me warily, as if suddenly realizing gossiping about his employer's family might not be the smartest idea.

I offered gossipy encouragement. "I think some family member even went to prison for something."

"Yeah. Uncle Bo."

Uncle? "*You're* a Braxton or Zollinger?"

"Zack Braxton."

I did a mental head slap. I should have guessed he was family. They were tighter knit than bulletproof underwear. They might grumble about each other, but Braxtons took care of their own and closed ranks against outsiders.

"So who are *you?*" he challenged.

I wasn't about to identify myself as a person who had helped send Uncle Bo to that prison. I hastily changed the subject. "I don't suppose you know of a furniture store with prices more suitable for someone on a tight budget?"

"There's Reece's Thrift Furniture out on Monroe. They have cheap stuff." Said with appropriate Braxton disdain, of course. He might resent having to work here, but

120

Braxtons stood up for Braxtons. They shared an admirable family unity. Except I've been the unfortunate target of that unity.

"Okay. Thanks."

I scurried to the stairs but paused at the top step to glance back. Zack Braxton was wide awake now. He watched me with an eyebrow-scrunched speculation that made my twitch of alarm jump to a full-blown shiver. I liked him better when he was asleep, making boyishly vulnerable snorts and whistles. Now he looked every inch a Braxton. And not at all vulnerable.

***

I located Reese's Furniture, but the faintly musty smell of their beds and mattresses turned me off right at the door. I found a couple other places and finally, about mid-afternoon, a store with a fresh, new-furniture scent and fairly reasonable prices. I was looking at sofas on my way to the mattress area, trying to decide if there was any way I could afford both, when a helpful saleswoman suggested a sleeper-sofa. Hey, great idea! She opened one up for me, and I tried the mattress and gave it a Goldilocks seal of approval. We arranged for delivery the following day.

On the way home I stopped at a hardware store for some gardening tools. I also spotted a pocket knife almost like one Mac had lost a while back and bought it for him. After that I went into a big, all-purpose drugstore to pick up some of that expensive pink hand cream I sometimes indulge in, although I had to drive out to the far end of the parking lot to find a space big enough for the motorhome.

I was trying to figure out how to get a jar of the cream off a top shelf when a commotion a couple of aisles away stopped me. I peered around the end of the shelves to see what was going on.

A stoop-shouldered older woman in baggy clothes and shoes run over at the heels was yelling at a clerk about ignoring her, and the clerk was looking at her as if she'd like to de-materialize her on the spot. In lieu of that, the clerk suddenly turned and stalked off. The older woman lifted the bottle of heartburn remedy in her hand as if she were about to hurl it at the departing clerk. I rushed up to see if I could calm her. I knew the feeling. I'd wanted to throw something at an unhelpful clerk a time or two myself. But it's the kind of thing that gets you labeled senile and trucked off to an old-folks home.

"Hey, is everything okay?" I asked, even though I could see that everything obviously was not okay. "Can I help you with something?"

She glanced down at me. Even stooped, she was considerably taller than I am. Her blue eyes behind heavy glasses in cat-eye frames still sparked with indignation, but then she did a double take. "Ivy?"

I squinted up at her.

"Don't you recognize me?" She sounded delighted now. She straightened to her full height and yanked off the glasses. "It's me! Tammy. Tasha. I'm in costume."

I blinked, backed off a step and looked at her more closely. Okay, underneath the padding, baggy clothes and gray wig, I could see a bare hint of the tall, youthful neighbor back on Madison Street. I asked the obvious question. "Why?"

"This is my new acting role! I wear all this padding on my body and putty-stuff on my face. To make me wrinkled and saggy all over."

All I could do was again ask, "Why?" And point out, "This isn't exactly a stage."

"You don't have to be on a stage to act. This is the role I told you about, the one that's all hush-hush. Dr. Dennington is running an experiment to see how old people are treated differently than younger ones in the commercial world. She's going to do a paper or book or something on it."

"Maybe she intends to blackmail the stores that do badly. There are laws about age discrimination."

Tasha blinked, appalled. "Dr. Dennington wouldn't do *that*. She's a wonderful woman." Pause. "But she could, couldn't she?"

"You could be wearing a video camera to record what happens. You can get miniature ones that look like a pen. Or even like a button that pokes through a regular buttonhole."

"Ivy, what a devious mind you have," Tasha scolded, even as fresh interest sparked in her eyes. "No wonder you found a body in your bathtub."

I didn't see the connection, but maybe I am a bit devious these days. Comes with the territory when someone is out to make roadkill out of you. "So why didn't she just hire an older woman?" I asked. "*I* could tell her how we're sometimes invisible and get treated differently."

"Because she wants to see if the exact same person gets treated differently, depending on if she's young or old. I came in yesterday as myself and got treated very nicely here. The clerk spent extra time checking to see if they ever carried a particular brand of pills for cramps. Then I came back like this today—" She held out her hands and I could see that even they were in disguise, with dark age spots painted on the skin and fingernails yellowed. "And the clerk kept waiting on other people instead of me, and, when she finally did get to me, she got all irritated because I wanted a specific laxative I couldn't remember the name of. Dr. Denington said that was something an older person might do. And the clerk just made me so angry! Old people shouldn't be treated differently. I had no idea."

Welcome to the world of invisible LOLs.

"Well, you're doing very well at it." This, I realized, was what she'd been doing that first evening I arrived back on Madison Street, when I'd seen Eric and an older woman I'd assumed was his grandmother out walking together. Tasha had been practicing for this role. I gave her arm a squeeze. Her tense muscles still felt primed for action. She could have nailed that clerk. Maybe I should have let her do it. "I didn't recognize you at all. I really thought you were an old woman."

"Thanks." Tasha replaced the heartburn medication on the shelf, rearranged her baggy clothes and went into her stooped-over stance again. "Okay, I'm off to the cosmetics department. I was over there yesterday buying mascara and eyeliner. The clerk was very helpful. Let's see how she is today when I want to buy—what did blush used to be called?"

"Rouge?"

"That's it." The gleam in Tasha's eyes suggested this clerk had better get it right.

"Try not to throw anything," I advised.

"Okay. But maybe, if she's really obnoxious, I could just, you know, *accidentally* stumble into her and knock her flat. We old people are so unsteady on our feet, you know."

Hmmm. A technique I might keep in mind. "You're a bit devious yourself, Tasha."

We grinned at each other. She shuffled off to the cosmetics department, and I headed for the exit.

After I got outside I realized I hadn't bought the pink hand cream after all, but I didn't go back in. I shouldn't be spending money on a non-necessity anyway. I was going to need more furniture.

I intended to stop at a grocery store, but there weren't any parking spaces big enough for the motorhome, so I passed that up. But it made me think. Was it time to trade the motorhome in on a car, a nice little gas-efficient compact? I had, after all, made the decision to stay here. At least the semi-decision. I was buying furniture and garden tools. So I probably no longer needed a motorhome.

But getting rid of it would take away one more escape hatch . . .

***

I was still feeling uneasy about the encounter with

young Zack Braxton in the furniture store when I headed out to the RV park to give Mac his new knife. By going into the store, had I let what Dix calls my mutant curiosity gene lead me somewhere I shouldn't have gone? Maybe as soon as I left the store Zack had rushed upstairs to describe me to Dirk and Emily, and they'd mention to other Braxtons the odd fact that an old lady was suspiciously curious about the family and knew about a connection with Zollingers too. And then someone would hit on it. *That must be the old woman who nailed Bo at the trial!*

I know what both Dix and Mac would say. *Back off.* But if we were going to tie the Braxtons to Lillian Hunnicutt's murder, a hands-off approach wasn't going to work.

I found Mac tossing horseshoes with a couple of senior-age guys. He introduced me and they invited me to join their game. I think they were just being polite and thought I'd politely decline, but I didn't.

I have no idea why, since my coordination on most athletic endeavors equals that of your average garden slug, and I'd never even picked up a horseshoe until a few months ago, but on some days I can toss a horseshoe as if it were a guided missile. Other days, I can't wrap that horseshoe around the target stake any more than I could hit the moon with it. What would today be? We made up two teams, RV park Bob and me on one team, Mac and RV park George on the other.

It took a few practice tosses to get a feel for this horseshoe pit, but then I hit two ringers in a row. Hey, one of my hot-arm days! My partner, in red-plaid shorts and a golfer's hat, applauded, obviously surprised. My unorthodox toss, which makes the horseshoe somersault along the route, looks as if it couldn't possibly work, so it surprises everyone when it does. Including me. Partner Bob got one leaner and then threw one that looked as if he'd been aiming at a stake just west of Texas. Mac threw a leaner and then a ringer, although it was iffy until they stuck a ruler across the two ends of the horseshoe, and it didn't touch the stake. His partner made a couple of no-score throws, although they were close enough to measure.

"I feel like I've been pool-sharked," Mac's partner, George, grumbled when the game was over and he was on the losing side. He looked at Mac. "How come you didn't tell us she could throw like a pro?"

Mac graciously didn't mention my differing days of competence. "Just be glad Ivy isn't a gambling woman or she'd have cleaned us out," he said.

My partner Bob turned to me. "How about golf? We're going out to the Sunland course tomorrow morning. Would you like to come along?"

He apparently assumed my talent for horseshoes translated into an equal competence at knocking a little white ball around, but I had to tell him that I might as well try to hit Pennsylvania with a peanut as get that ball into a hole in the ground. I kept to myself my personal and no doubt unpopular view of golf, that it's about as interesting, and productive, as trying to catch flies with a toilet plunger. Though I suppose I might have a more positive view of golf if I were better at it.

With the impressive victory at horseshoes, my spirits lifted as Mac and I sauntered away from the horseshoe pit. I gave him the new knife, and he was delighted with it. I could even look at my encounter with Zack Braxton from a more relaxed perspective. He probably had no idea who I was and couldn't care less. He'd probably been watching me there at the top of the stairs only to see if I was going to go squeal to Dirk and Emily about his sleeping on the job. He probably never even mentioned this snappy older woman to them.

I dodged the fact that there were a lot of optimistic *probablys* in there.

I distracted myself by telling Mac on the way back to his motorhome about encountering neighbor Tasha and what she was doing in her old-lady costume, then asked him, "How did the research for your new article go?"

"Not great. Actually, I need to get your opinion on it before I go any farther."

"Oh?" We often discussed Mac's articles, but I couldn't remember his ever wanting my opinion on deciding whether he should actually do a specific article.

He'd left the air conditioning on in the motorhome, and the coach was delightfully cool. He poured lemonade into glasses and handed me one. We sat at the little dinette.

"The thing is, it isn't an article I'm actually *planning*. Though I might pick up something I can use along the way," Mac said. "What I'm thinking is that we need to get an inside track on the Braxtons and what they're up to. They're going to be suspicious if we just start snooping around and asking questions. However, if I ask questions as a magazine writer, we might make it work."

"You mean, come right out and ask questions openly? Not sneak around?"

"Yes."

That twitch I'd had in the Braxton's furniture store re-twitched. "That's getting into dangerous territory."

"Exactly."

We both contemplated the dangers for a lemonade-drinking couple of minutes.

"But we don't have to deliver the killers to the police all neatly hog-tied, case solved," I pointed out. "All we have to do is find out enough to convince them the Braxtons and Zollingers are solid suspects in Lillian Hunnicutt's murder so they'll start investigating."

Mac nodded. "Good. I'm a little short on hog-tying experience."

"So all we have to do is figure out an appropriate subject for an article. Something they'll want to talk about."

"Something that gives no indication of what we're really interested in."

"How about something to do with one of their businesses?" I suggested. A little uneasily I added, "I was in Braxton Furniture today. I met a young guy named Zack Braxton. He said Bo Zollinger was his uncle, and the store owner was Drake Braxton's son."

"You *talked* to him about the Braxton's connection with murder?" Mac looked at me as if I'd just dropped a spider in his lemonade.

"It wasn't an *in-depth* conversation. He was kind of smart-alecky, and the subject of Bo's imprisonment just kind of . . . came up."

"Let's stay away from Braxton Furniture," Mac muttered.

Good idea. Although maybe they had store security photos of me and were even now e-mailing or Facebooking them all across cyberspace to other Braxtons and Zollingers.

"Actually, there isn't any reason for you to go along when I ask questions," Mac said. "I've always done interviews alone anyway. So—"

I didn't get into an argument about my non-participation. I just ignored it. "How about looking into Braxton Enterprises?"

"Nothing on the internet about them. I looked this morning. And it's too vague. We need a more specific, out-in-the-open subject."

"How about those horses out at that country place where they were having the barbecue? They were quite elegant looking."

"Elegant horses," Mac repeated thoughtfully. "That might work. Do you know anything about horses?"

"I used to ride a neighbor's horse when I was a kid. I can tell the front end from the back end."

"Good. You're the expert then."

CHAPTER 12

So that was how we found ourselves driving slowly under the *Braxton* arch at the country place on Wednesday morning. Three horses with coats polished to a metallic gleam grazed on the other side of the white board fence. I'd call them *brown,* but there was probably some more elegant horsy term for the color. The horses really were elegant, even aristocratic looking, with sculpted heads and manes that looked as if they'd had a double dose of Miracle-Gro. The chubby ponies were in the same pasture, one of them teasing a larger horse by playfully nipping at a hind leg. Which the larger horse, apparently good-natured and tolerant of the smaller pest, ignored.

We hadn't called ahead for an appointment. As Mac pointed out, better they didn't have a chance to turn us down. Whoever "they" were. I wasn't in full disguise. It's easier to disguise a young woman as an old woman, like Tasha did, than the other way around. But I'd borrowed a floppy sunhat and oversized sunglasses from her and hoped for the best.

We drove on through the area where all the vehicles had been parked for the barbecue and around to the rear of the house. A young woman was working another brown horse in a circular corral between the red barn and sprawling white stable. A new-looking, oversized blue horse trailer stood alongside the corral. We parked and watched the willowy, pony-tailed girl as she guided the horse through a complicated pattern of circles and turns. She wore a protective helmet, but she sat the horse as if she were a princess in a rocking chair. Both horse and rider seemed to glide along. I was impressed. I'd always bounced like a ping-pong ball at anything faster than a walk on the neighbor's horse. Although this horse seemed to have a smoother gait than the ones I'd ridden. At least that was what I told myself in defense of my past riding bobbles.

We got out of the pickup and walked over to the white rail fence. The young woman circled the arena and stopped by us.

"Hi," she called, her smile friendly. "Are you looking for someone?"

Mac climbed up on the fence. I followed. He handed her a business card. She was younger than I'd first realized, not over twelve or thirteen.

"I write articles for various magazines, and I'm interested in doing something on horse farms in this area," Mac said. "You have some exceptional looking animals. Would someone have time to talk to us about them?"

Her face lit up. "Sure! I'd love to. Do you know anything about Paso Finos?"

"Not a thing."

She dismounted and stuck her hand between the boards. "I'm Beth Braxton. We have ten Paso Finos now, including the new filly born a couple weeks ago. Her name is Braxton's Silver Princess. Grandma always puts Braxton in the name. For publicity, you know, so when the winner's name is called at a show everyone knows where the horse came from even if you don't still own it."

Beth Braxton. Sylvia Braxton Haldebrand's daughter. She'd told Mac that one of her daughters lived with a grandmother. This girl might be young, but she was taller than I am, and her offer of a handshake seemed surprisingly mature.

"Mac MacPherson." Mac shook her hand and then motioned to me. "This is my assistant. She'll be taking notes."

Assistant? Taking notes? I didn't know whether to be pleased at a promotion or indignant at a demotion. Okay, whatever. I found an old scratchpad in my purse and waved it at her to certify myself as note-taker.

Beth tugged off the helmet. "Paso Finos are awesome animals—as you can see!" She affectionately patted the neck of the horse she'd been riding. He was sweating lightly and exuded a not unpleasant scent of warm horse. "Lots of people have never heard of them, but the breed goes way back and started from Barb and Andalusian horses down in the Caribbean islands, plus some gaited Spanish Jennet blood too."

I looked at my hand after she let it go. It didn't feel contaminated, but it did feel . . . strange. Even though she was too young to be involved in any Ivy-roadkill project, and she seemed bubbly and friendly, she *was* a Braxton. I guess I'd always suspected that the touch of a Braxton would leave a lurid stain, but my hand looked quite normal. Though a bit horsy smelling.

"They're not large animals, usually under fifteen-two," Beth added.

Mac smiled. "Interpretation?"

"Fifteen-two hands tall at the withers." Beth pointed to the high point on the horse's back, almost under the saddle horn. "A hand is four inches." In spite of her maturity, she gave a teenage-ish giggle. "That's just the way you measure horses. Weird, huh?"

"Not any weirder than nautical measurements like knots and fathoms," Mac said.

"Do you want photos? Our Braxton Handy Ann won both her halter and trail horse classes when I showed her at the Southern Missouri Regional Show a few weeks ago." She talked at gallop speed, as if afraid we might disappear before she could tell us all about Paso Finos. "And our new filly is awesome. I can't wait to start showing her. Grandma just got us a new horse trailer."

"Yes, I'll need photos. My camera's in the pickup."

"Do you take care of the animals here?" I asked in hopes of getting into something more helpful than the oddities of measurements. "Or maybe your dad or someone else in the family does that?"

"Oh, I wish I could do it." She wrinkled her nose. "I'd rather take care of horses than go to school. But Grandma says I have to get an education. Of course I *want* an education, so I can be a veterinarian. Grandma has a vet school in Colorado picked out for me."

"You take a bus and go to school in town now?" Mac

asked.

"I go to a private school. Grandma usually takes me. I can't even get a driver's license for *years* yet." Teenage groan.

"Do you have a Grandpa?" Mac asked.

"He died before I was born. But Grandma has pictures of him. He dug oil wells. She has an old one with oil spouting out of a well and splashing all over him."

Oil wells. That explained where some Braxton money had come from. Although Drake seemed to be making plenty on his own.

"Grandma says he liked race horses, and he won her in a bet on a horse race. But I think she's just making that up. People don't *win* people," she scoffed. "But I'm glad she loves horses, like I do."

"All the horses here belong to her?" Mac asked.

"Yeah, but I do the training and showing. Wayne, he's the foreman, manages the farm, the cattle and stuff. Well, he does some of the horse training too," she admitted, apparently too honest to claim it all for herself. "Dad doesn't even *like* horses. No one does, except Grandma and me. Uncle Drake calls them a big money suck."

For a moment I felt guilty taking advantage of Beth's chatty innocence, but that didn't stop me from asking, "What does your dad do?"

"He's working for Uncle Drake now." She broke off the chatter. "Oh, hey, I'm sure it's okay if I talk to you, but I'd better go ask Grandma." Beth draped the reins around a board and climbed over the fence with youthful energy and agility. "Be back in minute!" she called over her shoulder as she dashed toward the house.

Asking Grandma's permission was admirable, but I was uneasy when I saw Beth had Mac's card clutched in her hand. There was nothing to give my name away, but, in the Braxtons' murderous search for me, they may have run across Mac's name too. I felt a panicky impulse to jump in the pickup and *run*. But I got a firm grip on the arena fence and rejected that thought. We might be in dangerous Braxton territory, but that's where we had to be to get any information.

"What do you think?" Mac asked. "Can we find out anything useful here?"

"I don't want to get this girl in trouble. We need to be careful what we ask her."

Mac nodded, but when Beth returned, she bubbled with eagerness to talk.

"Grandma will be out in a few minutes. She has to look you over. She just had another birthday, and you know how old people fuss and worry about strangers. Like there's a zombie or vampire behind every—"

Her face flushed as she apparently just then realized *old people* was *our* generation, but what I was thinking was that maybe Grandma saw any stranger as a potential boogeyman because some Braxtons *are* boogeymen. Or did Grandma even know that about her family? Maybe not, if she was wrapped up in horses and grandchildren. It must have been her I'd seen dancing with a toddler balanced on her feet at the barbecue.

"I didn't mean—I *mean* Grandma's really neat! Mom says she's old-fashioned as an eight-track tape, whatever that is, but she knows all about horse bloodlines and stuff. She's teaching me to play chess too."

We were getting way off track here, but Mac went with the tangent. "Do you like chess?"

Beth wrinkled her nose again. "Well, actually, it's kind of boring. But Grandma says if I can beat her three times, I can get a tattoo. I know she thinks she's safe with that, because I've never beaten her so far. But I'm going to!"

"What kind of tattoo?" I asked, mildly apprehensive as I considered the bizarre tattoos I saw everywhere.

"A butterfly on my ankle. A purple one. Or maybe a horse head."

As tattoos went, those didn't sound too bad, but this conversation wasn't getting us anywhere. Beth apparently thought so too, although her idea of keeping the conversation on-track was telling us about horses.

An important point about Paso Finos, she said, was that they didn't trot like other horses. They had this much smoother gait in which each foot struck the ground separately. (Hey, I was right! It was a different gait.) The slowest form was called the *paso fino*, like the horses themselves. A little faster gait, about the speed of a trot, was the *paso corto*. The fastest was the *paso largo*. I had to ask her how to spell those words, and she knew.

"They're all just like floating on air!" she added."

She rushed on, enthusing about how the animals were noted for being sure-footed and intelligent. They made especially fine trail horses, both in show ring trail-horse classes and out on real trails. She wanted to enter an endurance race with one next summer.

She glanced at me every once in a while, probably to see if I was taking notes. I'd started out just scribbling meaningless words. *Pretty horses. Nice girl. Bubbly.* But Beth really knew her stuff and I started taking notes for real. Maybe Mac actually could do a magazine article with this information.

When she finally slowed down, I asked, "If no one else in the family likes horses and cattle, what do they like?" I kept an eye on the rear door of the house as I asked. We probably didn't have much time before Grandma arrived. She might not be so chatty.

"Oh, you know. Boring stuff. My sister is getting married this fall, so all she's interested in is a wedding dress Grandma's having made for her, and where to go on her honeymoon and all that." Beth wrinkled her nose with disinterest in wedding details. "My cousin Zack is into gaming big time—"

"He *gambles*?"

Beth gave me one of those what-planet-do-you-live-on looks that I get way too often. "Not gambling. *Gaming.* Video games."

"Oh."

"Uncle Drake likes antique cars. There's a bunch of them over in the barn." She flicked a thumb in that direction.

My mind leaped away from how behind the times I was in teen-speak and grabbed onto *antique cars*. The man who'd managed Bottom Buck Barney's for Bo Zollinger had a collection of antique cars back then. Had Drake Braxton managed to latch onto the expensive collection after both Bo and the manager of his used-car business wound up in prison?

"My cousin Deena is a podiatrist. She collects dolls, but only ones with real looking feet. Because that's what podiatrists like you know. *Feet.*" Beth's can-you-believe-it? tone suggested how far down both dolls and feet were on her scale of importance. "My cousin Sam has a computer store—"

"Zollinger Brothers Computers?" I put in casually.

"Yeah. His brother, my cousin Tyler, they're twins, used to be in the store too, but Grandma helped Sam buy Tyler's half, and Tyler's working for Uncle Drake too now."

By now, all these cousins and uncles were colliding in my head, like cars in a demolition derby, but I figured we needed to grab any available information, even if it might seem irrelevant at the moment.

"Does Tyler have a family?" I asked.

"He was married, but now he just has girlfriends." Beth giggled. "Way too many girlfriends, Grandma says. The last one had blue hair. It looked really neat."

"Are you going to get blue hair?" I asked her.

"Are you kidding? Grandma'd freak out."

"It sounds like a very caring, close-knit family," Mac said.

"Grandma says that's what wrong with the world today, that families don't stick together like they used to."

I saw Grandma come out of the house, and I snuck in one more important question. "What kind of business does your uncle Drake have?"

"Umm . . . I'm not sure. It's down in Arkansas or Illinois or somewhere. Tyler used some of Grandma's money he got from selling out to Sam to buy a plane, and he and Uncle Drake are always flying around to meetings and stuff. Aunt Iris goes too, sometimes. Tyler said he'd take me up sometime, but he's never done it. I didn't see anyone in the family for a while, when Mom and Dad got divorced, but then Grandma said I should live here and go to the River Hills Academy. Do you want to take a picture of Rascal before I put him away?"

I had more questions about Drake's business, but Grandma Braxton was only a few yards away now. Although she apparently spent a lot of money on family, horses and private school for Beth, wedding dress for the sister, helping Sam buy out his brother's interest in the computer company, probably podiatry school for Deena, it looked as if she didn't splurge on herself. Mom-style jeans, faded at the knees and baggy around the hips. Shapeless plaid shirt. Gray hair frizzed into a too-tight perm. Scuffed cowboy boots. A build that had probably been petite when she was younger but had now gone a little dumpy.

I headed for the pickup to get Mac's camera . . . running errands, that's what we assistants do . . . and Grandma and Mac were shaking hands when I got back. I heard a kind of far-off whinnying sound, and Beth giggled as she unclipped a cell phone from her waist.

"My cousin Sam put the horse whinny ringer on the phone for me." She looked at the screen, thumbed in a quick response and put the phone away. "He wrote some kind of special program for Grandma's computer too, so she can keep track of all our horses' bloodlines."

Clever Sam, with all sorts of talent and resources with technological equipment. Had he also been helpful using technology to keep track of my whereabouts?

Up close, Grandma wasn't stooped, like Tasha's version of an older woman, but she didn't appear to be making any effort to look younger than she was. Her face was rosy-cheeked with senior good health, but it hadn't been Botoxed of wrinkles. Flour smudged her jeans. Maybe she wore cowboy boots even when baking cookies? But the diamond studs in her ears were big enough to act as beacons for lost ships, so she apparently spent some money on herself. Or maybe they were a long-ago gift from oil-well-digging Grandpa Braxton.

Beth introduced me to her grandmother, making an assumption and calling me Mrs. MacPherson. I started to correct her, but I caught myself. I certainly didn't want to give my real name. Mac gave me a quick wink, apparently not objecting to instant acquisition of a wife.

Grandma looked at Mac's card that Beth had given her, then asked him bluntly, "Do you have identification?"

The question obviously startled Mac, as it did me. He reached for his wallet. "I have a driver's license—"

"No, I mean identification that says you really are a magazine writer, not just someone snooping around asking nosy questions."

I thought she had us there, because we *were* snooping, but Mac went over to the pickup and came back with a manila envelope of clippings. He was prepared to show he really was a published writer. Good thinking. Mrs. Braxton took her time looking through the clippings and asking questions. Apparently his magazine-writing history passed inspection because she put everything back in the envelope and handed it to him.

"Thank you."

She obviously didn't intend to explain further, but Beth seemed suddenly uneasy that Mac might take offense at this scrutiny and decide not to write about her horses.

"Oh, Grandma, it's okay. Mr. MacPherson isn't like that creep who worked here a few days and then tried to steal one of Uncle Drake's cars out of the barn."

"I don't have a specific assignment to do an article on Paso Finos, so at this point I can't say in which magazine it might appear," Mac said. "I'd planned to write the article about horse farms in this area in general, but now I think I'll do it solely on the Braxton Paso Finos."

Grandma Braxton nodded as if that pleased her. She didn't smile, but she sounded somewhat more approachable when she said, "Perhaps I do tend to be overly cautious. But, as Beth mentioned, we recently had an unpleasant situation with a man I hired for yard work. He didn't get one of the antique cars, but he did make off with a valuable show saddle."

I let out the breath I didn't realize I'd been holding.

Yes, Grandma was suspicious, but, blessedly, not suspicious of what we were actually doing.

"Can I go get Storm now so Mr. MacPherson can take a picture of him?" Beth asked. "He's our stud," she added to Mac.

"Find Wayne and let him do it," Grandma said. Beth ran off in the direction of the stable. Grandma's fond gaze followed her. "Beth is very good with the horses, and Storm is well mannered, but I don't think she's old enough to handle a stud yet."

While Beth was looking for the foreman, Mac asked questions about why Mrs. Braxton had chosen Paso Finos as the breed to raise and show, and what her own background was with horses. I kept my mouth shut and took notes. She must have been at her son's trial and heard me testify against him, but at the moment, invisibility, with the aid of an oversized sunhat and sunglasses, seemed to be working.

Wayne, the foreman, brought the stud out, and Beth got the mare with the new filly. I couldn't tell if the filly was "awesome," but she was cute and frisky. Mac took dozens of digital photos. Of the horses and Beth riding them, of course, but also the farm buildings and the new horse trailer and Grandma Braxton herself. She fussed a little about putting on some nicer clothes for photos, but Mac assured her this image was exactly what he was looking for, a real working horsewoman. He told her he'd show her a copy of the article before he sent it anywhere for publication. Good. That gave us reason to return if we needed to do more snooping.

We were just finishing up when a vehicle roared

down the driveway, big and black, with tinted windows, blocky but sleek, and as menacing as a tank. Even I, with my limited vehicle-identification skills, could tell it was a big-bucks Hummer. It skidded to a stop next to the corral. Two men got out. I didn't recognize the one in ostrich-leather boots and cowboy hat, but, even though I hadn't seen him since the trial, I knew the driver instantly. The appearance of someone threatening to turn you into roadkill does tend to stick in your memory. Drake Braxton. Big and beefy, heavy-set, thick-necked, beady-eyed. More menacing than the oversized vehicle he was driving.

I looked for a hole to crawl into. A tall building to hide behind. Nothing. I ducked my head and made myself busy stuffing the scratch pad in my purse and hoping for a full cloak of invisibility. One that covered Mac too.

Grandma Braxton scowled at her son. "I swear, I am going to have speed bumps installed on that driveway. Big ones."

"You do that, Mom. And the axle on that Corvette of yours will be the first casualty. Your driving makes mine look like a snail next to a race horse." Drake gave her a jovial smile even though I heard a caustic edge to the words.

"At least I'm not racking up speeding tickets."

Drake looked as if he were about to make a retort, but he managed to keep smiling even as he gritted his jaw. He turned to the man with him. "Is your mother like this? When I'm old and gray, mine will probably still be telling me to eat my vegetables and wipe my feet at the door."

The exchange between Drake and Grandma Braxton

could be affectionate family teasing. Drake was trying to make it look that way, but that sharp edge to the conversation suggested some real animosity.

"How come you're here today?" Grandma added. "No business trip?"

"Look, Mom, I know you're unhappy because I didn't make it to your birthday barbecue, and Tyler couldn't be here either, because I needed him to pilot the plane. I'm sorry about that. But you know how important these meetings are—"

"Of course. Business comes first." Congenial words. Sarcastic tone. A crack in the Braxton family solidarity? Interesting. "You used to put family first, but now—"

"I said I'm sorry. We won't keep you from whatever you're doing," Drake said stiffly. His gaze flicked over both Mac and me without interest, ranking our level of importance down there with the horse droppings in the corral. Good. Where Drake was concerned, that was exactly where I wanted my level of importance to be. "We're just here to look at the '75 Thunderbird. I'm thinking about trading it on a Porsche Mr. Rawlings here has available."

My mouth opened to say something. He had a '75 Thunderbird out in the barn? Oh, I'd like to see it. My old Thunderbird was a '75, and I still had nostalgic feelings about it. But Mac silenced me with a jab of elbow.

Rescued before my curiosity got us in trouble. *Thank you, Mac.* That Thunderbird I remembered so fondly was the very one the Braxtons had tried to blow up down in Arkansas. My showing interest in this Thunderbird might light a dangerous bulb in Drake's memory.

"You're not thinking about putting another car in there, I hope," Grandma said. "You never said anything about keeping all those cars in there all this time."

"No, Mom. When I get the Porsche, it won't be sitting in the barn. I'll be driving it."

"I wish you'd just get all the cars out of there. Sam needs the space for his new boat."

Sam. It took me a moment to organize the demolition derby of family names in my head. Sam, the twin brother of Tyler, now sole owner of Zollinger Brothers Computers, both sons of Bo Zollinger.

"You bought Sam a new boat?" Drake asked.

"Sam works hard, but he puts family first," Grandma Braxton snapped. "And we need more space in the barn for hay too."

"More hay for more horses? At least the cars just sit there. Not eating truckloads of expensive hay or producing more truckloads of manure." As if suddenly realizing the cowboy-booted Mr. Rawlings might take offense at this attitude toward horses, Drake laughed and added, "Just kidding, of course. The horses are great for the kids."

"Uncle Drake, this is Mr. MacPherson," Beth interrupted. "He's going to write a story about our horses for a magazine. With lots of pictures."

An introduction was the last thing we wanted, but I knew Beth was trying to distract Drake and protect her beloved horses from his "money suck" attitude about them.

The introduction startled Mac too, but he managed a

quick recovery "A beautiful establishment Mrs. Braxton has here. With a very accomplished young horsewoman assisting."

Drake nodded, but he was looking at us now. Really *looking*. At Mac for a moment, then at me for a much longer moment, and I didn't feel at all invisible. His expression didn't register recognition. He surely wasn't expecting to see *me* here. But there was definitely a puzzled, do-I-know-this-old-lady? wrinkle across his forehead. Was he seeing me behind the sunglasses? Had my invisibility fallen away like the flabby pounds on some woman in a TV weight-loss ad?

"This is Mrs. MacPherson," Beth said, as if even she caught something beyond the normal in her uncle's gaze. "She helps him with notes and research."

"Thanks again," Mac said. "Nice meeting you," he added to Drake and then spun me around as if I were a rusty mannequin.

Surely Drake wouldn't remember where he'd seen me, I assured myself during what seemed a mile-long hike to the pickup. All little old ladies look alike, right? Unless you keep a photo of a specific one on your nightstand, and every night you look at it and vow *You're roadkill, lady. I'm gonna get you.*

We got in the pickup. Mac turned it around and headed down the driveway as sedately as any geezer sightseer. I risked a peek back over the seat. Drake Braxton and his cowboy-hatted friend had started around the corral to get to the barn.

Big flood of relief. I was forgotten.

But then Drake turned and looked back at our departing pickup. From this distance I couldn't see the expression on his beefy face, so all I could do was wonder:

Was he still trying to remember why I looked vaguely familiar?

Or was he thinking, *hey, didn't we kill that old lady once already?*

CHAPTER 13

"I take it that was the notorious Drake Braxton?" Mac said when we were back on the main road.

"In person." One of Drake's sons and one of Bo's sons had been with him that day he threatened me at the courthouse. I doubt I'd recognize either of them, but I'd know Drake if I saw him across the room at a thousand-thug convention.

"I got the impression that Mrs. Braxton wasn't any too happy about Drake's new business, whatever it is," Mac said.

"Is there any way we can take advantage of that?"

"I'll have to think about it. Do you think he recognized you?"

"I'm not sure."

Although I was sure I might be smarter if I filled the gas tank on the motorhome and made a run for it rather than buying new furniture for the house and planting myself here.

But this was *home*. And I couldn't let the Braxtons get away with killing Lillian.

"I wonder what kind of business Drake could have over in Arkansas or Illinois?" I asked. He'd been into construction and land development with his Braxton

Construction business when I tangled with the clan before.

"I'll do some more digging on the internet," Mac said.

***

We had an unexpected surprise back at the house, and this time it was a *nice* surprise. I ran across the street and through the open gate. Magnolia dropped the plastic bag of clothes she was carrying from motorhome to house and threw out her arms.

"Ivy!" She enfolded me in one of her BFF hugs. Best friends forever, in grand-niece Sandy's current vocabulary. It had been months since we'd seen each other.

"I'm so glad to see you!" I said a bit breathlessly. When Magnolia hugs, you know you've been hugged. "But I had no idea you were coming. What are you doing here? How long are you staying?"

"It just seemed like a good time to come home."

Magnolia was in one of her usual voluminous, swirly outfits that tend to magnify rather than conceal her imposing shape. The oversized flowers printed on it echoed her name. Her hair piled high atop her head was gray now, not one of her usual more flamboyant shades of pink or red. Ah, but Magnolia's gray was nothing like my inconspicuous possum gray; hers had a definite glitter that on closer inspection I realized came from some kind of spray-on stuff. Could I do that? Looked great on her. Although on me it would probably have people wondering if I'd acquired some virulent new version of dandruff.

"We may be here for some time," she added.

"You've given up on finding more members of your family/?"

"I've decided using the internet may be the way to do family research these days, and I can do that from here."

"You know how to use a computer now?" I asked doubtfully.

"No. But how difficult can it be?" She waved a dismissive hand. Magnolia is never shy about meeting new challenges. This is the woman who, with no previous experience, joined a chorus line out in Colorado and shimmied her way to a spectacular performance. "Oh, I'm just so glad to be home! You are too, aren't you?"

"The neighborhood has changed since I left. So many houses are vacant or rentals now. I'm not sure anyone I knew is still here."

"What we need is a good barbecue to get everyone together," Magnolia declared. "I'll get on it right away. Oh, I didn't have a chance to tell you, but after you called, our mail finally caught up with us. That same company made an offer on our place."

"What do you and Geoff think?"

Behind us, Magnolia's husband Geoff and Mac were shaking hands and talking motorhome gas mileage. They were good friends too, but they didn't go way back the way Magnolia and I did. Geoff is a contrast to Magnolia's flamboyance; he's compact and wiry and a little reserved. But underneath that mild-mannered and rather colorless exterior, he's solid as a battleship anchor, and admirably tolerant of Magnolia's quirks. If Magnolia wanted to look for family on the moon, Geoff would surely start inquiring about rocket rides.

Another dismissive wave from Magnolia now. "We've discussed it, and Geoff says it's a generous offer. But I can't imagine our actually *selling*. You're not, are you?" Her eyebrows, full-figured as the rest of her, lifted in mild alarm.

"I just today bought a new sleeper-sofa for the house," I assured her. The implication, of course, being that no one who buys a sleeper-sofa is on the move. I sneaked a side glance at Mac. I really should tell him before—

Too late. A van with the furniture store's name on the side was right now turning into my driveway. I headed across the street. "Hey, come over for dinner this evening, okay?" I called back to Magnolia. "We have a lot to talk about."

Mac caught up with me. "What's with the furniture store van? They must have the wrong address."

Two men were already opening rear doors and letting down a ramp on the van.

"They're delivering something I bought."

"You're buying *furniture*?"

"A sleeper-sofa. It's more practical than getting a new mattress for the bed. Now I'll have a sofa and a bed too."

"Very practical," he muttered. Approving words, but the feeling behind them was about as enthusiastic as if I'd announced I'd sent the Braxtons a housewarming invitation. I knew he saw the acquisition of furniture as my putting down ever deeper roots on Madison Street. Well, he was right.

I hurried on ahead and got the house unlocked and door open for the delivery men. It took only a few minutes for the husky guys to deposit the plastic draped sofa on the far side of the living room. That wasn't where the old sofa had been, but I thought this was a better location for sleeping.

"Enjoy your new sofa," one of the men said as he handed me the delivery ticket. He glanced around the otherwise empty room. "And if you need more furniture, be sure to keep Laurance's in mind."

"Oh, I will. Thank you."

I followed the men out to make sure they hauled off everything the saleswoman had agreed to with my purchase of the sofa. Although I have to admit I'd been a bit fuzzy with her about the smell aspect. One man scrunched up his face and the other coughed when they picked up the mattress, and they both looked at me as if wondering how this inconspicuous little old lady had managed to imbue her furniture with such an odor.

"There was a dead person in my bathtub," I explained.

They looked at each other, and I could tell they were skeptical about this as an explanation for the smell. But finally one man muttered, "If you say so," and they trundled off without asking questions.

After they also loaded the old sofa and chair in the van, I gave them a nice, well-deserved tip. It was only after they were gone that I realized I should have bargained for inclusion of the old drapes and mannequin head. Now the head sat there like some macabre growth sprouting in my weed-patch, and the drapes smelled as if something had died in them. Which was too close to the truth for comfort, of course. When I went back inside, Mac had the plastic covering stripped off the sofa and Koop was doing a prowl-by inspection.

The light blue sofa went nicely with the darker blue carpet, although it also looked a little lonely as the sole piece of furniture in the room. I'd left the house fully furnished, but by now everything had disappeared. Maybe Lillian Hunnicutt had a sideline selling used furniture?

"I'm going out to the motorhome for some bedding and get everything ready so I can sleep in here tonight."

"You're sure that's a good idea?" Mac asked.

"That's what I bought the sleeper-sofa for."

"You could move the motorhome out to the RV park and stay there. It might be better to keep out of sight until we get something to take the Braxtons out of action."

Maybe I should do that. Meeting Zack Braxton yesterday had rattled me, and going eye-to-eye with Drake Braxton today made me feel as if I'd stepped into a rattlesnake pit.

But I immediately dumped the idea of hiding out at the RV park. This was my *home*, and I'd let the Braxtons keep me away from it much too long. Tonight I was staying in it. Though I might consider some kind of defense system, just in case.

Apparently picking up on my negative response to his suggestion without my voicing it, Mac said, "I'll head on out to the RV park, then."

"You'll come back for the dinner I'm cooking for Magnolia and Geoff later?"

He hesitated, as if he might be going to decline, which was an uneasy reminder that our relationship had changed. I was home. He wasn't. But, after not seeing Magnolia and Geoff for so long, skipping dinner with them would be rude and Mac wasn't like that. He finally said, "Sure. I'll be here."

***

I piled the sofa cushions in a corner of the living room and pulled out the concealed mattress that made a bed. It was queen size, same as the bed in the motorhome, so my old sheets and blankets would fit fine. I intended to fold it up again, but Koop curled up in the middle of the mattress, and I didn't want to disturb him. I moved his cat bed into the house—occasionally he does like to sleep in it—along with his sack of dry cat food. There wasn't a regular clothes closet in the living room, of course, so I stuffed as many clothes in the little coat closet by the front door as it would hold. By then I was really into moving mode and carted stuff from motorhome to house until it was time to start dinner. Soon I'd have a big decision to make: should I sell the motorhome and buy a car? Or keep it in case I needed a fast escape in the middle of the night?

I decided on meat loaf and baked potatoes for dinner. On impulse I went down the street to invite Tasha and Eric.

I found Eric working in the yard outside the shop. Their back yard was almost a jungle of trees, green leaves spreading a cooling canopy overhead, more shade from the tall hedge running from house to garage. He was putting the motorcycle-handlebar horns on the cow and said Tasha was at a downtown department store being an old lady again today.

"So, yeah, dinner would be great! Tasha comes home really tired so she'll be glad not to have to cook. She says being an old lady is hard work."

Tell me about it.

I circled the close to life-size cow. I couldn't tell where the slabs of rough metal it was made of may have originated. "Do you ever paint your creations?" I asked.

"Not usually." He stepped back to contemplate the cow. "But I've been thinking Matilda here needs paint."

Matilda. Yes indeed. "What color did you have in mind?"

More reflection. "Purple, I think."

My arms prickled. *Beware the purple cow,* my fortune cookie had warned, which seemed an odd coincidence, with Eric now thinking about painting Matilda purple. "Black and white might be nice," I suggested. "I've seen big black and white cows."

"No, Matilda is definitely purple."

I felt a . . . what's that fancy word? Frisson. Yes, I felt a definite frisson of uneasiness. But what possible harm could the junk sculpture of a purple cow do? Besides, I don't believe in fortune cookies.

I decided I should stop and tell Magnolia about Lillian Hunnicutt's body in my bathtub so she wouldn't have the shock of learning about it over dinner. She was shocked, but not really surprised.

"If anyone is going to find a dead body in her bathtub, it would be you," she declared.

Magnolia isn't one to hide her opinions, but neither does she tend to be snarky. I decided to take the statement as a compliment.

"Thank you."

"The police are investigating?" she asked.

"I think she was killed because the Braxtons thought she was me, but the police don't seem inclined to think that way. They're focusing on someone from her past who had it in for her."

"What about Mac?"

"He thinks I should pick up and leave before they kill me too."

"He could be right, you know."

The possibility of my demise here on Madison Street seems to be a recurring theme.

***

Mac showed up first, and he made lemonade out of the fresh lemons he'd brought. Eric and Tasha arrived next, then Magnolia and Geoff.

It was a great evening. Mac offered the blessing at the dinner table. I think Eric and Tasha were surprised, but they didn't seem uncomfortable with it. I murmured an "Amen," and, after a moment, Eric did too.

The meat loaf turned out juicy and tasty, the baked potatoes soft and fluffy. Tasha shared some of her experiences as an older woman and declared that every young person should be required to try it for a day or two, just to know what being old was like. We stayed away from the subjects of dead bodies, murder, and Braxtons. Mac mentioned spending the afternoon helping a woman at the RV park look for her lost cat, which he found meowing in the garden shed behind her travel trailer. Mac's a good guy; helping people is the kind of thing he does. Even though I suspected this woman had stuffed the cat in the shed herself, just so she could enlist Mac's help. She'd given him a big plastic sack of homemade chocolate-chip cookies for his help. *The way to a man's heart is through his stomach.*

Fortunately, Mac likes cheesecake even better than chocolate chip cookies, and mine was a big hit. After dinner and dishes we sat around the table still talking. Actually, given that my furniture consisted of one sofa, there was nowhere else for any crowd larger than two to sit. On the way out, heading home, Eric spotted the mannequin head.

He stopped short. "Hey, look at that!"

I jumped on the opportunity. "Would you like to have it?"

"Yes!" He ran out to the garden area and came back clutching the head to his chest as if it were some long-lost treasure. "Wow, this is great!"

I didn't want to discourage this unexpected opportunity for disposal of the head, but I had to ask, "What can you do with it?"

"I don't know. I've never had a head to work with before."

"There's a picture of Elvis. Would you like to have that too?" I asked.

"I would!" Tasha said.

Hey, maybe I was on a roll here. "There's also that pile of old drapes," I offered hopefully. "They might be good for . . . something."

"Umm, no thanks," Tasha said.

Well, two out of three wasn't bad. Maybe if I spread the drapes over the garden area they'd smother the weeds.

Magnolia and Geoff left a few minutes after Eric and Tasha, Magnolia calling back, "Don't forget, potluck and barbecue Friday night. Tell anyone you see."

I'd make peach cobbler, I decided. That's what I'd taken to that barbecue where I met Mac. Maybe it would make him feel nostalgic about our meeting. I'd also wear that beautiful pendant of turquoise and silver he'd given me. Our relationship needed a jump-start. Then I gave myself a mental thumping. Going our separate ways was a foregone conclusion now, wasn't it?

Mac stayed for a last cup of coffee out under the maple tree. We didn't talk much, which wasn't unusual. We often enjoy a companionable silence. But this was different, a definite rift. Eventually, Mac slapped his thighs and stood up. He gave me a goodnight peck on the cheek. *Don't overdo it,* I grumbled silently.

Even if there was a rift between us, I was pleased that I could finally sleep in the house. I made up the bed in the sofa, intending to slide into it right away, but I decided there was one more job to take care of. Mac would probably scoff. So would Officer DeLora. I determinedly set about figuring how to do it anyway.

Paint would work best, but it was too late to drive to the store. What else would work? Syrup? Why not!

The project took longer than I figured, of course. The gallon jug of syrup—bigger than I needed when I bought it, but there'd been this great sale at a store back in California— was right there in the cupboard of the motorhome, but it took me a while to locate a suitable plastic bucket and a length of hefty string. Then it took even longer to figure out the logistics of my plan. That Home Alone kid was better at this than I was.

I surveyed the results when I was done. Okay, it would never qualify as high-tech home defense, and Mac would no doubt shake his head in skepticism or exasperation, but I could go to bed feeling reasonably safe and secure.

No Braxtons would be sneaking in unannounced or unscathed tonight.

CHAPTER 14

I windmilled my arms, appreciating the luxury of space, before slipping into my new bed. The left-behind air conditioner, although it now sounded a little like an asthmatic lion, cooled the sleeping area to where I didn't need windows open, which reinforced my feeling of security. The mattress on the sleeper-sofa was just right when I stretched out on it, not too hard, not too soft. Koop looped himself into a furry horseshoe around my head, and I quickly drifted off to sleep.

Deep, sweet, dreamless sleep. In my own home at last.

***

Something wakened me. I didn't know what, but my body went frozen-fish stiff and my nerves flashed warning signals. A noise. The asthmatic-lion air conditioner? That, but something more. A window breaking and a thud of Braxton feet? No. An ominous creak in the kitchen?

Something more, much more. Strange lights flickering at the uncurtained windows. Koop standing on the back of the sofa, electrified fur ridging his arched back. An ominous feeling that something had rumbled right through my body, with vibrations lingering like the aftershocks of an earthquake. And my ears, with a world-shattering thunder still echoing in them.

I jumped out of the bed and stumbled to the window. I stared out in disbelief.

The motorhome . . . Dense black smoke billowed upward, flames whipping within the dark cloud. Tongues of flame spurted out the windows. A roaring inferno raged behind them. Pieces of flaming debris littered the yard, more spiraling down like falling fireworks. A larger chunk of something . . . a piece of the motorhome *roof*? . . . blazed on the ground. The maple tree flamed a fiery torch within the billowing smoke.

I stood there paralyzed, momentarily unable to comprehend the reality of what was happening. The snarl of the fire amped up even as I watched. Now it was the roar of an oncoming train. Something whizzed toward the house as if shooting out of a 3D movie, and I automatically ducked. It thudded against the house

I fumbled for my cell phone on the cardboard box I'd set beside the sofa to use as a nightstand. Flames lit the room and flickering shadows danced on the far wall. Koop clawed his way under the bed. I punched in the 911 numbers and garbled a yell: *Fire!* An explosion . . . *another* explosion? . . . rocked the house and I clutched the sofa. A fireball spewed out the top of the motorhome where the roof had once been.

I gave the address, dropped the phone and ran for the back door, fumbled with the lock and yanked the door open. There was a hose out back. Maybe I could save—

The deluge hit my head. A thick tide sloshed over me. It ran into my eyes, dripped down my cheeks, rolled down my neck. I froze. Something sticky had blasted out of the motorhome?

No.

I groaned. My booby trap. Meant for villainous Braxtons, but indiscriminately dumping a sticky avalanche on whoever happened to open the door. *Whoever* right now being *me.*

I stepped outside, frantically trying to see through the syrupy veil.

Black smoke, evil as a snake fattened on prey, churned toward the starlit sky. An acrid scent filled the night air. Shards of broken glass glittered on the ground. I pawed at my eyes again. The syrup was in my eyelashes. In my eyebrows. In my hair. It plastered the pajamas to my body. I blinked and my eyelids stuck together. I pried them open with sticky fingers.

Something hissed within the burning motorhome. A crash. Sparks blasted through windows that no longer existed.

Braxtons! They'd tried to do it before, planting a dynamite bomb under my Thunderbird down in Arkansas. They hadn't succeeded then. Now they had.

I leaned against the corner of the house as the full truth hit me. They'd been after more, of course. *Me.* Drake Braxton might be too busy to go to his mother's birthday barbecue, but he still had plenty of time for a little arson and murder. I was supposed to be in that blazing firestorm, supposed to be dead by now.

Lord, thank you for looking out for me! Thank you

for bringing me safely inside the house tonight.

I ran for the hose coiled by the faucet in the back yard. I turned the faucet on full force, blasted myself in the face to wash off syrup, then dragged the hose toward the house. Smoke curled from the siding where that 3D shot had hit it.

Someone yelled my name. Geoff ran into the yard.

"I'm over here!" I glubbed back. It's not easy to yell with watered-down syrup still trying to glue your lips together.

Stupid hose caught on something. I dropped it and waved my arms at Geoff. Syrup ran down my raised arms and over my elbows and wrists and puddled in my underarms. I put my arms down to grab the hose again, and my elbows stuck to my body as if I were in a syrupy straightjacket.

How much syrup had I put *in* that booby trap? Oh, yeah. A full gallon, because I hadn't used any out of the jug yet. But it felt like even more than that, like barrels of syrup spreading over my body. It ran down my legs. My knees stuck together.

"You okay?" Geoff asked when he ran up to me. Irrelevantly, I noticed that big flowers sprigged his pajamas. I love Magnolia dearly, and I know she likes to emphasize her name by displaying magnolias everywhere, but sometimes she does overdo them just a teensy bit. He touched my shoulder and yanked his hand back. He looked at his sticky fingers. "Did the explosion hit you?"

"No. I'm okay. It's just syrup."

More shadowy figures moved out on the street. Shouts. Sharp wail of siren in the distance.

Geoff is a get-things-done man, and, though he gave me a puzzled look, he wasn't about to waste time asking for a syrup explanation. He ran around behind me and unkinked the hose. I didn't bother aiming the stream of water at the motorhome. I wasn't going to have to make some momentous decision about keeping or selling it after all. My home on wheels was a goner. I blasted the side of the house instead. Heat from the burning motorhome scorched my skin. Blessedly I hadn't cozied the motorhome up to the house. It was on the far side of the tree and driveway, or the explosion would have blasted right through the house. And me. I offered another heartfelt *Thank you, Lord.*

"We need more hose!" Geoff yelled.

"On the other side of the house."

Something exploded on the far side of the motorhome, and the blaze sagged in that direction. A tire? Yes. Another tire blew out on this side, and the back end drooped like some wounded monster. Someone I didn't recognize grabbed a chair from under the flaming tree and beat at flames in the dry grass.

Eric arrived in pajama bottoms and bare feet. He grabbed the hose out of my hands and arced the stream up to the eaves, to a curl of smoke I hadn't seen. Geoff aimed the other hose at the roof.

A fire truck with siren blaring roared up. Firemen jumped out, yelling and dragging out hoses. More sirens. A police car skidded up. Another firetruck. An ambulance.

"Nobody's hurt," I called when the EMTs jumped out. "No one was in the motorhome."

The EMTs and a police officer ran over anyway. They wanted to check me out, but I said I was fine, no injuries, just a little sticky. The police officer wanted to question me, but I asked if it could wait a few minutes. My brain felt sticky too.

"Okay, but don't walk around out here in your bare feet," the officer warned. "There's a lot of broken glass."

I definitely didn't want to get cut and bleed. What we didn't need here was a fainting Eric. Though at the moment he looked like one of those superhero figures, muscled shoulders and chest glinting copper in flame-light as he hit the burning chunk of motorhome roof on the ground with a blast from the hose.

Huge streams of water from the fire hoses dwarfed the sprays from my garden hoses as they blasted the motorhome and burning tree. Smoke and steam hissed and billowed. The skeleton of the motorhome, like some metal zombie walking through fire, began to emerge through the flames and smoke.

Tasha ran up to me. She was in ragged jeans and sweatshirt, flip-flops on her feet. She grabbed my shoulders and bent over to peer in my face. "Ivy, are you okay? What happened?"

"Braxtons."

"Braxtons?" she repeated.

I hadn't told her about the Braxtons and how I'd been running from them for almost three years and how they'd killed the dead woman in my bathtub thinking she was me. I gave her a ragged version of that now.

"They rigged my car so it would blow up when I started the engine down in Arkansas. It didn't work then, but this time they got it right."

"We heard the blast, but I never thought. . . You really think someone did this *deliberately*?"

"They thought I was there in the motorhome. So they blew it up."

Tasha's wrinkled forehead suggested she didn't fully believe me, but I'd been right about a dead body in the bathtub, so she didn't want to dismiss my wild story now. She tried to pat my back, but her hand stuck.

"Ivy, are you bleeding? Is that *blood*?" She yanked her hand free and looked at it in horror.

"No, it's just syrup," I said. "I didn't get it all hosed off."

"Syrup?"

"Imitation maple."

She licked a fingertip and nodded agreement.

"I put it in my booby trap. In case the Braxtons tried to get in the house," I explained. "But then I forgot about the booby trap and opened the door myself."

She didn't question my setting a booby trap. Apparently she figured booby traps were within my normal range of activity. Instead she asked, "Ivy, have you told the police about these Braxtons?"

"I told Officer DeLora earlier, but the police apparently think Lillian Hunnicutt was hiding from someone in her past, and that person found and killed her. She had kind of a . . . troubled past." That seemed an inoffensive way to put it.

As it turned out I had a chance to tell my version of Lillian's death to another officer. I was sitting on the back steps by then. Stuck to the steps, actually, watered-down syrup puddled around me. I could go inside and clean up . . . if I could get myself unstuck . . . but there's something morbidly hypnotizing about watching three years of your life go up in flames and smoke.

But I didn't go up in flames. Once more you were looking out for me, weren't you Lord? Thanks! Koop and I were okay. I'd earlier gotten quite a few important items out of the motorhome, and belongings are mostly expendable anyway.

The smoke wasn't black now, nor was it billowing. It drifted lazily from the motorhome in an almost gentle, white-ish cloud. Some of the tree branches made skeletal silhouettes against the night sky, but the tree no longer blazed. Only an occasional flame flared within the metal skeleton of the motorhome, and it was quickly zapped by the firemen. Kitchen stove and refrigerator had morphed into blobs now.

The police officer approached. "You're the owner?"

I swiped the pajama sleeve across my mouth. My hair seemed to have trapped a vast reservoir of syrup and was releasing it in measured dribbles. Putting a whole new spin on *having a bad hair day.*

"Yes. Ivy Malone."

Tasha was still with me, but the officer said he'd like to speak to me alone, and she said she'd go make sure Eric was okay. I didn't rush into the full story of what this was all about, figuring that would only make the officer suspect I was in shock and suffering paranoid delusions about Braxton thugs planting bombs. Although, after we got through the basic information, I brought up the fact that the police were right now investigating the murder of a woman I'd found dead in the bathtub of my house.

The officer stood with one foot braced on the bottom step, notebook on his thigh as he scribbled in it. He looked up. He'd obviously heard about that case, although he apparently hadn't yet connected it with this location. "That was here?"

"They thought they were killing me then. When they realized they'd gotten the wrong person, they tried again tonight. Except I'd moved into the house."

"I see. And 'they' are—?"

"Braxtons. Drake Braxton, specifically. The same people who planted a dynamite bomb under my car a few years ago down in Arkansas. It seems to be a favored technique with them."

"You think they planted dynamite under your motorhome and that's what caused the explosion and fire?" He sounded as skeptical as if I'd just claimed little green aliens had nuked the motorhome with some outer-space weapon.

I wasn't about to back down even if he was skeptical. "Yes. They've tried other ways to kill me too."

"But you just happened to move into the house tonight."

"I've been planning to move into the house ever since I got here, but I didn't have any furniture until today," I explained.

"And these Braxtons that you think did this. They're—what? A gang or organization?"

"A family. It was Drake Braxton who originally threatened me. But the whole family is in on it." I gave him other names and how they'd been trying ever since the trial to find and eliminate me.

More skepticism. The fact that I was a barefoot LOL, covered with remnants of a gallon of syrup plastering me to a step, probably didn't enhance my credibility. But I determinedly went on to tell him how I'd personally encountered a young Braxton at Braxton Furniture yesterday and then Drake Braxton at the horse farm today, and that those encounters may have precipitated tonight's raid.

"I see. And did either of these Braxtons threaten you at these encounters?"

"No. But Drake Braxton may have recognized me. Your crime scene investigators will be able to tell what caused the explosion, won't they?"

"Yes, I'm sure they will." No skepticism there, although the statement seemed to suggest something that wasn't necessarily reassuring. He finally commented on my sticky state. "You seem to be covered in some sort of . . . viscid substance."

"It was in my booby trap," I explained once more. "I

was afraid the Braxtons might try to get in the house, so I set this booby trap with a bucket of syrup above the door. But I accidentally tripped the trap myself."

"Ah. I see. A booby trap." He gave me a *get-out-the-nets-guys, we've-got-a-live-one-on-the-loose-here* look. "Did you hear anything or see anyone running away from the scene either before or after the explosion?"

"No. I was asleep. The bomb they set under my Thunderbird was rigged to explode when the ignition was turned on, but they must have done it differently here." I thought about Beth Braxton mentioning Cousin Sam's expertise with electronic gadgets and software. "One member of the family is an electronics expert, so they may have set an electronic timing device that would go off after they were away from the scene."

"Was the motorhome unlocked?"

"I don't think so. Although. . ." It could have been, I had to admit. I'd been in and out of the motorhome numerous times, moving stuff over to the house, and that last time, with my arms full of sheets and pillows, I could have forgotten to lock it. "But they didn't have to get inside to put dynamite underneath."

"I'm sure our experts will figure it all out."

He thanked me and then went on to question Tasha, Eric, and Geoff. Tasha came back to the steps after he was finished with her. I invited her to sit down beside me, but she said she'd stand. The puddle of watery syrup on the step around me may have been a deterrent.

"I'm not sure he believed me," I said. "What did he

ask you?"

"About what I observed when I got here. If we'd seen anyone suspicious looking." She hesitated momentarily. "He also asked a lot of questions about what we'd observed of your daily activities and, umm, mental state. If we'd observed incidents of confusion or forgetfulness."

"What do you tell him?"

"That I'd never seen any confusion or forgetfulness. And if you say these Braxtons did this because they're out to get you, *I* believe it," she declared almost fiercely. Which suggested she also thought the officer didn't believe me.

Magnolia rushed up then, her body covered in a voluminous bathrobe, her usually highly styled hair blowing loose around her face. The mask she always wore over her eyes at night dangled on a cord around her neck.

"Are you all right?" she gasped, hand on her chest. Magnolia is not a running person, but she'd run from the house over here. "What in the world happened?"

I explained once more.

Magnolia didn't make any doubtful noises. She knows my history with the Braxtons. She peered at me anxiously. "Are you all right?"

"I'm fine. Geoff's around here somewhere. He's been spraying the roof down so the fire wouldn't spread to the house."

Magnolia patted her chest and took deep breaths. She wears ear plugs, but apparently she'd remembered to yank them out before running over here. With the plugs in, she'd once slept through a two-bear attack on a garbage can right outside their motorhome in Wyoming, so it wasn't surprising she'd missed the initial explosion tonight.

So I had to ask, "What woke you up?"

"I got up to go to the bathroom. I realized Geoff wasn't there, and then I looked out and saw what was going on over here. Oh, Ivy, maybe you shouldn't have come home! Maybe even after all this time it's too dangerous for you here." She was concerned enough that she apparently hadn't even noticed she was wearing mismatched slippers, one of hers and one of Geoff's. "Does Mac know about this?"

"Not yet."

Should I call him? I wanted to. But there was nothing he could do now except give me a comforting hug, and that would be a little messy in my current syrupy condition. And maybe what he'd give me would be a scolding for not moving out to the RV park.

"I'm going inside and take a shower," I announced.

***

Koop followed me into the bathroom. I intended to wait until I got out of the shower to call Mac, but instead I just washed off one ear and punched his name on the contact list on my non-smart cell phone. Even if he scolded, I needed to talk to him. He answered on the second ring. I sat on the edge of the tub. Koop had already claimed a surveillance spot on the closed toilet seat.

"What's wrong?" Mac demanded.

I didn't bother to ask how he knew something was wrong. Even in the best of times, we don't tend to call each

173

other to whisper sweet nothings in the middle of the night. Or crow about how many points we just made on some Facebook game. Although I was curious— "Do you leave your phone turned on all night?"

"When I'm worried about you, Ivy, yes I do." He repeated his question. "What's wrong?"

"I'm fine. Just a minute while I get some syrup out of my ear." I dabbed at my ear with a washcloth and picked up the phone again. "Are you still there?"

"You want to tell me why you have syrup in your ear?"

"It's a, umm, long story."

"How about if I come over, and you can tell me all about it?"

You have to love a man who's willing to rouse himself out of bed in the middle of the night when all he knows is that you have syrup in your ear. "Thank you. I'd appreciate that."

I showered and then dressed in the same jeans and T-shirt I'd taken off when I went to bed. By the time I was through in the bathroom, Tasha had cleaned up both the kitchen floor and the sticky steps. The police car was gone, and one fire truck rumbled away as I stepped outside. The motorhome was now just a stark skeleton squatting on a burned-out chassis, like the bones of some angular dinosaur. The tires were burned down to bare wheels. A scent like soggy, burned garbage mixed with a chemical tang hung in the air. A fireman from a smaller fire-fighting unit came over and said he'd remain on duty all night in case of a flare-up.

I thanked him, and he also said investigation into cause of the fire would start first thing in the morning.

"I think you should come spend the night with us," Magnolia said.

"Or with us," Tasha added.

"Thanks, but Mac will be here in a few minutes."

No one left until Mac arrived, however. The stars were already fading into a paler blue in the eastern sky when he parked his pickup out on the street and picked his way through the fallen debris littering the yard. We surveyed the ruins together.

"I guess I should have listened to you and moved the motorhome over to your RV park."

Mac didn't say *I told you so.* He simply wrapped his arms around me. "I'm just glad you'd moved into the house."

We stood that way for a minute until I said, "Thanks for coming."

"About that syrup in your ear. . .?"

"The booby trap I set for the Braxtons worked on me."

He didn't question my setting a booby trap. I'm not sure it's a good thing when people see nothing unusual about someone setting a booby trap; just another day in the life of Ivy Malone.

"Do you think the Braxtons did this?" I asked.

"That would be my first guess, yes."

We walked around to the far side of the motorhome. I told him how I figured the Braxtons had rigged dynamite to explode under the motorhome, same as they'd done to my

175

Thunderbird down in Arkansas. Although, looking at the skeletal remains now, I didn't see any big hole blasted up through the floor. The motorhome door lay on the ground at least a dozen feet from the burned-out wreckage. The explosion had blown it right off the hinges.

"Looks as if the Braxtons weren't skimpy with their dynamite," I said. "Drake probably deducts it as a business expense for Braxton Construction."

Mac nodded, but he tilted his head thoughtfully. "The way the door blew off, it almost looks as if the explosion came from inside rather than under the motorhome. Not that I'm any expert on explosions," he added.

Unfortunately, the Braxtons were.

CHAPTER 15

A couple hours later, the guy who'd stayed all night watching for flare-ups drove off and two guys in bulky suits started plowing through the blackened ruins of the motorhome. Mac commented that the materials used in construction of an RV could be more hazardous than in a regular house, which probably explained their heavy-duty gear. One man had a camera and took photos from all angles inside and outside.

Another police officer arrived and questioned me, and I was pleased that he circled the motorhome with yellow crime scene tape before he left. Then a man from some state agency dealing with fires and arson arrived. Mac wandered over to Magnolia and Geoff's yard while I was once more being questioned. I spotted Eric and Tasha going over there a little later too.

I sat on the back steps of the house as the investigator asked all kinds of questions. When was the motorhome last driven? Was the air conditioner in working condition and when was it last used? Had I cooked on the kitchen stove last evening? Were there any problems with it? How about electric or propane problems? Had I moved all my belongings into the house or had I lost everything in the fire?

Was there insurance? What time was I last in the motorhome? Why had I moved into the house? And about a zillion more questions about both the motorhome and me.

A question about why I hadn't lived in the house for almost three years finally gave me an opening to tell him about my hostile relationship with the Braxton clan, including how they'd dumped the body of the woman they thought was me in the bathtub. I left out the part about getting caught in my own booby trap. Not really relevant, I assured myself.

The man made no comment and showed no reaction to any of my statements, so I couldn't tell if he was taking me seriously or reserving a space for me in the loony bin. Did these guys have special training in facial and body control? Stoneface 101, attendance required. He merely said he appreciated my helpfulness and, with the usual request that if I thought of anything more to call him, he gave me his card when he left.

Mac returned as soon as the man was gone. The day was already warm, and we went into the kitchen for lemonade. I could see now that the side of the house facing the motorhome had more damage than I'd earlier realized. I gave Mac a rundown on what the investigator had asked.

"Some of the questions seemed irrelevant, but I suppose it's all routine procedure in an arson case," I said.

"Probably."

Something about his reserved answer made me ask, "You think there may be something more going on here?"

"We'll just have to wait and see."

Magnolia, Geoff, Tasha and Eric trooped across the street en masse. I could tell they had something on their collective minds. Magnolia announced what it was.

"This latest incident has us all worried. We think it's too dangerous for you to stay here in the house alone."

Mac said, "Ivy could—"

I interrupted him. "I think—"

Tasha interrupted both of us. "We've talked it over and decided the best solution is for you to move in with us temporarily. We'll clean out our extra bedroom and there'll be plenty of room."

I was momentarily taken back by this. *They'd* decided? Hey, I might be an LOL, but my brain functions hadn't deteriorated to turnip level yet. I didn't need decisions made for me.

Another thought instantly overrode that ungracious reaction. *God will provide.* God's provision is something I've always believed in, and God was providing now through the caring of good friends.

"We discussed your coming to our house," Magnolia said, "but then we all decided you'd be safer with Eric and Tasha. Their house isn't right across the street like ours—"

"And we're thinking the Braxtons don't know that you're friends with us, so they wouldn't have any reason to look for you at our place," Tasha added.

No one mentioned Eric's body-guard physique, but I figured that also played a part in the decision.

I studied the four of them watching me anxiously. No, five anxious watchers because Mac's concerned eyes watched too. I was just ready to say okay when Mac touched my arm.

"Could I talk to you for a minute?"

He pushed me around to the other side of the burned-out hulk. "Look, it's great that Eric and Tasha are willing to provide a place for you to stay. But I think you should reconsider staying on Madison Street at all. The Braxtons aren't likely to give up, you know, and sooner or later they will figure out where you are. I think you should get far away from here. *Now.*"

"My motorhome isn't exactly in traveling condition," I pointed out. As if to emphasize that fact, a dangling chunk of black stuff fell off and clunked at our feet.

"We could get married."

For a moment I was indignant at the sound of that. As if marrying me would be some big sacrifice! But I quickly chucked that reaction. Mac didn't mean it that way. At the moment, he was worried, and definitely not in romance mode. So I honestly took some time to consider that choice.

But finally I brought up the bottom line in my thinking. "If I run away now, even if we got married, the Braxtons will always be after me. I'll be running for the rest of my life. Always looking under the motorhome for dynamite. Constantly trying to hide my trail so they won't find me. Forever wondering what new and improved method of doing me in—and maybe you too!—they might come up with. I can't live that way."

Mac nodded slowly. "Okay, then. We'll concentrate

on nailing the Braxtons. That's our goal." He didn't sound happy about it, just resigned.

We went back to the foursome waiting by the house, and I thanked Eric and Tasha for their invitation. "Koop can come too, I hope?"

"Of course."

Thank you once more, Lord. Thank you for friends who care.

"What about the Friday night barbecue?" Tasha asked. "Is it still on?"

Magnolia lifted her magnificent eyebrows. "Of course."

Eric and Tasha went home to get the bedroom ready. The rest of us loaded my minimal belongings into Mac's pickup and hauled them over to my temporary new residence. I wondered if the Braxtons were somehow watching, frustrated that I'd again escaped their clutches. But the fact that I *had* escaped was mildly reassuring. They hadn't been watching closely enough to know that I wasn't in the motorhome last night. Hopefully, even if Mac was worried, this move would escape their attention too.

On the way through to the bedroom at Eric and Tasha's house, I noted that Elvis had a new home on the wall of the living room. A tin-can-lid frame had replaced the broken plastic one. It went nicely with Elvis's curl-of-lip smile.

The bedroom was small but certainly adequate. A narrow bed stood along the inside wall, beside it a nightstand and a chest of drawers. Some small creations of Eric's filled a table along the opposite wall, the all-too-familiar mannequin head there as well. Apparently Eric hadn't figured out a use for it yet. The one window looked out on the back yard, where the purple cow with its motorcycle-handle horns stood under the heavy shade of that jungle of oak and maple. A wheelbarrow full of discarded pieces of metal stood under one tree. Or maybe they were valuable parts destined to become Ockunzzi Originals. It was hard to tell, given Eric's quirky creativity.

Koop, cool cat that he is, gave the room a quick inspection, batted at a cat made of bolts and screws, with oversized metal-washer eyes, then turned his attention to what was really important. Washing his hind leg.

Mac went back to the RV park, and I settled down with insurance papers on both motorhome and house. Blessedly, the box of my most important papers was among the items I'd carried into the house before the fire. I called the insurance people, and they said they'd send someone out. I also called both the police officer and the arson investigator and left messages to let them know where I was, in case they needed to contact me.

All was quiet at the motorhome the rest of the day. I assumed there was lab work on the fire to be done. No more officials came around to ask questions. I organized my belongings in the bedroom a little better. That night, the bed was comfortable, and Koop curled up beside me, but I tossed and turned restlessly. Had my move to Tasha and Eric's bedroom been noted by the Braxton's? Was this putting Tasha and Eric in danger too? I kept feeling as if someone was watching me. Were Braxtons lurking around outside, planning their next assault? Or maybe it was just that mannequin's head watching me. I quickly scoffed at that. Mannequins have no seeing abilities. But I got up and turned the head to face the wall and finally went to sleep.

The next morning, when I strolled down to the house to see if anything was going on, the scent of barbecued motorhome still hung heavy in the air. I thanked the good Lord again that I wasn't barbecued along with it. Then I noticed that the crime scene tape was gone. I thought that odd, but maybe some kid had made off with it because he wanted something cool to drape in his room.

While I contemplated the possibilities, Officer DeLora showed up. Her red hair was solidly gelled in place this morning, but she was in jeans and T-shirt rather than police uniform, and she wasn't driving an official car.

"Ivy, are you all right?" she asked as we met while circling the burned-out hulk from opposite directions.

"I'm fine. I was in the house when it happened. Are you working on this case?"

"No, but I heard about it. I'm not on Lillian Hunnicutt's case either." She didn't comment on that other than to clamp her jaw momentarily, which suggested this was not her choice. "I'm working on some burglaries out on the south side of town. But I'm off today."

"Would you like to come inside and have some ice water? It's all I have here. I'm staying with Eric and Tasha for now."

She nodded. "I'm glad you won't be here alone."

We went inside, and I found a couple of glasses still in the cupboard. I filled them with ice and water, and we sat at the kitchen table.

Wondering why she was here, if this wasn't her case, and this was her day off, I asked, "They're doing lab work on cause of the explosion and fire?"

"From what I've heard that won't be necessary."

I didn't like the sound of that.

"They know the cause of the explosion," she explained. "The investigation isn't complete, but the preliminary report indicates it was an accident."

"Accident? The Braxtons dynamite my motorhome, and they're calling it an *accident*?"

"The kitchen stove was considerably damaged, of course, but the investigators could determine that two of the burners were turned on. That let propane escape into the interior of the motorhome. When the refrigerator or hot water heater automatically turned on sometime in the night, the spark set off explosion of the propane."

I sat there assimilating all that. It didn't take long. "No dynamite planted under the motorhome?"

"No dynamite anywhere. That's definite. There was considerable damage to the floor, but it all came from above, not below."

More assimilation. "So what they're saying is that I'm a forgetful old lady who turned on the stove burners but didn't light them, and the ensuing explosion just happened by itself. The Braxtons didn't have anything to do with it."

I remembered Tasha saying the police officer had

asked about my mental condition and forgetfulness, and I'd certainly felt the arson guy's skepticism about my Braxton claims. Now I understood the removal of the crime scene tape. No crime, just an accident.

"As you probably saw yourself, the explosion blew the door off the motorhome," Officer DeLora added. "They could tell it was locked."

"Locked, suggesting—?"

"That no one had gotten inside." Officer DeLora stood up as if she were restless. She jiggled the ice in her glass. "I probably shouldn't be telling you any of this, but . . ." She left her reason for doing so drift off.

"So if no one got inside, that strengthens their theory that I left the burners on myself."

"That's apparently the thinking, yes."

"But even if the door was locked, that doesn't necessarily mean the Braxtons didn't get inside," I argued. "It's a multi-talented family. One of them could have picked the lock." Hadn't Mac said that the computer store had a safe and locks section?

"That's possible."

I ran with the idea. "Then whatever Braxton it was slipped inside to turn on the stove burners knowing the escaping propane would explode sooner or later. They didn't have to figure a way to set it off. A perfect blow-up-Ivy scheme, which would look like something I'd accidentally done myself. And then he locked the door when he went out."

"You think they'd come inside even thinking you

were sleeping there?"

"Why not? It wouldn't take more than a few seconds. They probably figured that at my age I wouldn't wake up even if they took time for a snack from the refrigerator. And even if I did wake up, I wasn't likely to storm out of the bedroom with an assault rifle."

But my scenario of Braxtons sneaking into the motorhome wilted even as I expanded on it. Maybe the investigators were right. I couldn't think why I'd have left the stove burners turned on, but maybe I had. The stove in this older motorhome didn't have some automatic shutoff to prevent escaping propane if a burner wasn't lit. Maybe I *was* simply a forgetful little old lady now, accidentally responsible for destroying my own motorhome. It was a disturbing and dismaying thought, the kind that makes lurking thoughts wake up the dark dragon of senility.

Officer DeLora and I both clinked ice in our glasses for a contemplative couple of minutes. Finally I said, "I appreciate your coming and telling me all this. Is this an official visit?"

"No. I'm here on my own."

"Would your superior officers approve?"

"Probably not."

That sat there like roadkill between us until I finally said, "So why *are* you here?"

"I saw some statistics the other day. A couple years ago, the rate for murder cases solved in the US was just under sixty-five percent."

"So?"

"That means thirty-five percent went *un*solved. I'm afraid the dead body in your tub is going to be among that thirty-five percent. And then there's . . . something else about your motorhome fire."

Her reluctant tone told me the "something else" was not good. A mental window suddenly opened on an ominous new possibility. One that I guessed had already occurred to Mac.

"Let me guess. The authorities are considering the possibility that this wasn't an accident," I said. "Though not because they're giving any credibility to my claim of Braxton involvement. They're thinking that it could be a set-up, that I did it myself to get the insurance payoff on the motorhome, and tried to make it look like a forgetful-little-old-lady accident. Insurance fraud."

"No one seems to think you're lacking anything in the mental department."

"Which suggests I'm clever enough to try insurance fraud."

She made a reluctant nod of head.

"But I could just be forgetful! I mean, I set a booby-trap for the Braxtons and then forgot and caught myself in it. I practically drowned in the syrup."

Then I broke off. Hey, wait a minute. Did I really want to prove that I'm a few chocolate chips short on my mental cookie? I jumped to a different line of defense. "So you think you're going to pry a confession out of me and raise your status in the department? Maybe make detective?"

"You're a *suspicious* little old lady, aren't you?" she

snapped back.

Yeah, and not being fair, either. "I'm sorry. I appreciate your coming and telling me all this. What's the current thinking on Lillian Hunnicutt's body in my bathtub now?"

"There's a 'person of interest' in the case. Someone she had a hair-pulling incident with at a homeless shelter several months ago. They're trying to locate that person now."

My being so off-base about dynamite planted under the motorhome no doubt undermined whatever minimal credibility my accusations about the Braxtons killing Lillian Hunnicutt may have had. I felt as if I'd run into a concrete wall. Fallen into a bottomless pit.

Okay, maybe that was a little melodramatic, but it was a real setback realizing the Braxtons weren't even a footnote on law enforcement's agenda.

Not in Lillian Hunnicutt's death. Not in destruction of my motorhome. Not in their determination to make roadkill out of me.

It was an updated version of David and Goliath. Me vs. the Braxtons. And I didn't even have a slingshot.

CHAPTER 16

"But I do."

I was so lost in my woe-is-me party, and Officer DeLora's comment was so far from what I expected, that I simply gave a dumbfounded, "You do what?"

"I do believe the Braxtons have been trying to track you down and kill you ever since the trial. I do believe Braxton people killed Lillian Hunnicutt thinking she was you. And I do believe they were the brainpower behind the explosion in your motorhome."

I was glad to hear that, but— "Why?"

"For one thing, because I looked up the records of Beaumont Zollinger's trial. Your testimony was powerful and right on target. You were threatened before the trial, but you had the courage to testify anyway. You came up with the gun he used in the murder and provided evidence about illegal activity in his business dealings. The defense tried to discredit you as a witness and couldn't do it. If prosecutors gave out gold stars, you'd get one."

"So you don't think I'm a paranoid crackpot with an oversized imagination?"

"No." She gave me a frowning appraisal. "Although I don't think coming back here and putting yourself right smack in the middle of Braxton territory was the smartest move in the world."

That was the blunt, no-nonsense Officer DeLora I knew.

"Okay, I appreciate your believing the Braxtons have been out to get me and that they killed Lillian Hunnicutt and blew up my motorhome, but what good is it? You're not working on either case, and apparently no one else is listening to me."

"I figure, even if I also think it's not a real smart move, that you're going to be out there like some over-aged Nancy Drew investigating this yourself."

I wasn't about to admit that, but an ever-present aversion to dishonesty kept me from denying it. I got up and added ice to our glasses.

"So one reason I'm here is that I think you need someone looking out for you. Someone to see that you don't get yourself killed." Officer DeLora tilted her head and narrowed her eyes. "Or that you don't kill anyone."

"I wouldn't do that!" I protested indignantly. Although, I had to admit, accidents do happen, and Braxton preservation isn't high on my priority list. But I'd never deliberately harm anyone.

Officer DeLora didn't comment on my protest. "Actually, I did a little investigating on my own already." She looked around as if wary some disapproving superior in the police department might leap out from under the sink.

"And found out what?"

"Well, not enough to warrant an arrest, unfortunately. Not even enough to make the Braxton name familiar to law enforcement. But enough to suggest that Drake Braxton might not make it into model-citizen category."

"In what way?"

"Irregularities in his construction business. Lawsuits on defects in buildings he's constructed. Various traffic citations. Some credit and IRS problems. Unpaid property taxes."

"I understand he has some new business in Arkansas or Illinois. From what I've seen, he must be doing quite well with it."

"Oh? I didn't run across that. What kind of business?"

"I don't know. I just happened to hear about it when we were . . . talking to some people a couple days ago."

Officer DeLora zeroed in on that, of course. "Talking to what people?"

"Drake Braxton's mother and a niece. But we weren't talking to them about Lillian Hunnicutt's death. Or about the explosion in my motorhome, either. I mean, the explosion hadn't even happened yet when we talked to them. Drake Braxton just happened to show up when Mac was getting information about the horses at the Braxton's horse farm for a magazine article. That's what Mac does, you know. He writes magazine articles. The mother and granddaughter are both horse lovers. Very nice people, even if they are Braxtons. They raise Paso Finos."

My overload of information didn't sidetrack Officer DeLora. "So you are investigating this on your own." She waited for me to say something, but I was suddenly very busy checking out a scar on the kitchen table.

"Doing a magazine article makes a nice cover for being nosy. Very clever of you to use that ploy." Officer DeLora's grumpy tone negated any compliment in the statement. She stood up. "Just be careful, Ivy. Really, really careful."

"Bo Zollinger, the man I testified against at the trial, is dead now. Did you know that?"

"No. How do you know that?"

"An FBI friend." I hurried on before she could question how I had an FBI friend. "He was killed in a prison fight several months ago. When I heard about it just a few days ago, I thought maybe it meant the family would drop their search-and-destroy plan for me. That maybe he was the one behind their bloodhound persistence in tracking me down, and behind Lillian Hunnicutt's murder too. And once he was dead they'd give up on their grudge against me."

"Do you think that now?" she asked.

My gaze followed hers out the window to the skeleton of my burned-out motorhome.

"No. Drake Braxton hasn't given up."

"Ivy, I should tell you that amateur investigation of murder and arson isn't *illegal* as long as you stay out of the way of the official investigation. But it is *not* a good idea."

I pointed out that there apparently wasn't going to be any further investigation into my motorhome explosion because it was now being called an accident. And the investigation on Lillian Hunnicutt's death was following an irrelevant rabbit trail.

She repeated her earlier words, "Just be careful, Ivy. Very, very careful. And I'll see what I can do to help on my end." She added a qualification. "In an unofficial capacity, of course. I'll give you my personal cell phone number."

I got out my cell phone and added her name and number to my contact list.

The Lord will provide. Now, with this promise of help from Officer DeLora, minimal as it was, he'd once more proved that. Mac was in this with me too, and I always had a direct prayer line to the Lord. I wasn't battling the Braxtons alone. Cancel the pity party.

On impulse I said, "Hey, you want to come to a potluck barbecue tonight? Right across the street, at Magnolia and Geoff's place. They're inviting everyone in the neighborhood, and you're kind of involved in the neighborhood."

Her head started to shake *no,* but then her face brightened. "Sure. Why not? I'll bring my new fresh tomato casserole."

"Great!"

I just hoped the Braxtons didn't decide to show up too.

I was heading back to Eric and Tasha's place when I saw the mail-lady coming my way. I hadn't yet received any mail here, but today she apparently had something for me. Now was my chance to find out what she knew about the unauthorized occupant of my house.

"Hi," I said as she stuffed a couple of envelopes in

my box. "I'm Ivy Malone. I lived here for years, but the house was rented while I've been away. But now I'm back."

"Hi. Nice to meet you. I'm Charlene. I would say, always nice to come home. This is my first day back after two-weeks down in Arkansas taking care of my grandkids, and I'm *really* glad to be home. But it looks as if coming home wasn't so nice for you." She jiggled a shoulder toward the burned relic of my motorhome. She was fifty-ish, with wiry gray hair, but she had great legs showing beneath her postal-uniform shorts. Maybe a benefit of all the walking she did on her postal route? "What happened?"

"Propane explosion. The cause is still under investigation," I added, though that was undoubtedly an overly optimistic statement, considering what Officer DeLora had said. "I wanted to ask you, were you delivering mail here last winter or spring? A woman about my age lived here then. I'm hoping maybe you knew her. I found her body in the upstairs bathroom. She'd been dead quite a while."

"How awful!" She shook her head. "No, I started this route just a couple months ago, after old Luke Morris died, and there's never been any mail for this address while I've been delivering here. She just . . . died in your bathtub?"

"No, she was murdered."

"My goodness, I leave for two weeks and come home to explosion and murder?"

"Madison Street is different than it used to be."

"It must be. I'm hearing a rumor that all the houses around here may be razed before long too."

"Some outfit called Radison Properties is trying to

buy up everything. No one seems sure what they intend to do. You've probably delivered mail from them to people here?" I tossed out hopefully, thinking she might have some inside information.

"I, uh, really can't discuss mail I deliver."

"Of course. Well, it was nice meeting you. Thanks for the mail."

She walked on to the next house on her nicely-toned legs, and I pulled my mail out of the box. I felt a little letdown. In the mystery and detective books I read, the clever sleuth always snags some vital bit of information from someone no one else thought to talk to. What did I snag? The information that I might have better legs if I walked more.

But I perked up when I looked at the mail. The two larger envelopes were from my mail-forwarding addresses, but the other one was from grand-niece Sandy. Back in my bedroom at Eric and Tasha's, I ripped her envelope open first.

Hey, Aunt Ivy, you're going to love this! Sandy had written. *You can put them anywhere, but the round one will fit just right around your belly button! Send me a selfie! Love, Sandy. P.S. Mom told you I'm writing a teen news column for the newspaper now, and I keep getting these lovelorn questions asking for advice. So maybe I'll have to ask* you *for advice!*

Yeah, right. As if I were experienced on lovelorn subjects. Then—oh, no!—I realized I'd been right about the ominous possibilities of Sandy's gift. Here it was: belly button adornment. Maybe big in Sandy's age group, not so much in the LOL world. But the envelope was flat, not lumpy. What did she have in mind for my belly button? I shook out the contents.

Stick-on tattoos. No, I did not want a tattoo on my bellybutton or any other portion of my anatomy. I'd just toss them and tell her— Then I looked at the tattoos more closely. Nothing ghastly. Just fluttering butterflies and cuddly kittens and cheerful daisies. I balanced the packet in my hand.

It wasn't as if a stick-on tattoo would be attached forever. The instructions said they'd come right off with rubbing alcohol or baby oil. And it wasn't as if anyone would actually *see* it.

Why not?

I opened the round one and followed instructions, positioning it in place and pressing it with a damp washcloth. A couple minutes later I removed the stick-on sheet and craned my neck over to see what I'd done.

Hey, it worked!

I felt an unexpected giddiness. No, I was not going to send Sandy a selfie. I'd heard all about how selfies sometimes mysteriously wind up plastered all over the internet, and an LOL with daisies decorating her belly-button might become Laugh of the Day. But now I was a woman walking around with a secret. Maybe even a woman of mystery. It gave me an unexpected bounce of confidence. I had a ring of daisies around my belly button!

So what was I going to do with this sudden boost of confidence?

CHAPTER 17

Tackle the Braxtons, of course. What was this business of Drake's that kept him so busy he didn't even go to his mother's birthday barbecue? Although not too busy to barbecue my motorhome, of course. Yes, his business definitely needed further investigation.

And I was going to do this how?

That upbeat confidence plunged into a nose-dive. I didn't have any great ideas. I didn't have a computer. I didn't even have wheels.

I still had feet and a phone, although at the moment I couldn't think what to do with either. I was alone in the house. Eric was working out at the gym today. He'd taken the bus to get there, because Tasha needed their one vehicle for her assignment checking out reaction to her old-woman persona at a trendy clothing boutique. They were taking a load of Eric's junk creations to a flea market at the fairgrounds tomorrow.

I opened my envelopes of mail from my forwarding boxes. An ad for hearing aids. A newsletter from a church I'd gone to while I was on the road. Mailings from a couple of charities I occasionally donate to. A couple of political pleas for money. Hardly worth the bother.

Go, Ivy, Go!

The eyes of the mannequin head watched me as I tossed the mail. Hey, hadn't I turned her face to the wall? But here she was, looking at me again. Okay, I'd give her something to look at. I flashed my belly button daisies at her.

About midafternoon, I heard the front door open and, after making sure my T-shirt covered my newly-enhanced mid-section, I went out to see who had come home.

Tasha plopped on the sofa and struggled out of her sturdy shoes. She finally got one off and flung it across the room. "I'm tired of being an old lady," she muttered.

Aren't we all.

"My back hurts and my feet hurt, and some teensy-tiny, size-two salesgirl turned up her nose and told me they never carried anything for my size or age group. And then she tried to rush me out the door before anyone, heaven forbid, thought I was an actual customer there."

She reached under her clothes and withdrew her bulging belly pad, plunked her heels on the bare floor, and stretched out with an I've-had-it whoosh of breath. I felt a moment of envy. It would be nice to be able to simply yank off some of my sags and bulges.

"But, you know, being old myself, even if it's only temporary, makes me think." Tasha kicked another shoe across the floor and eyed the baggy stockings. "It's depressing, being old."

"We're all going to get old. Unless we die young, of course," I pointed out.

"Yeah, right. We get saggy and baggy and tired and stiff. Everything hurts. Nothing works right. Your eyesight goes dim and your hearing wonky—" She paused and dug a wad of cotton out of one ear. "Sometimes it seems, when I'm in old mode, I can't even *taste* right."

"It's not that bad," I protested. I have no trouble tasting, although I've had some older friends who grumble that everything tastes like that flour and water paste we used to make when we were kids. With my glasses, I see okay. Although my hearing may be a smidgen questionable. Mac's too.

Sometimes we have odd conversations. He asks me a question. I, having heard, "Let's feet shout tonight," answer with, "Okay, but how do we get our feet to shout and why would we want to?" He gives me a strange, blank look because what he'd said was, "Let's eat out tonight." But eventually we get everything straightened out and laugh about it.

"And then after all that bad stuff, what happens?" Tasha answered her own question. "You top it off by *dying*."

I couldn't argue with that.

"It makes you wonder what comes after." She slumped farther down on the sofa. "If anything."

"The afterwards part bothers you?" I asked.

"I've never thought much about dying. I mean, it always seemed so far off. But now, like this—" She yanked off the wig and dangled it in front of her face as if looking for answers in its mousy-gray depths. "It doesn't seem so far away. What happens then, Ivy? Don't you worry about that?"

With the obvious implication that I was old; I should

be worried about death and afterwards. I could take the question as demeaning to my age, but I knew Tasha didn't mean it that way. She was truly troubled.

"No," I answered truthfully.

"No?"

"No," I repeated. "I don't look forward to what might be an unpleasant process of dying, but I don't worry about what comes afterward. Jesus came and died on the cross so we could move on to a forever life with him. 'For God so loved the world that he gave his one and only Son, that whoever believes in him shall not perish but have eternal life,'" I quoted from John 3:16.

"Up there flapping our wings and playing harps?" She gave a desultory arm flap of her own.

I couldn't help but laugh. "I don't know what eternal life will be like, but I know we don't turn into angels with wings, and I doubt the Lord would ever assign someone with my minimal musical talents to play the harp." Though I've always had this secret yearning to make a soulful wail with a saxophone. Maybe I can do that in eternity? "But the good news is that there will be a meaningful, even joyful, existence with him."

"For all of us?"

"Life with the Lord comes for those who've accepted Jesus as Savior."

She snagged a stocking with the toe of her other foot and dragged it off. "Eric's folks sent him to Sunday School some when he was a kid, but mine never did."

"Going to Sunday School and church isn't going to

get you into eternal life with the Lord. And not going won't keep you out. An eternal life with the Lord isn't something you can *earn*. It's our acceptance of Jesus as Savior."

"That seems really, uh. . ."

"Preachy?"

"I was going to say *narrow-minded*. It doesn't seem like that should be the *only* way to get there." She pulled off the other stocking. "Is it?"

"The Bible is pretty definite about that, so yes, the only way. It also has some pretty good 'stuff' for while we're living too. The Bible and prayer have helped me through some bad times over the years. My son's disappearance and my husband's death were the worst."

She gave me an interested glance but didn't pry for further information. "My folks splitting up when I was eleven was my worst. My dad got married again and had some more kids and I guess just forgot about me."

"Our heavenly father never forgets about us. You can talk to him yourself, you know."

"Me? You mean *pray*?" She said the word as if there might be something underhanded about it, like insider trading.

"Sure. You don't need a special code or password."

"Actually, things are pretty good now for Eric and me. Nothing awful that we need to pray about anyway."

"Then you should be thanking God for that."

"Though sometimes I feel as if we're . . . I don't know . . . missing out on something? Sometimes I wonder if spending your life pretending to be someone else has any value. Because when you get to the bottom line, that's what acting is. Pretending."

"You can talk to God about things like that."

"He cares about that kind of stuff?"

"Sure. I talk to him about most everything."

"Really?" She glanced at me as if looking for some new and improved communications equipment, but there wasn't any, of course. Prayer, blessedly, doesn't take any high-tech equipment, and even if your hearing goes wonky and your eyesight fades, you can still pray. "Well, I'll think about it."

Not exactly a life-changing acceptance of the Lord, but maybe a start. "If you and Eric ever want to come to church with Mac and me, we'd be glad to have you. Or if you want to talk to me about any of it, that'd be fine too."

"I'll think about it," she repeated. She stood up and extracted another blob of padding. "Right now I'm going to go take all this stuff off. Then I need to make something for the potluck and barbecue tonight."

"Eric hasn't come home yet. He won't miss the barbecue, will he?"

"After his workout he was going to help with a training session at the gym for the little kids. I have to go pick him up at five. We still have to get stuff loaded for the flea market tomorrow too."

Tasha went to her bedroom to undo being an old lady, and I went to mine where I had no choice but to continue being one. Still, as I'd told her, it wasn't as bad as she seemed to think. Not bad at all, in fact. I don't wake up in the morning feeling as if all that's left in life is worn-out leftovers. But life would also be a whole lot better if I could just banish the Braxtons from it.

I hadn't any way to do that at the moment, however, so I plastered on another tattoo. Which gave me the unexpected thought that I'd gotten a purple butterfly on my ankle before Beth Braxton did, and I hadn't had to beat Grandma Braxton at chess to do it. Hey, yeah, sometimes there are unexpected benefits to being in the older generation! And just to take further advantage of this particular benefit, I put a blue kitten on my other ankle.

I didn't have any peaches to make the cobbler I'd planned, so I baked a pan of brownies while Tasha went to get Eric at the gym. When she got home, she made a macaroni and cheese casserole. I hadn't heard from Mac all day, but when we trooped over to Geoff and Magnolia's back yard, he was there. With a nice platter of deviled eggs. I wondered if he'd notice my fake tattoos.

He was talking to one of the widow/divorcee types who seem drawn to him like teenagers to a rock star, but he excused himself and came over to me. "I've been on the internet all day. I think we need to take a trip," he said in a low, almost conspiratorial whisper.

"A trip? Where?"

He didn't have a chance to answer because Magnolia tapped him with her golden wand. She always does special outfits for her barbecue get-togethers, and she was in fairy godmother mode this evening, complete with glittery tiara and that wand. "There's this girl over here who's writing a novel—she says it's over a thousand pages now!—and I told her you know all about these things."

Mac rolled his eyes, but he followed her toward a young woman with spiky black hair, earrings that looked like nails jabbed through her ears, and tattoos covering her arms from wrists to shoulders. Not stick-on ones like mine. At our first meeting, Magnolia had thrown Mac and me together like tossed salad, but I guess she now considers us, if not welded at the hip, at least comfortably knit at the elbow. I hadn't confided to her that our couple-hood has been unraveling ever since I decided to come back to Madison Street.

"Talk to you later," Mac said over his shoulder to me, leaving me to wonder if this trip he had in mind was a jaunt to a new Chinese restaurant, or if it was some sneaky new plot to take me far away from Madison Street, maybe away from Missouri entirely.

The crowd in Magnolia's back yard wasn't as large as their gatherings used to be, but there were more people than I expected. Geoff's barbecued chicken and burgers scented the air like a carnivore's dream. I wandered around introducing myself to people, mostly renters. I asked if they'd known the "renter" in my house before she became the body in the bathtub. Most had already been interviewed by the police, but no one had ever exchanged more than a few words with her. There was plenty of sympathy about my burned motorhome, but I detoured answering questions about cause of the fire.

No one noticed my ankle decorations. Although,

admittedly, they were inconspicuous compared to Tattooed Girl's fully-covered arms. I thought about flinging a foot in the air to get mine out where they'd be more visible, or maybe even flashing my daisy-encircled belly button. But I didn't do either, of course. Okay, call me boring, but I'm just not a foot-flinging or belly-button-flashing sort of person.

Then I spotted Ed and Marie Daggitt, the neighbors who used to raise such a great garden but whose house was empty now.

"It's so good to see you!" Marie said as we hugged. "You just seemed to drop off the edge of the earth. Where in the world have you been all this time?"

"Oh, just traveling around. But it looks as if I won't be doing that anymore." I made a no-big-deal wave in the direction of the motorhome. It wasn't visible from Magnolia's back yard, but the Daggitts must have seen it from the street. "Will you be living here again?"

"We have an apartment in Kansas City now," Ed said. "We just came to see what was going on with the house."

"Renter problems?"

"No, we sold it. Just like a lot of others have done, to that company over in Illinois."

"Radison Properties?"

"That's the one. But we've been in touch with old Mrs. Cumberland . . . you remember her?"

I nodded. Sweet elderly woman with a sweet little bulldog whose slobber, unfortunately, could be measured in gallons.

"She's in assisted living now. But she didn't receive the payoff she was supposed to get on her house, just a letter saying there would be an 'unfortunate delay' in the payment. Assisting living can be expensive, and she was counting on that money. She's afraid she may wind up out on the street."

"Has she contacted them since the letter?"

"She's tried to, but her calls are never returned."

"Sounds as if she may need a lawyer," I said.

"That's what we think too. But she's in no financial position to hire one, of course. I'm guessing Radison Properties is counting on that. Sometimes I'm afraid we're dealing with a bunch of shysters."

"That's too bad. I've been considering their offer on my place, but this makes me wonder."

"We're wondering too, but we've already sold. That's why we're here. We were afraid maybe they'd already torn the house down, even though we haven't received our payoff yet."

"But it isn't torn down and the payment isn't even due yet for a month yet," Marie reminded him. "And the Burdishes got their payoff right on time, remember? And now they're living in Florida."

"Yeah, that's right." Ed gave me an apologetic smile. "I suppose I'm just getting impatient. Maybe a little paranoid too. Don't let me change your mind if you want to sell. They're offering good prices, and Madison Street isn't improving with age."

"Did you ever meet a representative of Radison Properties in person when you were dealing with them?"

206

"No. Everything was handled by mail or Fed Ex, and it was real easy."

"Okay, thanks."

The evening turned out to be fun. Good food. Some impromptu guitar playing by Tattooed Girl. She had a nice voice, and I was actually familiar with some of her songs. Officer DeLora showed up, and her tomato casserole was great. I heard several people ask for the recipe. She was in jeans and big dangly earrings, her hair loose and swingy. She didn't look like a cop, but I saw her working the crowd from a cop's perspective, checking everyone out.

My brownies were ordinary but disappeared quickly. Magnolia made unexpected use of that wand when Tattooed Girl's boyfriend got a little unruly. She gave him a tap on the head that was more like a whack, which was when I realized the wand was actually a metal rod that Geoff had painted gold for her. Unruly Guy blinked and sat down and wasn't unruly any more. Tattooed Girl was admiring Officer DeLora's dangly earrings at the time.

But I was still impatient for it to be over. I wanted to find out what this trip was that Mac thought we should take.

CHAPTER 18

We finally had a few minutes alone when Mac walked back to Eric and Tasha's with me. They'd gone home early to get the pickup loaded for tomorrow's flea market.

"So what is this trip you think we should take?" I admit the question came out grumpy. I was still suspicious it was just some get-Ivy-out-of-town trick.

"To a place called Heart of Home Hill down in Arkansas."

"You want to go see a hill?"

"It's not just a *hill.* I've been digging around on the internet and found it. I think it's the name of a nursing home or assisted living or retirement home, something like that."

"And you think we should go there because one or more of us should be in a place like this?" I inquired.

"I think we should take a look at it because it's owned by something called Braxton Brothers."

I stopped short, my snarky attitude doing a 180 right there in the middle of the street. "You think this may be Drake Braxton's new business? The source of money for his interest in Porsches and swimming-pool-sized house additions?"

"I don't know. There's no website with photos or information. You'd think they'd be promoting the place, but

I found it only because I decided to search for Braxton property ownership in some nearby states. I can't see how it could have anything to do with the Braxtons murdering Lillian Hunnicutt or burning your motorhome, but you never know."

"Where is it, exactly?"

"In or near a small town called Daniel Springs in the Ozark Mountains. I'll show you."

Mac got out his phone, brought up a map of Arkansas and then zeroed in on the appropriate area, which was southeast of Fayetteville. "We'll probably have to take the motorhome. It's going to be more than a one-day trip."

That wasn't as cozy a situation as his suggestion might imply. When being away from home was necessary another time, Mac graciously gave me the bedroom and slept on the sofa himself. But after seeing the map I had a better idea.

"Woodston, where my niece DeeAnn lives, is on the opposite side of Fayetteville . . . remember, you visited me there once? . . . but Daniel Springs shouldn't be all that far from Woodston." I keep in touch with DeeAnn and grand-niece Sandy, but I haven't seen them since I drove away from Woodston in the motorhome I'd just then acquired, but which was now a warped skeleton in my driveway. "Maybe we could spend a night with them, take the next day to investigate this Heart of Home place, and spend another night with them on the way home."

"Would they mind spur-of-the-moment guests?"

"I'll see."

My phone doesn't provide maps like Mac's, but it does all that I ask of a phone, which is make phone calls. DeeAnn answered on the third ring, and she was delighted with the prospect of visitors. I told her we'd be there sometime tomorrow.

At the last minute, before going to bed, I went out and talked to Tasha. I figured my LOL invisibility might need a little upgrading for this venture into Braxton territory.

***

Next morning, when Mac picked me up for breakfast at McDonalds, Tasha and Eric had already left with their load of bargains for the flea market. We took turns driving after we were headed down to Arkansas. I made a suggestion on the way that we not elaborate to DeeAnn and Mike why we were visiting Heart of Home Hill. They aren't freak-out type people, but the idea of our prowling around in Braxton territory might arouse a dormant freak gene. Mac agreed.

As soon as we pulled into the yard at their home beside Little Tom Lake later that day, Sandy, in crop top and shorts, ran out to meet us with hugs. Their enormous dog Baby was with her. He gave me a slurpy welcome. I don't know if this was because he remembered me or because he's eager to slurp almost anyone. Sandy's friend, Skye, who'd been living with them since I was here before, was temporarily visiting her mother in New York. I already knew, from photos, that Sandy had grown into a very nice looking young lady, and now I also saw she'd outgrown me by half a head. She noticed my ankle tattoos right away.

"Aunt Ivy, you did it!" she squealed. "They look

awesome!"

She bent over to look at my ankles. Mac looked then too. My ankles haven't been inspected with so much interest in the past twenty years.

"Did you do the other one too? The one for your belly-button?" Sandy asked.

"You can tattoo your *belly-button?*" Mac asked.

Sandy interpreted the tone of his question correctly. "Oh, Mac, don't be so horrified," she scolded. "They're fakes! Just a transfer thing that goes on your skin. And it's *around* your belly-button, not in it."

"I can take them off any time," I assured him.

"Okay, let's see the belly-button one," Mac said.

Now I was the horrified one. "No way."

"That isn't fair," Mac said. He seemed to have developed a certain enthusiasm for this now. "To get a fake tattoo and then keep it a big secret."

I made a pointed glance at *his* tattoo, the real one of the blue motorcycle on his forearm. It might be viewable, but he'd always been less than forthcoming about it. The glance made him back off and become busy getting our overnight bags out of the pickup.

Sandy wasn't giving up yet, however. "You could put on your bikini and show—"

"Sandy Harrington, you know very well I don't own a bikini!"

"Then maybe it's time you got—"

"Okay, that's it," I said. "No more talk about tattoos or bikinis or belly-buttons. None. Zip. The subject is *finis.*"

Sandy looked mildly downcast. "Are you mad because I sent them to you?"

I gave her another hug. "Of course not, sweetie. Actually, they are fun." I put out my foot, and we both admired my ankle butterfly again.

"I had a couple of dolphins on my shoulder. They were fun too, but after a while, I was really glad I wasn't stuck with them for life."

"Me too." Sometimes I wonder about all the girls I see now with permanent designs everywhere, from nape of neck to small of back to depth of cleavage. How are all those astrological designs and tangled vines and mysterious faces going to look when wrinkles and cellulite and gravity get hold of them?

"I'm really glad you're here," Sandy said as we went arm-in-arm to the house, Mac following, Baby galumphing on ahead. "Mom said she didn't think you were coming just for a visit. She thought you might have a big announcement to make." She cast a meaningful glance over her shoulder at Mac.

"No big announcement."

"I don't understand you two. It seems about time—"

"Another subject that is not open for discussion," I told her. "Unless you want to give me a detailed rundown on your romance life."

"Sure," she said. "I kind of like this guy on my gymnastics team. But then there's this terrific guy who lifeguards at—"

"Never mind," I muttered at this backfire of my

212

challenge.

Although, over dinner, the news about my blown-up-and-burned motorhome did come across as a big announcement, but of a different sort than I knew they were all hoping for.

"Braxtons," DeeAnn said, an accusation not a question. "Oh, I don't like you being in the same state, let alone the same *city*, with them. Why don't you—"

I knew DeeAnn had started to suggest I come stay with them, but the Braxtons had found me here once. Which was when they'd tried to dynamite both my Thunderbird and me into the next county. At least I was sure it was them, even though they'd never been officially tied to it. Braxtons are slippery as greased pigs at squirming their way out of things.

DeeAnn apparently registered that problem with the Braxtons and altered the suggestion. "Maybe you could use the insurance money to buy another motorhome and get away from Madison Street again."

Mike nodded. "You could update too. The newer ones have those nice tip-outs for more space. We can help out if you need something extra to swing a deal."

"Thanks. That's really sweet of you, but I'm still, umm, considering my options." I never thought I'd use that grandiose sounding phrase, but there it was. "What we're doing on this trip is looking at a place called Heart of Home Hill over at Daniel Springs. Then we'll be back here again tomorrow night. Have you ever heard of it?"

DeeAnn and Mike hadn't, but, surprisingly, Sandy

had. "My friend Carla's folks are trying to find a good place for her grandma's sister to live, and I'm sure that's a place they looked at. Carla went along and said it was really *gross*. Dirty and smelled like week-old soup, and there was this big, heart-shaped *monstrosity* out front, all cracked and scabby looking, like some enormous creature had keeled over and *died* there."

DeeAnn and Mike didn't ask questions about why we were going to look at Heart of Home Hill, which was a relief because that meant we didn't have to fudge and tell them Mac was thinking about writing a magazine article about the place. Although he *is* always looking for subjects for magazine articles, so it wouldn't have been a real untruth anyway.

We had a fun evening visiting with them. Sandy showed me some of her teen-advice columns from the newspaper. I got the bedroom I'd stayed in before, the one with the big old four-poster bed, braided rugs, and the beautiful watercolor of an empty cross that always gives me goosebumps. Mac got the bedroom farther down the hall. Next morning, after we all went to early church, the extra 7:30 service the church holds during summer months, I changed to the outfit I'd decided on for today: loose, baggy top, elastic-waist pants, and shoes so sensible they could pass an IQ test.

***

I was familiar, from the time I'd lived with DeeAnn and Mike, with the route as far as Fayetteville, but I'd never been farther east into the Ozark Mountains. It was

214

breathtaking country, wild and beautiful. The roads wound through deep ravines and around mountains heavily forested with oak and hickory, the trees on the highest ridges showing just a tinge of glorious fall colors to come. Creeks with waterfalls, a bridge over a river, a fish hatchery, some quaint small towns I wished we had time to stop and explore.

"Maybe we can come another time just for fun," I suggested.

Mac had no comment, and I was reminded again that our relationship now had a cut-off date, the day when I remained on Madison Street and Mac didn't. That gave me a pang, but I determinedly reminded myself that I should contact the insurance company again. I needed that money from the motorhome for a car. I'd have no transportation after Mac left.

We found the turnoff to Daniel Springs, and then the old brick buildings of the town itself. It looked as if it were trying to be a touristy town, with colorful paintings on store windows and banners across the street about a bluegrass festival. From the absence of traffic, the tourist appeal didn't appear wildly successful, however. We didn't see a Heart of Home Hill sign, or a cracked heart, and Mac finally had to ask someone for directions. I asked Mac if we could first stop at a station and fill the gas tank. Although what I really needed, of course, was the restroom for my makeover.

I took along my bag with items I'd borrowed from Tasha.

CHAPTER 19

The restroom was clean but tiny, and I banged elbows and knees and even my chin as I squirmed into the items borrowed from Tasha. Afterward, the reflection in the small mirror showed my transformation wasn't nearly as total as Tasha's, but I looked less like me now. I hurried back to the pickup and slipped inside.

Mac gave me a look. "I'm sorry, but I'm afraid you're in the wrong—" He broke off and peered closer. "*Ivy?*"

Hey, great! If it took Mac a second look to identify me, I'd surely fool any Braxtons skulking around Heart of Home Hill. Tasha's wig covered my head, the hair longer and whiter than my own possum gray. A wide-brimmed purple hat flopped over my right eye, rose-tinted sunglasses with big purple frames hid the other eye, and padding inserted at various places changed my shape. Not exactly a flattering look, but I was going for disguise, not a fashion statement.

"I don't want to take a chance on Drake Braxton recognizing me if we run into him again," I explained.

Mac cast a surreptitious glance at my lumpy body. "Good job."

So, following directions, we turned onto a paved but

narrow road leading south out of town to . . . yes, indeedy, a hill. A beautiful setting, actually. Grand old oak trees scattered on the grassy slope, a picturesque road winding up the hill, a Southern-plantation style building looming on top. It certainly didn't look, as Sandy's friend had labeled it, *gross*.

A favorable first impression that deteriorated rapidly as we bumped across the pot-holed parking lot next to the building. Up close, the white paint was weathered and peeling like dead skin. The columns across the front retained some of their original grandeur, but various malignant looking additions to the sides and back of the building took away any semblance of elegance. The landscaping, overgrown and unkempt, might charitably be described as "natural."

Definitely gross.

And there, just as Sandy had said, was the huge red heart looming out front. Probably not a great idea even when originally stuck out there, apparently to give some significance to the Heart of Home Hill name, and now, with paint faded and concrete cracked and scabby, almost macabre.

The parking lot held a few cars, employees perhaps, or maybe visitors on this Sunday afternoon. Out back, five people in wheelchairs occupied a concrete patio. It was not an animated group.

"This is Drake Braxton's new business venture that keeps him so busy?" Mac asked doubtfully. "Why would he and that nephew with the plane fly down here for meetings?"

Good question. "It doesn't look as if he could be getting rich off it." I adjusted the brim of the hat lower on my eye. "So how are we doing this? You're writing a magazine article, and I'm your assistant?"

Mac grabbed his camera and I, as assistant, dug out my notebook and pen, and we approached the front entrance. I put my foot carefully on the bottom step, partly because it was cracked and warped, partly because my padding had an unanticipated tendency to make a continental shift when I moved. I gave it a surreptitious adjustment. How did Tasha keep everything in place? She hadn't mentioned this particular problem.

Inside, several people slumped on two saggy sofas watched a large-screen TV, and more people sat around two card tables. All but two were women. One woman suddenly reached across the table and snatched another woman's cards with a screech of "Cheat!" The two women stood up, glared at each other, and then they sat down and the game went on. A carpet underfoot wasn't threadbare, but it looked old enough to have known some Confederate boots. It could also, I decided as I peered closer, use a good cleaning.

Maybe Drake Braxton was making a tidy profit off this place by cutting corners on everything from maintenance to employees to meals? Although that didn't explain his flying trips. There was definitely an old-soup scent, heavy on the cabbage. A door on the left opened to a small office where a middle-aged woman sat behind a desk looking at a computer screen. She appeared to be concentrating hard, and I thought that was a good sign until

218

Mac muttered, "Facebook game," about the sounds coming from the computer. She wasn't so engrossed in the game that she missed our arrival, however. She stood up when we stepped through the doorway.

"Hello, may I help you?" She sounded pleasant enough. "Are you visiting one of our residents today?"

"No, we're here to—" Mac paused as if recalculating how he wanted to present this magazine-article proposal so it wouldn't sound as if he planned an exposé of the place. Which, after hearing a thud from somewhere beyond the group area, then another screech from the card players, I was beginning to think was what was needed.

The woman ignored the noise. She gave Mac a friendly smile, but her expression turned puzzled and a little wary when she looked at me. Was something wrong? I looked down and was horrified to see that something had shifted again. Now, where there should be only two bumps, there were definitely *four*. I hastily turned my back, pretended to look out the window, and shoved everything back into place.

The woman spoke to Mac. "You're looking for a place for your mother, perhaps?"

I whipped around . . . oh, oh, another shift, which I covered with folded arms. I glared at her with my one usable eye. She thought I was Mac's *mother*? I opened my mouth for an indignant objection, but I closed it when Mac smoothly took advantage of the situation and switched directions.

"Yes, Mother needs a new home. We were

wondering about a tour. Would that be possible?"

"Yes, of course. I'm Linette Magnuson, and you are—?"

"I'm Oliver MacPherson and Mother is—" He paused as if undecided how to identify me. He hadn't actually misstated his own name. Oliver is his middle name, although I've never known him to use it.

I had a middle name too, although I doubted Mac even knew it. A nice, ordinary one. "Anne," I said and left Mrs. Magnuson to supply whatever last name she thought appropriate.

I still wasn't enamored with the idea of being Mother, but at least I didn't have to take notes. I did a shoulder jiggle to get everything aligned, stuffed my notebook back in my purse and concentrated on Mother mode. I added a hint of limp as we left the office, which I thought was a nice touch until I realized it shifted my hip padding into an improbable pregnant look. I elbowed it back in place. How *did* Tasha manage this stuff? Mrs. Magnuson led us to an elevator tucked around behind the office, and Mac, ever the thoughtful "son," helped me into it with a hand on my elbow and a sly bump of hip against mine. As the elevator creaked upward, Mrs. Magnuson went on at great length about what a wonderful place Heart of Home Hill was. Activities for the residents, nutritionally balanced meals, a wonderfully caring live-in nurse.

"Perhaps we could speak with her?" Mac suggested.

"Actually, today is a rare exception, and she isn't here. She had a family emergency."

"You're the manager here?" I asked in my best old-mother squeak.

"Oh, no, I'm the office secretary. Mr. Braxton is our manager."

She didn't say anything about our meeting the manager, but I wiped my suddenly-damp hands on my padded thighs, half panicky that Drake Braxton would appear when the elevator door opened and target us with something more deadly than old soup.

"Mr. Braxton isn't here today," Mrs. Magnuson added. She smiled in a magnanimous way. "He works so hard that he does deserve an occasional day off."

An absent nurse. An absent manager. Which left a woman playing Facebook games running the place while the residents fought it out in a card game. Hmm.

"Is that Arnold Braxton?" Mac asked, smoothly inventing a name on the spot rather than using Drake's name.

"No, our Mr. Braxton is Dwayne."

Dwayne Braxton, Beth's father. That fit. She'd said he worked for Drake. Mrs. Magnuson expounded on his wonderful qualities as a manager while she unlocked a door to the left of the elevator. It was an unexpectedly pleasant room with a big window looking out on an expansive view of wooded hills and a cozy kitchen area tucked into one corner.

"For times when a resident wants a snack or light meal on her own," Mrs. Magnuson said. "We value our residents' needs, whether they want privacy or social interaction." She opened a bathroom door. "We have showers only, no bathtubs. We're very conscientious about the safety of our residents here."

Are showers safer than tubs? I wasn't sure. But probably cheaper.

There was also a desk, a twin-sized bed, a TV, and a tiny closet.

"This is the room Mother would have?" Mac asked.

That question hadn't occurred to me, but it was a shrewd one, because it made Mrs. Magnuson admit, "No, this room is already spoken for." Smoothly she added, "The available room is being cleaned and renovated right now."

But when we went back out to the hall just as a resident was coming out of her room, I got a peek inside it. Much different than the airy, nicely furnished room we'd just exited. Drab walls and a tiny window with a view of the peeling wall of one of those ugly additions, bed with a couple of bricks propping up one corner. What we'd just seen, I was reasonably certain, was a room reserved strictly for show purposes.

As we went back downstairs, Mrs. Magnuson and Mac discussed "Mother's" needs as if "Mother" wasn't present. I resisted an urge to kick some shins and stomp some toes. In the dining room, which Mac said he wanted to see, the old-soup scent was heavier than ever, but Mrs. Magnuson blithely ignored it and talked about the wonderful meals Heart of Home provided.

Beside a tablecloth with old stains, I asked, "What is that awful smell?"

Mrs. Magnuson patted my hand. "You smell

something?" she said, with a look at Mac that sympathized with his having to deal with a mother who had smell hallucinations and undoubtedly other peculiarities as well.

But Mac unhelpfully said, "I smell it too."

Mrs. Magnuson touched her chest and breathed deeply. "You know, now that you mention it, I do too. Perhaps an accident in the kitchen. I'll check with them right away."

I decided to take advantage of my position as the cantankerous mother who says whatever happens to come into her head. "What about the yard?" I asked. "Doesn't anyone ever trim the bushes or paint anything?"

"We're had a bit of a problem with the maintenance people this summer, so I must apologize that we do have a deferred maintenance situation at the moment."

Hmm. I'll have to remember that one. Sometimes my housework is in a "deferred maintenance" status.

Back at the office, Mac inquired about rates and Mrs. Magnuson gave him a price sheet. He asked about ownership, if some big corporation with far-off offices owned the Home, and was informed that this was a "family-owned enterprise."

"The owners visit often and are as concerned and caring about all our residents as they are about older members of their own family," she assured him.

"Well, we'll keep Heart of Home in mind," Mac said. "We do have some other places to look at. I want the best for Mother."

Mrs. Magnuson gave me another look. I smiled at

her. I had everything back in place now. It might be only will power holding it there, but I do have will power.

"Perhaps you're thinking of something a bit more upscale?" Mrs. Magnuson suggested almost delicately.

"Perhaps," Mac said.

"I do know of another property that might interest you." She dug in a drawer and produced a brochure. "It's a different type of living arrangement, a condo building, in which residents will each own their own units. But with so many amenities! One- or two-bedroom units. *Two* swimming pools, one indoor, one outdoor, plus a hot tub. Full dining service with a French chef. Tennis courts, workout room, everything to provide an active senior lifestyle." She gave my Doughboy shape a sideways glance. "Or, if someone prefers a less active lifestyle, there's a library and a cozy recreation room for playing cards or just relaxing. Plus organized outings to various events and places. All at a very reasonable price."

"That sounds wonderful," I said.

"You mean you buy a unit rather than rent?" Mac asked.

"Yes, which is why we don't mention it to everyone." With that same hint of delicacy she added, "Actually, it's an *investment* as well as a fantastic lifestyle. You become a part of the company itself, which means you share in the company profits *and* you have the right to purchase a condo at a fantastic price! Of course, a certain income level is one of the requirements of ownership. Would that be a problem?"

"It's never been so far." Mac managed to sound not *affronted* by the question, just mildly disdainful of it. "Although I prefer not to flaunt my assets or income."

Good comment, Mac. Just in case this woman happened to look out and spot that old Toyota pickup. It looks well past its flaunting days. Actually, I have no idea what Mac's income is. Sometimes he's frugal, sometimes spendy, both in situations that have always seemed appropriate at the time.

Mrs. Magnuson smiled as if he'd given the perfect answer. "Of course. And, for someone as astute as yourself, this is the perfect time to get in on the ground floor! Because, as an investor in the company, you're entitled to buy a unit in Phase One at half the price they will be when the project is completed. Can you believe it, *half* price, for a place like Camelot Golden Age Condos!"

"That's cash?" Mac asked.

"Complete information about both the company investment and condo purchase is covered at the informational seminars, and you can get individual details in a meeting with one of the personal counselors at that time. The seminars are held in various locations, so I'm sure there's one that's convenient for you."

"But I couldn't live there right away if we bought one, because it isn't finished?" I fussed.

"The project isn't ready for occupancy quite yet, no. But that's why it's such a marvelous opportunity! The lucky buyers will have both a lovely place to live in the near future *and* a wonderful investment in the company." Mrs.

Magnuson moved a step closer and lowered her voice. "Although I wouldn't wait, if I were you. There are only so many slots available, and I understand that Phase One is almost sold out."

"Is this place near here where we could see it?" Mac asked.

"As I mentioned, there are informational seminars in various cities, with a lovely complimentary dinner. There's even an opportunity to *win* a condo outright!" Mrs. Magnuson put the brochure in Mac's hand and closed his fingers around it. "This will tell you everything you need to know."

"This is owned by the same company that owns Heart of Home?" I asked.

"The family is dedicated to projects that benefit seniors. In fact, some older members of the family plan to live in Camelot Golden Age Condos themselves."

Blunt Mother had another question. "You get a commission if you sell us one?"

"I don't handle sales directly, no, but my name is stamped on the back of the brochure and you might mention it when you talk to a counselor at a seminar. But it's such an incredible opportunity that I hope you get in on it whether or not you mention my name."

"Okay, well, thanks, Mrs. Magnuson," Mac said. "We certainly appreciate your time and information."

We went back out to the pickup. I glanced through the glossy brochure as we took the winding road down the hill. Camelot Golden Age Condos. Very slickly done. An artist's rendition of an impressive building with balconies and windows. Outdoor pool glittering in sunshine, large building for the indoor pool, expansive lawns, elegant landscaping. Other views were artist's renditions of condo interiors with sleek woodwork, upscale appliances and airy rooms. There were also artist-rendition people, older but toned and tanned, playing tennis and golf, working out on various machines and lounging in front of an enormous fireplace. There were a few actual photos of beautiful landscaping, lovely trees, a man-made waterfall, and an elegant sign.

"What do you think now?" I asked Mac. I squirmed in the seat. My willpower was apparently fading because the padding felt as if it were doing another continental shift. "Is this new place Drake Braxton's golden goose laying Porsche eggs?"

"Sounds as if it could be."

"I wonder if the 'informational seminars' are the meetings Drake and his nephew fly around to?"

"I'd guess 'informational seminar' is a nice euphemism for a hard-sell sales pitch. And don't forget the 'complimentary dinner,'" Mac said.

I studied the fine print in the brochure. No Braxton name anywhere, just the rather uninformative statement that this was a Camelot Golden Age property. The location wasn't specified, other than a general statement that it was in the "banana belt of the Midwest." There was a number to call for dates and locations of the informational seminars.

"You never found anything like this when you were

searching for Braxton-owned property?"

"No. But I'll look again using the Camelot Golden Age name."

"Do you think this is on the up-and-up?" I asked finally.

"I question whether anything the Braxtons do is on the up-and-up."

"Including Beth Braxton and the Paso Fino horses?" I asked with a feeling of dismay. Beth and her grandma seemed sweet, and I certainly didn't want to think of them as involved in anything nefarious.

"They may be the exception to the rule," Mac granted. "But I'm beginning to see that the Braxtons hide behind any number of company names."

He asked if I wanted to stop at the same gas-station restroom to undo my makeover, but, with the brochure in my hand, apprehension jabbed me. As if we might turn a corner and run head on into Drake Braxton in his Hummer at any moment. I suddenly wanted to get out of Daniel Springs *now*. Mac cooperated, and we whipped right on through town, and it wasn't until the second small town farther along the road that we stopped at another gas station.

***

That evening I realized, as I should have before, that DeeAnn and Mike, and Sandy too, thought we'd gone to see Heart of Home Hill because we were actually thinking about living in a retirement home. And, helpful people that they are, they had a slug of other brochures for us to study. I gave them a real semi-explanation, which brought out their concerns, of course. I assured them we hadn't left a trail at Heart of Home Hill for any murderous Braxtons to follow.

We had another good evening, this time a steak cookout on the patio, and next morning DeeAnn's homemade cinnamon rolls for breakfast. She even packed a lunch for us, and at noon we stopped at a roadside rest area to eat it. I was leafing through the various brochures while we ate, thinking how wonderful they all made old age sound, if we were only living in their particular establishment.

I was looking at the Camelot Golden Age Condos brochure again when I saw something I hadn't noticed before in one of the actual photos. I adjusted my glasses and looked again. Could it be? No, surely not . . . but it was!

"Mac, look at this."

CHAPTER 20

Mac scooted over and looked at the photo I was tapping. "So?"

"Don't you recognize those trees?"

"Why would I recognize them? They're just trees. Pretty trees," he granted.

"It isn't an artist's rendition like most of the others. It's an actual photo."

"I can see that."

"Mac, those are the magnolia trees in Magnolia and Geoff's yard when they're in full bloom!"

"Why would their trees be in a brochure for the Braxton's condos?" Mac scoffed. He pulled the brochure over, took another look and shook his head.

"Look at the shape of the tree there on the left. It's a profile of Nixon's face! It was there when I left Madison Street, and I noticed it again as soon as I got back." I traced the outline for him. "There, can you see it now? How many magnolia trees are shaped like Nixon?"

"If you squint and hold your head just right and use a lot of imagination, there might be some small resemblance to a face," Mac said, clearly not convinced.

"You look when we get back home and you'll see it. Those are Magnolia's magnolias."

***

I reminded him of this when we drove down Madison Street late that afternoon. He still couldn't see anything unique about that tree in Magnolia and Geoff's yard. They were beautiful trees, yes, but just trees, no Nixon profile lurking among them. He parked at Eric and Tasha's place, and I grabbed his hand and determinedly led him back down the street for a better look. Magnolia came out to see what we were looking at. I pointed out the shape of the tree to her also, although I didn't mention the photo in the Camelot Golden Age Condos brochure. Mac and Magnolia both studied the trees the same way they'd look at a package of beans. All exactly alike.

"The forehead is a little more rounded than it used to be, but it's *there*," I insisted.

Magnolia frowned. "Ivy, I don't think this is a good thing, your seeing presidents and celebrity faces everywhere. Remember John Wayne?"

"I don't see them everywhere," I protested. And that blotch on a sidewalk in a little town in Arizona did bear a remarkable resemblance to John Wayne, even if Magnolia and two passers-by couldn't see it and one of them made that little twirly gesture at her head when they walked away. "Nixon's profile is definitely in that tree."

Mac squinted at the trees. "Well, if I close one eye and tilt my head just right, and stand on my left foot—"

"Maybe if you stood on your head," Magnolia suggested with facetious helpfulness.

They were making fun of me, gently, of course, but I

felt totally frustrated. "Oh, forget it," was what I muttered, but what I was fuming was, *Why couldn't they see it? Nixon's nose was plain as that padding on my hips.*

"Oh, before I forget it, someone was here looking at the motorhome while you were gone," Magnolia said. "He took a lot of photos."

"The police or arson investigator?"

"The car had an insurance company name on the side."

Great! Maybe the motorhome insurance money would be coming soon. Although I still hadn't heard anything from the house insurance people, and that one side of the house definitely needed an overhaul.

Mac and I walked in silence back toward the parked pickup. Finally Mac said, "I'm sorry I can't see it."

"It's probably not important anyway."

"But maybe it is. Maybe really important. Let's do some supposing here. Some what-iffing."

"About what?"

"A company called Radison Properties is trying to buy up everything on and around Madison Street. Right?"

"That isn't what-iffing. They're actually doing it."

"But who is Radison Properties? Braxtons are using several names for their businesses. Braxton Enterprises and Braxton Construction and Braxton Furniture. Zollinger Computers for the computer store. Braxton Brothers down in Arkansas. Suppose they set up another business, with a totally different name—"

Before Mac could get wherever he was going with

this, Magnolia yoo-hooed us back.

"Something else I forgot to tell you. Ed called earlier today. You remember Ed and Marie who used to live here? They were at the barbecue."

"Yes, I talked to them. Why did he call?"

"He and Marie drove over to Illinois to that Radison Properties address in Springfield. Ed decided he wanted to talk to them in person about the deal on their house. And they found that it isn't a real business address at all. It's just one of those mail forwarding outfits like you and we use."

No doubt some legitimate businesses use such services rather than maintaining an expensive office, but still. . .

"He said if anyone decides to sell to them, they'd better be really careful." Magnolia segued into another subject without pause. "I'm going to tell Geoff we need to get these trees trimmed. They're getting all out of shape."

She didn't mention it, but I had to wonder if perhaps she finally *had* seen Nixon's profile in her tree. From this angle, no Nixon was visible, but if you looked really close at that tree in the middle—

Forget it, Ivy! No face, no ears. Nothing. It's just a tree.

I thought Mac was going to head on back to the RV park, but instead, when we got to his pickup, he said, "I think we should consider this some more."

"Consider what? My tendency to see things that aren't there?" The question was a little grumpy, but I was alarmed that for a minute I had seen Obama's ears in that tree. Is it normal to see presidential body parts in the local flora? Maybe not. But then, I sometimes think *normal* is highly over-rated.

"No. To do some more what-iffing," Mac said.

"Okay."

We went inside. I fixed lemonade, took a glass out to Eric working in his shop and heard his report about a great day at the flea market. With all the trees out there, the shady back yard was cooler than the house. Mac was studying the brochure for Camelot Golden Age Condos when I returned and sat down beside him on the sofa in the living room.

"I can't see Nixon in that tree, either in the photo or in Magnolia's yard," Mac said. He sounded regretful. "I just can't. But I can see a similarity in the size and general arrangement of the trees. I think this photo may very well be of Magnolia and Geoff's trees."

"So the Braxtons set up a new company and call it Radison Properties. What's that got to do with a photo of Magnolia's trees in this brochure?" I said, still a little grumpy.

"The Braxtons wanted something real in a photo so the brochure promoting Camelot Golden Age Condos wasn't all 'artist's conception' stuff. Magnolia's trees looked great so they used a picture of them. I doubt they figured anyone would ever recognize *trees*."

"So where did they get a photo of Magnolia's trees?"

"They were in the area trying to kill you, so they just snapped a picture."

Such as, *Hey, wait a minute, Brax, before you pull*

the trigger on the old lady. I gotta get a picture of these here trees. I pointed to another actual photo. "If they were just snapping photos in the area, there isn't any manmade waterfall like that around here."

"It's from somewhere else, then, maybe a stock photo off the internet." Mac sounded impatient. "They just wanted photos that looked good. And real. Not an artist's rendering."

"There's this one of the nice sign." I pointed to the photo of the elegantly carved sign. Camelot Golden Age Condos – Gracious Senior Living. "That didn't come off the internet. It's a real sign."

"Anyone can have a sign made and take a photo of it. It could be sitting in Drake Braxton's back yard."

"So exactly what is it we're supposing?"

"Suppose one of the Braxtons is keeping an occasional eye on your place, watching for you to show up, and they see possibilities in an area that looks like it's slipping downhill. A good area in which to buy up property. That big swampy area where nothing has been built is available too."

"And has been for a long time. Probably because nothing *can* be built there. There are a zillion extra regulations on doing anything with something designated as wetland property."

"Drake Braxton figures he can get around that. He comes up with this plan for a fancy condo project here. Maybe, *maybe,*" he stressed, "it starts out as a legitimate idea for a project."

"He sets up Radison Properties and starts buying places."

"Right. He also sets up Camelot Golden Age Properties as a company. But then he runs short of money, so he invests in a fancy brochure with lots of artist's renderings of a beautiful setup. He does some sales pitch meetings to get people to buy into the project before it's built so he can keep it going. He uses money coming in from those deals not to actually start building anything but to buy more properties and upgrade his own lifestyle."

I expanded on Mac's what-if's. "But then he realizes that, rather than actually building anything, there's easier money to be made by selling investors a portion of the business as an investment, sweetening the deal with an 'opportunity' to buy a condo at a bargain price."

Mac nodded. "Or maybe he never intended to build anything. Maybe it's all been a scam from the beginning. He was buying the Madison Street properties in case the legitimacy of the project was questioned, so it would look like the condo project was really in the works, just a little behind schedule. Now he's gone big-time with 'informational seminars' in several states, probably figuring on expanding all over the country. With dinner, and, of course, that extra draw of the chance to win a free condo. And using money from new investors to pay dividends to earlier investors, so they think they've made a great investment. A Ponzi-type scheme."

"Could he get away with that?"

"Con men have gotten away with schemes much

more grandiose than that. I couldn't find any projects that Braxton Construction has going locally, but Drake Braxton is getting money somewhere to finance Hummers and Porsches and expensive house additions. He may be cutting enough corners at Heart of Home to provide some profit, but not enough to finance the lifestyle he likes."

True. "But what would it all have to do with killing Lillian Hunnicutt and blowing up my motorhome?"

"Nothing. Braxtons are capable of more than one criminal project at a time. Multi-tasking."

"Is Heart of Home Hill connected with it?" I was the one who'd noticed the similarity between Magnolia's magnolias and the trees in the brochure photo Mrs. Magnuson had given us, but the enormity of the scheme Mac was 'supposing' was more than I'd ever imagined.

"I don't think it has anything to do with Heart of Home, other than that after prospective clients look at that place and decide it's a dump, Drake Braxton comes up with the bigger-and-better idea for Camelot Golden Age Condos. Along with the buy-into-the-company investment scheme for his own bigger and better profits."

"But it's possible it *isn't* a scam. Maybe the Braxtons *are* selling pieces of a real business and have a real condo project going somewhere."

"Maybe they do. It's also possible there's really a Tooth Fairy. And if there is, the Braxtons would probably figure out how to make a buck off used teeth."

"There's nothing in the brochure to suggest the condo project is here on Madison Street. Apparently they aren't doing any sales pitches around here."

"It's easier to make a project sound glamorous from a distance, and they don't want someone up close looking at the site and seeing there aren't any signs of a condo project in progress. So they're keeping their pitches away from this area."

"Would anyone buy without actually seeing it?"

"Marguerite and I once went to a meeting, a *free dinner* meeting," Mac emphasized, "with a sales pitch for parcels in some big subdivision project down in Florida. With slick 'artist's renderings' of houses and roads and community buildings and people having fun on the beach. With a bargain price if we bought *now*."

"Did you?"

"No, but a lot of people did. I heard later it was all out in a swamp somewhere, and the only beach overlooked some stagnant water and alligators. Nothing was ever built, and the people promoting it wound up in deep trouble for interstate fraud. There are a lot more state and federal rules and regulations now to keep something like that from happening, but guys like Drake Braxton dodge or ignore rules and regulations. I'm going back to the motorhome and see what I can find out about Camelot Golden Age Condos on the internet."

"Can't you do that right here with your phone?"

"I could. But when I'm really looking for something I'd rather have a bigger, old-fashioned computer screen to look at. I'll be back later and we'll go to dinner somewhere."

Leaving me to consider the changes in my lifetime,

from when a computer was an awesome new invention to now. When a computer screen is old fashioned.

I pulled up my shirt tail and looked at my daisies. I might have a fake tattoo around my belly-button, but I was definitely behind the times otherwise.

***

Tasha got home a little later. She'd spent the day on a temp job in an office, but she'd be returning to her old-lady disguise project next week. I returned the wig and padding I'd borrowed from her. She was on the sofa, one foot in her lap so she could rub it. Oh, to be so young and flexible!

"I wanted to ask— I had a real problem keeping the padding from shifting around. Do you ever have trouble with that?"

Tasha laughed. "I did at first, but then I learned how to tape it in place. I should have told you about that." Then she turned gloomy. "But lately I've just been letting it sag or shift. When you're *old* it doesn't seem to matter. People don't see you anyway, unless you really get in their face."

Oh, yes, the invisible LOL scenario. I was familiar with it.

"I'm not sure I want to do any more of it." She picked up the hip pad I'd returned to her and looked at it as if it were a snake. "It's depressing, the people I encounter."

"But surely you've run across some people who are nice to older women."

"Oh, yeah, a few. A woman at one cosmetics counter went to a lot of trouble to find a blush that would look good on older skin. And a guy at an ice cream store told me they

239

offered a senior discount, but he wasn't sure I was old enough to be eligible. I knew he was kidding, but it was fun anyway. And he gave me an extra scoop."

"And what you're doing is worthwhile. Maybe when this woman publishes her results, it will actually make a difference in how some businesses and individuals perceive older people. You're using your acting ability for a good cause."

She gave me a cause-smause grimace. "Maybe it's just being old that depresses me. A friend was telling me today about a job opening she knew about. Good pay, more than I'm making pretending to be an old lady. Lots of tips."

"Waitressing?"

"Pole dancing."

Pole dancing! Which even I knew did not mean a few tastefully-clad girls twirling to old-fashioned polka music around a ribbon-bedecked pole.

"I could, you know, do it like I've done some other jobs. Just make it an acting job. *Acting* like I'm a pole dancer, not *being* one."

It seemed a rather fine distinction, but all I said was, "Are you going to do it?"

"I don't know. I keep thinking, what if God's watching? Do I want him to see me pole dancing?"

"Do you?"

"I don't think so."

***

That evening Mac and I went to the Chinese place with the red dragon. Mac ordered Mongolian chicken and I decided on shrimp chow mein. He spread a few pages he'd printed off the internet on the table.

I glanced through them. "They look like the same pictures that are in the brochure. Including Magnolia's trees."

No comment from Mac on the trees, with or without Nixon's profile. "The website doesn't spell out details about investing in the company along with buying a condo, although it several times mentions a 'remarkable investment opportunity.' It's mostly pushing people to come to one of their 'informational seminars.' Which is where they hit you with the hard sell and put the pen in your hand so you can sign on the line."

"So where and when are these seminars?"

"The closest one the website lists within the next few days is up in Minnesota, a St. Paul suburb. It's this coming Thursday evening. I think they're targeting people in cold weather areas where what they're calling 'the banana belt of the Midwest' would look appealing as a place to live."

"Actually, I've never heard of a banana belt in the Midwest."

Mac pointed to a line on one of the pages he'd printed out. "You have now. It sounds like a wonderful place."

"How long would it take to drive up to where this seminar is being held?"

"I figure we should allow a day and a half."

"Plus a day and a half back. It's a long way to go for a free dinner."

"But don't forget the chance to win a free condo! I

really think Oliver MacPherson and Mother Anne should look into this awesome opportunity. And see what the Braxtons are up to."

So Mac brought up the reservation form and filled it in. It asked various personal questions, including income range, which Mac dodged by answering "private information." Before our dinner was finished, he had an e-mail reply confirming our reservation for the Thursday night dinner and seminar in Minnesota.

This time it seemed more than ever likely we'd actually encounter some in-person Braxtons, so before we left I borrowed the wig and padding from Tasha again.

This time I added a roll of duct tape, indispensable for all kinds of do-it-yourself projects. No more four where there should be only two.

CHAPTER 21

We headed out in Mac's motorhome the next
morning, Koop included. He's been in Mac's motorhome
before and settled into a favorite spot in the bathroom sink.
We stayed that night in an RV park in southern Minnesota.
Mac generously gave me the comfortable bedroom, while he
slept on the sofa. He said the sofa was comfortable too, but
I figured, to be fair, the next night we should trade places.

The "seminar" was scheduled for a meeting room in
a three-story motel that looked fairly high-class when we
drove by the following day. A waterfall burbled out front.
With a half day to spare, we had lunch at Mickey's Dining
Car, a well-known 1930s art-deco diner with jukeboxes and
great food. We drove by the impressive Cathedral of St. Paul
and then toured Fort Snelling, the historical site of an 1820s
military outpost. We laughed and had fun, a mini-vacation,
although my nerves amped up when we dressed for the
dinner. This did *not*, I kept telling myself, bear any
similarities to the last meal served a convict before sentence
is carried out.

This time I used strategically placed strips of duct
tape to fasten the padding firmly in place, and everything felt
as steady as if it were surgically implanted when we walked
across the parking lot from the motorhome to the conference

room. I psyched myself up along the way. Okay, Braxtons, bring it on! We're going to nail you! Mac had a small digital recorder in his pocket to get their spiel down word for word. Dinner was scheduled for 6:00, "informational seminar" to follow. I wondered if they locked the door in case anyone tried to just eat and run. I didn't let myself think what they did if they discovered their least-favorite LOL in there chowing down on their free steak.

Quite a few people were waiting in the hallway outside the door when we arrived. They looked like average people, not wealthy but probably financially capable of making a reasonable-sized investment. Mac, gregarious as always, quickly started up a conversation with an older couple. They said they wanted a warmer place to live than their home north of St. Paul, but they didn't want to move too far from their grandchildren. They figured the banana belt of Camelot Golden Age Condos would be just right.

"I've not quite sure where that banana belt is," Mac said. "I've never heard of it before."

"I guess that's one of the things we'll find out tonight." The man sounded jovial, even eager. "I'm looking forward to lounging in that indoor pool instead of shoveling snow all winter."

"I understand that you have to invest in the company in order to purchase a condo," Mac said.

"Sounds good to me. Given what we're getting off our money-market funds and bank CDs, I'll welcome a more profitable investment," the man said. "A friend of ours got in early on this, and he's been getting good payoffs on his investment."

These people were poised to buy. Wise investors? Or naïve innocents rushing down the trail to sucker-dom?

6:00 came, but the doors didn't open. Another ten minutes and a man in a dark suit stepped out and announced there would be a slight delay. Behind him, I could see long rows of tables with floral centerpieces and place settings on white tablecloths. I also got a glimpse of a podium up front, with a screen for a video or power-point presentation. Individual cubicles set up along the far side offered privacy for individual hard sells. Everything looked ready to go. But another ten minutes dragged by and nothing happened. Except I started to itch under the duct tape plastered to my skin. I discreetly wiggled an elbow to scratch it.

We overheard part of another discussion. One in which one of the men said he was beginning to wonder if Camelot Golden Age Condos was as good a deal as they tried to make it out to be. "One of those deals that, if it sounds too good to be true, probably isn't."

"I figure I can tell a good deal from a bad one," the other guy said. "They aren't going to put anything over on me."

My own thought was, *Famous last words.*

Then Mac got started talking to two older women, sisters. They were elegantly dressed, although it was an out-of-date elegance of taffeta and lace. At first they talked primly about wanting to get out of the big, drafty old house they'd lived in for thirty years and into a condo with less upkeep. But something in Mac's friendly manner apparently encouraged them to get more confidential with him. They edged closer and so did I.

"Actually, we're not planning to buy anything," the one with upswept hair confided. "We come to these things for the free dinners."

The other sister, in old-fashioned pearls and lacy blouse with a bow, giggled. "We sign up for anything where there's free food. Last week we did an open house—"

"Where the cocktail wiener things were a *disgrace*," Upswept Hair declared. "If we'd paid anything, I'd have demanded our money back."

"But the burgers at the car dealership were great. We were really tempted by that hybrid model they had on display."

I couldn't tell if they were elders living in genteel poverty and needed free meals, or eccentric rich ladies who could afford a hybrid car and just enjoyed caging free meals.

"We think this condo thing tonight is probably a rip-off. Worse than the time-share-in Hawaii hustle we went to a while back. Their luau dinner was fantastic, but I finally had to pretend a fainting spell to get away from that dreadful pushy salesman."

"So why are you suspicious of tonight's event?" Mac asked.

"After a while, you get a *feel* for these things." Upswept Hair nodded wisely. "You can just tell if they have something authentic to offer or if it's all bells and whistles hiding an expensive trap. Which it usually is."

"How'd you hear about tonight's event?"

"Ad in a local newspaper. That's where we find most of our events."

"We're thinking we'll try wedding receptions next," Pearls and Lacy Blouse said. "Who's going to know at a big wedding if you're an invited guest or not? And they won't be trying to sell us anything."

I didn't mention that I'd considered this myself a long time ago, when I was newly dismayed to find I'd aged into invisibility. Not that I'd ever actually done it. Yet.

"Well, uh, happy eating," Mac said finally.

Ten more minutes went by. People were getting restless. And, given the fact that these were all older people, tired of standing. A couple of benches along the wall were already filled. The itch under my tape got even itchier. What I wanted to do was raise my left arm and scratch like a chimpanzee with fleas, but I settled for edging to the side and surreptitiously rubbing my shoulder against the wall. Until a woman in a white linen pantsuit started giving me an odd look. By now I wasn't sure itching was much of an improvement over shifting body parts.

Grumbles rumbled through the group. A few people left. More, however, were apparently not yet ready to give up on a free dinner. I figured a free steak was the least of what the Braxtons owed me for my years of running and hiding from them. At 6:50 the man in dark suit stepped through the door again.

"I'm sorry to have to inform you that tonight's dinner and seminar have been cancelled. This is an unforeseen and most unfortunate circumstance which the management of this establishment highly regrets. It is, however, beyond our control and you should express your dissatisfaction to sponsors of the event."

"So where are they to express it to?" someone yelled.

"Yeah, what kind of a shyster outfits do you let come in here?"

More yells, and the man said, "One moment, please," and stepped back through the door. A few minutes later he reappeared, big smile. He held up a hand. "We realize what an inconvenience this is, and the management would like to make amends by offering you dinner in our main dining room. Just mention to the server that you were with the Camelot Golden Age group and your dinner will be discounted a full fifty percent."

That brought a mixed response: some applause, some grumbling.

"Interested?" Mac asked.

I shook my head. By now even my belly-button tattoo was itching, and there is no way to scratch your belly gracefully in public. Or even effectively, if it's under a big mound of padding. "We can fix something out in the motorhome."

Which we did. In the tiny bathroom, I yanked off the wig, ouched as I pulled off the duct tape, and scrubbed at the itchy strips on my skin with a washcloth. Then we had canned chili topped with grated cheese, and discussed tonight's odd no-show situation. Were the Braxtons up to something? Well, the Braxtons usually were up to something, we agreed, but this didn't seem planned. They were surely stuck with a big bill even though tonight hadn't produced any investors. Illness? Airplane disaster? We couldn't figure it out, but we decided we may as well start for home.

We drove a hundred or so miles before parking at a roadside rest area. I tried to get Mac to trade places with me, but he insisted I take the bedroom again. Koop chose to curl up with him this night. I got a fairly good night's sleep in spite of the noisy refrigerated truck that parked next to us most of the night, an aggravation familiar to on-the-road sleepers.

Neither Tasha nor Eric was at home when Mac dropped me off late the next day. I unpacked my overnight bag and then walked down to my old house to check for mail. Nothing. I felt restless, relieved that there hadn't been some dangerous confrontation with the Braxtons but also vaguely let down. I'd been all psyched up to get something definite to take to Officer DeLora about some nefarious scheme the family had going, and now everything just felt . . . unfinished. What was our next move? I couldn't think of one.

So what I did was find a bottle of rubbing alcohol and remove my ankle and belly-button adornments. Like Sandy had said about her temporary dolphin tattoos, they were fun for a while but I was glad I wasn't stuck with them for life.

Mac called. He said the guys at the RV park wanted me to come out for another round of horseshoes tomorrow, but I declined the invitation. My horseshoe-tossing talent is unreliable, and I decided I'd rather rest on my laurels than have an ignominious bad-horseshoe day. He said he intended to spend the next day working on the article about Grandma Braxton and the horses, and next week we'd take it out for her approval. I decided, if granddaughter Beth was there, I'd suggest the fake tattoos to her. Maybe Grandma would approve of that alternative, and maybe it would also make Beth decide that temporary was better than permanent. I'd point out that with temporary, she could change the designs as often as she wanted.

Sometimes I wonder about my life. I've turned into an LOL pushing fake tattoos?

Tasha and Eric still weren't home by the time I headed for bed. I locked everything up tight and watched out the window for a few minutes after turning the lights off. It occurred to me that if the Braxtons weren't up in Minnesota hard-selling non-existent condos, they could be right here on Madison Street stalking me again. The mannequin's head had fallen over. I set her upright but left her facing the wall.

On Saturday evening Mac brought over a rough draft of his article and we popped some popcorn and edited what he'd written. I figured Grandma Braxton would be delighted. The next morning we went to church. I invited Eric and Tasha to come along, but they'd already decided to spend the morning working out at the gym. More admirable than sleeping in, I granted, but a muscular body here wouldn't make much difference in eternity.

The message at church that morning was lively, about the pastor's experience buying a house "as is," which meant it had everything from "termites holding hands to keep the walls together," to a basement with a rat big enough to terrorize their cat. He compared this "as is" house with the Lord accepting us "as is," with all our flaws and shortcomings, that we don't have to try to remake ourselves before we come to him. I really wished Tasha and Eric had come.

By that evening I was still restless. Everything felt up in the air, as if I were waiting for the other shoe to fall. Although, with the Braxtons, it might be waiting for the next explosion to go off. Mac seemed to feel that way too. We spent some time at the horseshoe pit at his RV park that afternoon. I was glad no one else was there to see my performance. On this day, my horseshoes plunged to the ground as if they had a death wish.

And then at midmorning on Monday, while I was studying insurance papers again, Officer DeLora called. "Have you seen this morning's paper yet?" Her voice held a controlled excitement.

"No."

"Don't go anywhere. I'm coming right over."

CHAPTER 22

Officer DeLora didn't arrive with siren wailing, but she must have jammed the gas pedal to the floorboard to get here so fast. She ran up the front steps holding the newspaper and thrust it at me when I opened the door.

"Third page!"

The story may not have made the front page, but I sat down when I saw the headline.

Locals Caught in Investment Scheme Roundup.

With Drake Braxton's recognizable face, his hands cuffed behind him, in one of the photos. Before I could read any further, Mac was there, pounding on the door. He, too, had newspaper in hand.

"No wonder that dinner and sales pitch we went to was cancelled!" he said.

I raced through the article, then read it more slowly a second time. The gist of the article was that the FBI had been working on this case of investment fraud for months. Coordinated arrests had been made in Missouri, Minnesota, Wisconsin, Illinois, Kansas and Arkansas. The fraud was even bigger than what Mac and I had imagined, and it went far beyond Madison Street. Millions had been bilked out of investors on what they were calling a Ponzi type scheme,

252

paying early investors off with money from new investors. As I read, I realized the arrests in Minnesota must have come only minutes before we were scheduled to sit down to dinner and listen to their spiel.

I was familiar with many of the names listed. Drake Braxton, of course. Several other Braxtons, including Heart of Home manager Dwayne Braxton. That gave me a little pang. Did young Beth Braxton know about her father yet? Even the attorney in the family, Elton Braxton had been nabbed. Also Tyler Zollinger and various other Zollingers. Plus others with non-Braxton or Zollinger names.

There were also names I *didn't* see. Grandma Braxton wasn't there. Neither was Deena the Podiatrist or Drake Braxton's wife. Or Tyler's twin brother Sam. Or the young Zack Braxton I'd encountered at the furniture store. Did that mean they were uninvolved and innocent, or just that they hadn't been arrested yet?

The article didn't go into complete details about the fraud, but it did say unregistered securities were involved, as well as a network of investment pitches disguised as seminars, and sales of non-existent condos. Other heavyweight government agencies, the Securities and Exchange Commission and the Financial Industry Regulating Authority, were also involved.

I felt a little giddy. The Braxtons had gone *down*.

"You knew about this but just couldn't tell us?" I asked Officer DeLora.

She shook her head. "We're as surprised as anyone. If we call the FBI in and work with them on a case, we have some idea what they're doing. But they don't confide in us on a situation in which we're not involved, such as this one, even if it is in our area. And this takedown includes way more than our local area."

"So what happens now?" Mac asked.

"A trial eventually. Although I don't know where. Unless they reach some kind of plea bargain agreement. In any case, some of them are undoubtedly going to prison for a good, long stretch."

"Drake Braxton?" I asked hopefully.

"It looks as if he's a big wheel in the scheme, so I'd say yes," Officer DeLora said.

"Where are they?" Mac asked.

"We don't have that information, but I can tell you that none of them are being held here locally."

I figured that was also good news. In any circumstance, a Braxton several states away is preferable to a close-by Braxton. But, after a momentary glee, the bottom-line truth hammered me. Thinking I was Braxton-free was much too premature. "They may be caught, but they'll get out on bail."

With a frown, Officer DeLora agreed. "There's always that. Big money fraud is involved here, but these aren't no-bail type crimes."

"Which will give Drake Braxton plenty of time to take care of unfinished business with me before he gets sent up."

"He'll probably be too busy coping with all this to have time to worry about you," Officer DeLora said. "With the SEC and FIRA involved, some extremely large fines are probably in the offing. He'll have that to worry about, along with the shutdown of his business."

I knew Officer DeLora was trying to reassure me, but I pointed out what Mac had said a few days ago. "The Braxtons are experts at multi-tasking." And, considering how doggedly they'd trailed me, they'd no doubt set aside a few minutes to finish the job.

"What about the body in the bathtub?" Mac asked. "And Ivy's motor home? Will they get Drake and perhaps some other Braxtons on murder and arson charges too?"

"The FBI may not have run into those crimes, since they aren't connected with the interstate fraud, but this should make our local department look more closely at Braxton involvement in those cases," Officer DeLora said. She got a glint in her eye that matched the tightness of the bun in her hair. "In fact, I'm going to make sure that happens."

Officer DeLora left, and Mac and I looked at each other.

"I suppose you'll be leaving now that the Braxtons are taken care of," I said. Elvis was a little tilted on the wall now, and I went over to straighten his tin-can-lid frame. I would *not* get all teary because Mac was going.

But Mac didn't fail me.

"Not yet. As you said, it won't take them long to get out on bail." He glanced around the living room with its one-of-a-kind junkyard decorating scheme. "I know Eric and Tasha are concerned about you, and I have to wonder how safe you are here."

***

There were more articles in the newspaper and on TV over the next few days. The authorities had connected Radison Properties with the fraud. No explanation of why the name Radison had been used for the company purchasing properties around Madison Street, and no arrest of anyone by that name, but a complicated tangle of ownership through various companies led back to the Braxtons. None of the photos showed houses on Madison Street, but there was one of the swampy area they'd purchased, along with the facetious question, "Wanna buy a condo here?"

A home seller on Madison Street was quoted as saying he thought they may have had a legitimate project planned to start with, but it had morphed into a big scam. Iris Braxton, Drake's wife, whose name had been missing earlier, was also arrested. She'd been involved as both a bookkeeper and a "counselor."

Officer DeLora called and said some of the lower-echelon people involved in sales, people who were unrelated to the family and may not even have known they were pitching a phony scheme, were now out on bail. Drake Braxton and several other upper-level people hadn't yet made the much higher bail set for them and were still being held. Lawyer Elton Braxton, who either had more money available or knew his way around the system better, was out.

"But they'll all be out before long," I said. Grandma Braxton might be unhappy with the family and make them sit in jail for a while, but she'd undoubtedly bail them out soon.

Officer DeLora didn't argue that. "I'll call you as soon as they're released, so you can take appropriate steps," she said. She didn't specify what those "appropriate steps" might be, but Mac would no doubt tell me again that it was time to get out of town.

"Oh, something else," Officer DeLora added. "The 'person of interest' in the murder of the woman in your bathtub turns out to have an ironclad alibi. She was in jail from last November to this past May."

"Which means?"

"The Braxtons are definitely under greater scrutiny for her murder now. There is at least one interesting fingerprint that wasn't identified earlier but may be now that we have other fingerprints with which to compare it."

The fact that law enforcement was taking aim at the Braxtons was good news. But I couldn't let down my guard. The Braxtons were a many-tentacled clan.

The insurance company had the remains of the motorhome hauled away, and Mac moved his motorhome into the driveway at the house again. I had to admit I liked having him closer. We did more work on the interior of the house, cleaning and repainting. The headstone I'd chosen to mark an empty grave for Colin was set in place on the plot next to Harley. I didn't feel any lessening of grief when we visited it, but there was a gentle sense of closure.

That same day, we drove out by Drake Braxton's house. Work on the big addition appeared to have halted. Mac took the completed article to Grandma Braxton later that day, but I had to meet with the house insurance people and didn't go along. He didn't see Grandma, but Beth was working a horse in the corral and he left the envelope with her to pass on to her grandmother. Beth didn't say anything about the Braxton disaster, but Mac said she wasn't nearly as bubbly as before.

Much to my surprise at the speedy action, I received a check for the insurance payoff on the motorhome. It wasn't overly generous, definitely not in Hummer territory, but Mac helped me find a nice used Camry. Several years old, but only 59,000 miles on it.

So, life moved along, slowly but in relatively normal fashion. Some interested buyers came to look at Eric's purple cow. Tasha's next project in old-age disguise would be to see how a lone, older woman was treated in various restaurants, but that wouldn't start for several days yet. Now she had a temporary house-cleaning job.

In spite of the normalcy, I still had that uneasy, waiting-for-the-other-shoe-to-drop feeling. Then Officer DeLora called again, late in the afternoon. I stopped in the middle of cleaning Koop's litter box to answer the phone.

"Some bad news," she said. "Drake Braxton and the others still in custody have made their bail and will be released tomorrow."

"So I'd better run for cover?"

"Well, that's up to you, of course." She said it offhandedly, and with nonchalance added, "Although there is also some good news. As soon as Drake Braxton is released, he'll be immediately re-arrested." And finally she dropped the deliberate casualness and burst out with the best news. "And there's no way he's getting out on bail with the new charges against him!"

She'd taken a drama-queen way of announcing this, stretching it out, but I was too pleased to hear it to grumble about technique. "Re-arrested by whom for what?"

"By us. For murder. Your theory that the Braxtons had killed the woman in your tub thinking she was you finally got some serious attention. That previously unidentified fingerprint on the tub was compared with Drake Braxton's prints, which we didn't have before he was arrested by the FBI, and it matched. And DNA from a couple strands of hair in that blood on the chunk of carpet cut out of the bedroom floor also matched his. We didn't have his DNA before, either."

"Wow. I'm impressed. Good work!"

"I don't think we can tie Drake Braxton to arson on your motorhome," she added regretfully, "but the murder case against him is strong. This is all confidential information, of course. I'm telling you only so you can stop worrying that he's going to get out and come after you."

"Okay. And thank you! I really appreciate your going to bat on this. Now you can quit a winner and start life as a vegan chef."

Officer DeLora had too much self-control to actually sigh, but I heard an undercurrent of sigh in her voice when she said, "Not yet. I don't really get much credit on this. And I heard one officer say to another this morning, after he banged up the fender of a squad car, that he'd 'pulled a

DeLora.' So I still have to live with that. But I'm really glad that now you can feel safe."

We talked a minute more, and when the call ended the new feeling really began to sink in. It was over! For the first time since Bo Zollinger's trial almost three years ago, I didn't have to worry about a Braxton stalking or ambushing me. Koop gave me a strange look as I picked up the mannequin head and danced around the room with it. Safe!

Although that might mean something else not so wonderful. . .

The news about Drake Braxton's new arrest for murder hit the news right after he was released on bail the next day. Officer DeLora called to tell me he was in custody again, and I walked down the street to Mac's motorhome to tell him. He gave me a hug and said we should turn cartwheels in the street to celebrate. I was willing to give it a try, but then he said maybe we should settle for a celebratory dinner.

It was a great dinner at the Chinese restaurant that evening, fun and companionable, with joy and laughter. There were leftovers to take home, tangy sweet-and-sour chicken wings and pork fried rice. The waitress brought fortune cookies and a fresh pot of tea.

"So, free at last," Mac said.

"It's a good feeling," I said, although I noticed we weren't having any conversation about the future. "No Braxtons. No wondering about a bomb under my bed or a bullet through a window."

"You can also go anywhere you want now, do

whatever you want, without worrying that the Braxtons will track you down," Mac added.

"I also don't have a motorhome now, remember? But I don't need one. There's nowhere I want to go. I'm *home.*"

Mac cleared his throat and leaned forward, as if that were an opening he'd been waiting for. "I love you, you know. I'm thinking, we could get married, and then we could make our home traveling together. I like the freedom of being on the road and seeing new places."

I cleared my throat too. "I'm thinking, we could get married and live right here together. I like being in one place. Home. I love you too. You know."

Then we just sat there like two turtles with their heads drawn in, fortune cookies untouched, other words dangling unspoken between us.

If you loved me enough, you'd roam the world with me.

If you loved me enough, you'd make a home here with me.

The silence stretched out until Mac finally said, "I talked to Dan this morning." Dan is Mac's son who lives in Montana, the destination Mac hadn't reached when he detoured here to see me. It sounded like a change of subjects, but I knew it wasn't. "He's putting an addition on their house. I'm thinking I should head up there and help him get it done before winter. Snow sometimes comes early in Montana, you know."

No surprise. We'd both known this time of going our separate ways was coming, but I had to swallow a big lump of dismay. After I choked it down, I managed to say, "Yes, that's true. I'm sure he'll appreciate the help. I'm thinking, after that damaged wall on the house is repaired, I should get some more furniture before winter."

"The house is still rather empty," Mac agreed.

The waitress interrupted this little conversational dance. "Do you need containers?"

We both eyed the leftovers that didn't look nearly as appealing as they had a few minutes earlier.

"No, none for me," Mac said.

"I won't be needing any either."

No big argument, no angry hostility between us. On the drive back to Madison Street, our only conversation was about what a beautiful evening it was. Mac took me to Eric and Tasha's place and kissed me lightly at the door.

I went inside feeling unsettled but not devastated. Nothing, I reminded myself, was actually settled yet. We were stubborn but reasonable people. We loved each other. We'd talk about this again in the morning. Maybe we could compromise by living here on Madison Street and taking short, or even some longer trips in the motorhome together.

But next morning, the driveway was empty. Mac was gone.

CHAPTER 23

I stared at the empty space. An even larger empty space loomed inside me. Bereaved, forsaken, abandoned. Like the people in those "Left Behind" books, where all that remained of loved ones were the clothes they'd been wearing. There was even a glove lying alongside the driveway. A grease-and-grass-stained work glove. Mac's glove. I picked it up and felt the hollow emptiness where Mac's hand had been. I remembered how warm and good his hand had felt holding mine as we strolled together.

Then indignation flooded my empty space. Mac hadn't been whisked off, helpless to resist; he'd just picked up and left. And I was floundering in melodrama. Stubborn old geezer!

I marched back to my room at Tasha and Eric's house. I started to toss the glove in the trash basket but instead set it on the table by the mannequin's head. To remind myself that I didn't need Mac himself any more than I needed his old glove. I had a car, a cat, a sleeper-sofa, good friends, and my home. And the Lord, always the Lord.

Time to get on with life.

I briskly contacted the house insurance people again, and they told me to go ahead with bids on the repair work. Three construction outfits came in one day and wrote up quick bids. The repair work wasn't extensive, but I decided to wait until it was done before moving back into the house. I fixed loose handles on several cabinet doors and repaired a hinge myself. I could handle a screwdriver. A hammer too, if necessary.

I remembered some old song about getting along without you before I met you, and how the singer was gonna get along without you now. I determinedly hummed it. *I can get along without you, Mac MacPherson.* But I didn't feel like dancing to it.

Magnolia had bought a computer and, with her usual determination, was enthusiastically learning how to use it. She'd already found a new "cousin" in France, which meant their back yard needed some French touches to highlight the connection. I went with her to several nurseries to look for French shrubs. We couldn't find any French shrubs . . . in fact, the question rather mystified the salesclerk . . . but Magnolia lingered over an elf yard ornament. The clerk, a good saleswoman, said she thought it was a French elf. I doubted elves came with nationalistic connections, but its mischievous expression reminded me of Mac.

That was a problem. Way too many things reminded me of Mac. The color of the bathroom; that soft pink had been his idea. My denim shorts; he'd especially liked them. A whiff of garlic in spaghetti sauce even brought a twinge of nostalgia for all the garlic we'd shared.

I took Koop to the vet to have his shots updated. I helped Eric make some new wind chimes out of long bolts and shiny wheel lugs. We hung them all on a low branch near the shop, where they filled the back yard with musical tinkles. Someone gave Tasha a box of peaches and I canned them for her.

A week went by, and I didn't hear anything from Mac. I wondered if he'd made it up to Montana okay. I wondered if the motorhome was lying in a ditch on some backcountry road. I wondered if vultures were circling overhead.

Well, if they were, they'd better watch out. Mac is self-sufficient, capable, and practical, and any circling vulture might just wind up as vulture pot pie. If vultures are edible. I didn't know. But Mac would.

But I don't miss Mac. I repeat that to myself before breakfast, during lunch and after dinner, and maybe, oh, seventeen other times during the day. I figure if I say it enough times, sooner or later it will be true. I was frustrated with myself. Mac and I had been separated much longer than a week at various times, and I'd never suffered any pity-party separation pangs. But it was different this time, of course. This wasn't a meet-you-up-in-Oregon—or Arizona or Texas—type separation. This time Mac was as gone as if he'd stepped into another dimension.

Stubborn old geezer.

Meaning Mac, of course. Not *me*.

Okay, time to get that furniture I needed before I moved back into the house. I couldn't afford a houseful, so the sleeper-sofa could serve as both sofa and bed for a while yet, but I needed a recliner and curtains for the living room. An end table to replace the cardboard box by the sofa. A TV and a toaster that didn't throw slices of bread like a pitcher trying out for the World Series.

I went back to the store where I'd bought the sofa. I looked at recliners. I sat in recliners. I reclined in recliners. Nothing felt right. I looked at curtains. Too heavy. Too light. Too blue. Not blue enough. I looked at TVs. Too big. Too little. Lousy programs on all of them.

I returned to Madison Street without purchasing anything. I wandered the empty house feeling restless and fidgety. Everything was clean, repainted, scent-less. I wasn't ready to take a bath in the upstairs bathroom yet, but I could walk in there without cringing. The Braxtons were safely corralled in jail, out of my life for good. I should be singing with joy instead of moping around.

I planted myself beside the upstairs bedroom window and stared out at the blackened maple tree. It looked dark and skeletal, as if it had been hit with some devastating curse. But Geoff had assured me it would grow back, so no disaster there. I looked down at the fire-damaged wall of the house. It would be repaired soon. No disaster there, either.

But also no joy.

So, Ms. Ivy Malone, what's wrong here? How come you're dragging around like a slug in a puddle of molasses?

It didn't take a lightning-strike epiphany to answer that question. Mac was what was wrong. Specifically, *no Mac* was the problem.

But you're home, Ivy, I reminded myself. You're *home.*

Was I? Yes, it was a house that had once been home,

but, without Mac, it wasn't a home now. And all the furniture in the world wasn't going to make it home without him.

I instantly scoffed at that country-and-western song philosophy. Mac had never lived here. How could his not being here now keep it from being home?

It just did.

This was not good. It was even worse than seeing dead presidents in tomatoes and trees. I'm talking to myself. About missing Mac.

So what are you going to do about it?

Nothing. Absolutely nothing. I'm a sensible, independent LOL, not some lovesick, angst-driven teenager. To prove it, I went back to my bedroom at Tasha and Eric's place and plastered a fresh tattoo on my ankle.

Well, great. In my rush to prove something . . . although I wasn't quite sure what . . . I'd made a small misjudgment. Now I had an upside-down purple unicorn on my ankle.

And that was how I felt. As if my whole life had turned upside down. All because of Mac.

I was trying to decide if I wanted to undo the upside-down unicorn when three words thundered in my head. Yes, *thundered.*

Go, Ivy, go.

I looked around. Up. Down. Sideways. I even turned a slow circle and gave my chest a questioning thump. Who, me? Go where?

You know where. Go. To Mac.

This is even more not good. Now I'm hearing voices

in my head. I walked around again. *I'm home,* I reminded myself once more. This was no time to let that dreaded *s* word, *senile,* overtake me. Stop procrastinating, I told myself, and get busy picking out new furniture.

Go, Ivy, go.

I paused warily. Is that you, Lord?

Go. Now.

Okay, okay. I hear you. I suppose I could do that. I could drive up to Montana. Maybe I could talk some sense into him. But he could have stayed. Why should I have to make the first move? I'll think about it.

Go, Ivy, go.

A sign from the Lord? No, more than a sign. These were words ringing in my head.

But I'm free of the Braxtons now, I argued. I don't have to run and hide any more. Besides, I don't have a motorhome now. I can't just take off, like jumping off a cliff—

Jump, Ivy, jump!

How come I'm the one getting all this *go* and *jump* advice? You could yell at *him,* Lord. Tell that stubborn old geezer to come back to *me.* I offered appropriate words. Go, Mac, go.

Go, Ivy, go.

You're repeating yourself, Lord.

Go, Ivy, go.

I sighed. That's what the Lord has to do sometimes, isn't it? Repeat himself. Give us a gentle nudge. Maybe even a not-so-gentle shove.

Okay, okay, I'm going. But when will I be back?

No answer to that question. Just another *Go, Ivy, go.*

***

Grudgingly, remembering Tasha and Eric had said they'd tried to buy the house they were living in, I talked to them that evening. Although all the time we were talking I was thinking, I don't have to *sell* the house. I could rent or even just loan it to them. I mean, taking off after Mac might be just a wild goose chase. Maybe I'll want to turn around and come home.

Except it wasn't home without Mac.

It was a short talk with Eric and Tasha, no sales pitch involved. They were delighted. Yes, they'd like to buy the house. I reminded them that the upstairs carpet had a big hole in it and the scorched siding still needed repair. They said neither mattered. Eric had been offered a full-time job working with kids at the gym. Now he could take it. Tasha was rethinking acting as a lifetime endeavor; maybe she'd go back to school and learn a computer occupation. The money they'd saved was enough for a down payment on the house. We decided on monthly payments direct to me, so they wouldn't have to go through a bank to finance the purchase.

With the decision made, I wanted to jump in the car and go. Maybe before I changed my mind? Maybe I *should* give myself time to change my mind. . .

Go—

Never mind, Lord.

Tasha called a title company about setting up the

arrangement between us, and the soonest we could make an appointment was two days from now. At some point there would be documents to sign, but they said I could contact them later about where to send the papers. I started culling my belongings down to what I could stuff in the car. Tasha said they'd be glad to store whatever I didn't have room to take along now.

I had to tell Magnolia and Geoff what I was doing. If I expected argument, I didn't get it. Magnolia declared that she'd known ever since she introduced Mac and me that we belonged together. Geoff gave me a new U.S. map and we discussed the best route to Montana. I marked it in red on the map.

The red line was comforting, like a guideline for my life. Although I still had qualms and misgivings. Mac had never called. Maybe I should call him before I stepped off that cliff and left this life behind. Lord, you don't want me recklessly burning all my bridges behind me, do you? It occurred to me that I was mixing metaphors here, stepping off cliffs and burning bridges, but if the Lord noticed he didn't mention it. All I got were the same old words.

Go, Ivy, go.

Okay, Lord, I hear you. No need to shout.

We met with the title company and got the sale/purchase arranged. I jammed everything in the car that it would hold, leaving only a space on top for Koop's bed. I told Tasha not to bother storing what was left of my belongings; just donate them somewhere. I was jumping off the cliff, no bungee cord of belongings to yank me back.

Lorena McCourtney

CHAPTER 24

We planned a barbecue for my final evening on Madison Street, but, as it turned out, Tasha had to work. The psychologist sent her on one final, older-woman assignment, a visit to an upscale restaurant. A plumbing disaster sent Mike to the gym for an emergency cleanup job. Magnolia and Geoff both came down with digestive upsets from something at the buffet where they had lunch.

So here we were on our final evening on Madison Street, just Koop and me alone in my almost empty bedroom at Eric and Tasha's house, the red-lined map spread on the bed between us. I didn't have Mac's son's address, but how hard could it be to find someone in Wolf Junction, Montana? I also wondered how long it would take to get there. I couldn't just stop in a rest area or shopping center as I usually did when traveling in the motorhome. With the car, I'd have to stay in motels along the way. Maybe *I* would be the one lost on some backcountry road, vultures circling overhead.

Another gloomy unknown loomed. How would Mac react when I finally caught up with him? If he really felt a marrying kind of love, wouldn't he have stayed here with me?

Maybe he was dancing around his motorhome even now, rejoicing over his narrow escape from a marriage entanglement.

Maybe I should operate on the theory of absence makes love grow fonder and wait for him to come back. Wasn't rushing after him sending a desperate I-can't-live-without-you message?

Well, that was a problem. Because I seemed to be doing an excellent imitation of I-can't-live-without-you angst. Or maybe it wasn't an imitation.

Stubborn old geezer.

But when I caught up with him I wasn't going to tell him right off that I'd sold the house and have him feel some noble obligation to marry me. No way.

I looked out the back window, tempted not to wait until morning. Just jump in the car and take off tonight. Do it and get it over with.

I couldn't see the purple cow out there in the yard now. The yard light had gone out yesterday, and Eric hadn't had a chance to replace it yet. No moon or stars shone in the glimpse of cloud-covered sky between the trees. All I could see in the dark glass was my own reflection.

I stared at the dim reflection that seemed to emphasize every LOL wrinkle and gray hair, every sag in my baggy old sweatpants and T-shirt and *me*. It was nice to feel safe from murderous Braxtons, but I couldn't seem to get past this internal wavering about following the *Go, Ivy, go* directive. This was no time of life to rush into something wild and reckless. Did you consider my age, Lord, when you said *Go*? Maybe I should wait until—

Go, Ivy, go.

Do I now hear exasperation in the words?

Okay, okay, I'm going. I yanked the drapes shut.

Rather late, I realized I hadn't eaten anything, so I went out to the kitchen and fixed a grilled cheese sandwich in Tasha's big old cast-iron skillet. Should I make sandwiches for tomorrow? I couldn't just stop and fix lunch anytime. Another disadvantage of traveling without a motorhome.

I found a can of tuna and made two hefty sandwiches. I wrapped lettuce separately, added leftover potato salad, an orange, a couple of brownies and a Snickers bar, and tucked everything in the refrigerator. I decided to add some potato chips but managed to drop the package and then step on it. So then I had to get broom and dustpan out of the closet in the corner of the kitchen and clean up the mess I'd made.

It was early to go to bed, but I decided I might as well do it before I made any more messes. Although maybe I should call Mac first? I mean, if he'd changed his mind about marriage, this was going to be one awkward meeting when I caught up with him. Right up there with one of those embarrassing dreams when you find yourself strolling through a mall wearing nothing but pearl earrings and a pair of cowboy boots.

I plopped down on the living room sofa and eyed my cell phone. Yes, calling him was definitely the sensible thing to do. His number was right there at the top of my list of contacts. I poised a finger over the call button.

Go,Ivy—

Nag, nag, nag. I plunked the phone down, with maybe a bit more force than necessary, and went back to the bedroom. I brushed my teeth and stuffed everything except clean underthings for morning into my main form of luggage, plastic sacks. At the last minute I tossed Mac's old glove on top. I might as well give it back to him.

I heard the front door open and close. Good. I could tell Tasha or Eric goodbye tonight, pick up my phone in the living room, and leave before daybreak. Then the door opened and closed again. They must both be home now. A sudden thought unexpectedly dropped into my head, a fantastic idea for how Eric could use that mannequin's head. I grabbed it and headed for the living room. Koop followed.

In the hallway, I heard voices. I couldn't make out what they were saying, but it didn't sound like a conversation between Eric and Tasha. I paused a couple of feet from the living room door. From this angle I could see Tasha in her old-lady disguise on the sofa. She was pulling off a sturdy shoe. A carton of leftovers from the restaurant sat on the coffee table in front of her. Then the other person moved into view. Not Eric. Then another person. Two people . . . in black ski masks!

I eased backward a step.

It took me only a few seconds to recognize the short, slightly dumpy figure and scuffed boots on one of the ski-masked people. Grandma Braxton. Grandma Braxton with a *gun.* Another gun in the hand of the larger male figure standing behind her.

My nerves skittered frantically, and my supper turned into a toasted cheese tornado in my stomach.

I wasn't free of the Braxtons after all. Knock one, or even a half dozen of them down, and two more popped up. Eager to finish Drake's vow of turning me into roadkill. I'd procrastinated too long. Now two guns stood between me and Mac in Montana.

I clutched the mannequin head tighter and took a steadying breath. No need to go all doomsday yet. Montana and Mac were still a possibility. Just back away and call 911.

A great idea, except at that moment I could see my cell phone, right there on the end table where I'd plunked it down after thinking about calling Mac. As far out of reach as if I'd drop-kicked it to Montana.

Now what?

I pep-talked myself again. No need to panic. Just sneak out the back door, run over to Magnolia's, and call from there. Grandma Braxton was looking for me, so surely she'd ask questions rather than blast an unknown woman just sitting there on the sofa with one shoe off.

But before I could even start edging toward the door, Grandma stalked over and planted herself in front of Tasha like some short but menacing tower of doom. Her eyes glared through the slits in the ski mask.

"So. You're the woman who killed my son."

My feet froze to the floor. Grandma wasn't demanding to know my whereabouts. She thought Tasha in her old-lady disguise was *me*.

I expected Tasha to protest that the woman had made

a big mistake, that she had no idea who either Grandma or her son were, but instead Tasha mumbled a generic, "I didn't kill anyone."

"Oh yes you did. You framed him! If it weren't for you doing that, Bo wouldn't have been in prison. If he weren't in prison he wouldn't have been killed in a fight." With implacable Grandma logic, she raised the gun to target Tasha dead center and repeated her indictment. "It's your fault he's dead. You killed him."

She might be a horse-loving, cookie-baking grandma, but she had murder in her heart.

"He wasn't framed," Tasha protested. "There were lots of other witnesses besides me who testified at the trial."

Witnesses besides her? With a wave of panic, I realized what Tasha was doing. She was going along with Grandma's error. Pulling off her biggest acting job ever, pretending she was *me*. Protecting me.

I couldn't let her do that. I couldn't let herself get killed for me! This left no time for dashing over to Magnolia's to call 911. Grandma might pull the trigger on Tasha before I could get out the back door. I charged into the room. Koop prudently skedaddled the other direction.

I ignored the ski masks. "Oh, I'm sorry. I didn't know we had company."

Grandma took a step backwards.

"Who are you?" the big man behind her demanded.

"I'm Ivy Malone. Who are you?"

"No, she isn't. *I'm* Ivy Malone," Tasha declared. She gave me a perfectly acted glare. "Sis, you're all mixed up.

Are you off your medication again?" Then, her head turned away from Grandma and accomplice, she gave me an exaggerated wink.

I caught her message. If you can't beat 'em—and we couldn't beat 'em because *they* had the guns—confuse 'em.

"You're the one who needs medication, sister dear," I chided. "Who are these nice people?" To the ski-masked pair, I added, "Won't you take off your, umm, things, and stay a while? I'll fix a nice cup of tea."

I had no idea where we could go with this, and I doubted Tasha did either. Maybe we were only delaying the inevitable outcome. But at least we *were* delaying it. Maybe if we could delay long enough, Eric would come home.

"There's jasmine or chamomile," I said. "Or plain old green tea, of course."

"Why are you carrying that head?" Grandma demanded. She sounded suspicious, as if she thought it might be loaded with dynamite. I wished it were. A bomb would be a handy asset right now.

"Oh, I'm sorry. I should introduce you." I held up the head I still had clutched under my arm. "This is Imogene."

"My sister gets things so mixed up these days. She talks to that stupid mannequin's head as if it were a real person," Tasha complained.

"Imogene isn't stupid," I objected. "She may have a, umm, speech problem, but she still has *feelings*." I glared at Tasha and hugged both arms around "Imogene."

"I told you her name is Rosemary not Imogene,"

Tasha snapped.

"Let's get this over with," the guy growled. "They're both nuttier'n fruit cakes."

Tasha ignored him. "Usually she thinks she's me, but sometimes she gets even more mixed up. Like when she thinks she's Elizabeth Taylor and gets teary-eyed about all those husbands." Tasha rolled her eyes. She did an excellent eye-roll, very expressive.

I dragged up names from that place in the brain that stores useless information. Along with the words to Mairzy Doats, the list of Elizabeth Taylor's husbands was in there. I went a little dreamy. "Yes. Nicky Hilton, he was my first. Then Michael, of course, father of my children. And Mike Todd. Such very different Michaels." Big sigh. "Then, my great love, Richard—"

"Shut up," Grandma yelled. She waved the gun as if she wanted to shoot someone but she wasn't sure who. "Just shut up, both of you."

"Who did you say you were again, dearie?" I inquired.

"You know who I am! At least one of you knows me!" She yanked off the ski mask, and there she was, the same rosy-cheeked Grandma I'd seen that day at the farm. But a much more frustrated and angry one. Her glance whipped back and forth between Tasha and me.

I expected recognition to kick in when she got a better look at me. I'd managed to be invisible in the floppy sunhat and sunglasses that day at the farm, but surely she'd recognize me now. She'd seen me at the trial. Unpleasant thought: maybe I'd aged so much I was no longer recognizable.

"Surely you've seen a photo of the real Ivy Malone. Which is me." I stuck a thumb, the one that wasn't holding "Imogene," against my collarbone for emphasis.

"Sis, cut it out. How many times do I have to tell you? You're not Ivy. *I'm* Ivy." Tasha stood up, a little lopsided with one shoe on, one off. "I'm going to go find your pills."

"You're not going anywhere," the guy snapped. "Get back on the sofa. *Now.*"

Tasha dropped back to the sofa. It was old and squishy, and her weight bounced me upward. A rather frivolous bounce, considering the life-and-death situation we were in. Some other time I might have said *whee!* But not now.

Grandma kept her eyes flicking between Tasha and me, but she turned her head slightly to speak to the man behind her. "Have you ever seen a photo?"

"No. What difference does it make? We'll just get rid of both of them."

I still didn't know who he was, but he was definitely Braxton to the core. One more murder? No problem.

Although now Grandma's gun dipped slightly and she said, "I don't want to do that. I'm not an . . . indiscriminate killer."

"Of course you're not," I encouraged. "And your devotion to your son's memory is quite admirable."

The gun came back up. "I just want Ivy Malone dead.

280

Whichever one of you is her." She glared at us again.

"She'd have been dead a long time ago if Drake hadn't kept messing up," the guy muttered.

I ignored . . . at least pretended to ignore . . . this conversation about my hoped-for demise. "Imogene, we really need to get you some hair, don't we?" I smoothed the mannequin's bald head.

"You, get over on the sofa," Grandma commanded suddenly. She motioned to me with the gun. "I want to see the two of you together. I saw the real Ivy at the trial."

"We don't have time to sort out who's who," the guy said. "It doesn't matter anyway. We have to get rid of both of them. The one who isn't Ivy knows too much now. We can't leave her alive."

Grandma hesitated only momentarily before nodding agreement.

"You shoot the one on the right. I'll take the one on the left." The one on the left was me. His gun took deadly aim on my midsection. The grilled cheese sandwich went into tornado mode again. "Then we get out of here."

What Tasha and I had discussed one time flashed into my head. Death and what came after. Was I afraid? Not of what came after. But, looking down the barrel of the gun, I was definitely jittery about the unpleasant preliminaries facing me.

"No, we stick with the original plan," Grandma said. I felt a faint relief that she was still in charge. "If we shoot them here someone may hear and call the police before we can get away. We just walk them out to the car and take them to the farm. No one will ever find the bodies there."

Well, personally I didn't think much of either plan, but no one was asking my opinion. I had the impression the guy didn't want to do it that way, although it's difficult to read expression through a ski-mask.

All I could think of was delay.

"Where's Beth?" I asked. "Surely you didn't leave her home all alone tonight, did you?"

"No. She's with her mother for a few—"

"Grandma, don't *talk* to them," the guy said.

Grandma ignored him. "What do you know about Beth?" she demanded.

"I know all about you and your family." Tasha nodded knowingly, still in Ivy mode. "I make it a point to know all I can about people who are trying to kill me."

"Oh, nobody wants to kill you. You're not Ivy Malone," I grumbled to Tasha. To Grandma I said, "How'd you know that I, the real Ivy Malone, was here in this house, not in my own house?"

"Sis, if you can't remember who you are, I'm going to have to put a name tag on you," Tasha grumbled.

I thought Grandma was going to answer my question about knowing how I was here in this house instead of my own, but the guy interrupted before she could say anything.

"Grandma, don't *talk* to them." This time he sounded almost pleading. "Just—"

"I don't understand why you two are even here," I complained before he could demand a speeded-up shooting schedule. "It's Drake who's been after me all this time."

"After *me*," Tasha corrected.

"Oh yes. Drake was all for tracking you down after Bo went to prison," Grandma said. The scorn in her voice sounded as if I'd hit a hot button. "The whole family was at first. But he'd have quit a long time ago if it weren't for Sam and me."

Sam. I ran the name through my mental file of the Braxton clan. So this was Sam Zollinger, Bo's son, which would make him Grandma's grandson from her first marriage. His twin brother Tyler had joined the condo scheme and was in custody along with Drake now, but Sam was still in the computer store business, free to carry on with exterminate-Ivy schemes.

"But after he killed the wrong woman, we finally figured out Drake couldn't find his own foot in the shower," Sam said sourly.

"His big condo deal is more important to him than family," Grandma said.

A noxious sin, obviously. Family loyalty was everything to Grandma. Admirable in her protective attitude toward granddaughter Beth. Admirable in her generosity to both Beth and other family members. Not so admirable, at least from my admittedly prejudiced point of view, was her determination to avenge her son's death by killing me.

"Drake burned down my motorhome too?" I asked.

"*My* motorhome," Tasha said.

"No, that would be me," Sam said, apparently proud enough of that accomplishment to claim it.

"Very clever," I said. "How'd you get inside to turn

the stove on? The door was locked."

"I could've picked that lock in my sleep."

"But not too smart doing it when I wasn't even inside," Tasha observed.

"Drake was supposed to do it," Sam muttered. "But he was off running one of his stupid seminars."

"And he still thought I was going to pay his bail," Grandma added scornfully.

"Nothing is more important than family," Tasha declared righteously. "Family comes first."

"A family sticks together," I chimed in.

"But I finally figured it out." Grandma sounded grimly victorious. "Family or not, if you want something done right, you have to do it yourself."

Another opinion I could often share, although in this instance it did bring us to this rather unfortunate moment.

I suddenly realized that in my new position on the sofa, I was within inches of my cell phone sitting on the end table. If I could edge over and get hold of it, maybe I could—

I shifted a fraction of an inch toward the end table. Grandma noticed. Her gun swung a fraction of an inch in response.

Sam was getting impatient. "C'mon. We're wasting time. Let's get going. Stand up, both of you." Another motion with a gun.

I stood up, but I knew if they ever got us in their car, we'd be two dead Ivy's. I got a firm grip on the mannequin's neck.

I aimed for Sam. I didn't know which of them was

the more dangerous, but he was a bigger target. Throwing a mannequin head isn't like throwing a horseshoe at a stake. My skill is also unpredictable even in the best of situations. And this was not the best of situations.

But I gave it *my* best, along with a prayer. I threw. Hard.

It sailed across the room, but a mannequin head hurled by a nervous LOL does not travel at the speed or accuracy of a guided missile. Sam took a wild shot at it. He missed but the bullet thunked the ceiling and plaster rained down. The head sailed on in what seemed like agonizingly slow motion. But if anyone ever wants to know if Sam's skull is harder than a mannequin's head, it is.

The mannequin head exploded when it collided with Sam's nose. Mannequin shrapnel and blood flew everywhere. I ducked. Sam howled, threw up an arm to protect his injured nose, and his next shot went wild. He probably couldn't have hit the narrow chain holding the chandelier if he'd aimed for it, but without aim, it was a direct hit.

The chandelier crashed. Grandma, standing directly under it, crashed too, instantly entangled in wheel, chains, and copper-shaded bulbs. The wheel caught Sam on the shoulder and he staggered backward.

I was so astonished, I just stood there. But Tasha wasn't as frozen as I was. She threw something too. Her shoe. I don't think she aimed for Sam's most delicate masculine area, but that's where the shoe hit. He doubled over even as he pulled the trigger again.

A scream. Me? Yeah. But other screams too. Maybe Tasha. Maybe Grandma. Maybe Sam had a high-pitched scream of his own, considering where the shoe had hit.

I had a micro-thought about trying to grab Grandma's gun while she was incapacitated, but Sam, even with his nose gushing blood and his body bent from the shoe attack, was still shooting. He got a hit on one of the tin can lids in Elvis's frame, and Elvis crashed to the floor. Whatever happened to the good ol' six-shooter, where the bad guy ran out of bullets? This guy must be using a clip with fifteen or twenty bullets.

The glass-topped coffee table shattered. Stuffing blasted out of the sofa. Tasha threw again. This time it was the carton of leftovers. A medley of vegetables in sauce flowered in Sam's hair and ran into his eyes. He howled again.

"Run!" I yelled.

It wasn't until I blasted through the back door that I realized Tasha wasn't right behind me. I stopped short.

She must have run out the front door. Or maybe she was trapped in there with trigger-happy Sam. Or maybe she was shot!

I turned and stumbled back toward the living room.

CHAPTER 25

Another shot blasted before I reached the door to the living room. I cautiously peered one eye around the door frame.

Grandma Braxton was still on the floor, frantically trying to untangle herself from the web of the chandelier and, as far as I could tell, only enmeshing herself deeper. I couldn't see any injuries on her, but blood was splattered everywhere. On her. On the walls. On the floor. It had to be Sam's blood, didn't it, from where I'd hit him on the nose with the mannequin's head? But a heavier stain of blood soaked the sofa where Tasha had been sitting. *Had she been hit? Where was she? Where was Sam?*

Grandma let loose with a string of words I hoped she never used around Beth. "Get me out of here!" she screeched. A portion of vegetable medley decorated her hair too.

I winced when she targeted me with another torrent of un-grandmotherly words, but I wasn't about to do the good-Samaritan thing and help her out of the trap she was in. I grabbed my cell phone and stuck it in my pocket. On second thought, I also snatched up the gun that had flown out of Grandma's hand.

Go, Ivy, Go!

Now what? I hesitated for a moment. Run out the front door? That's where Tasha must have gone. Sam wasn't exactly in good running shape after both the mannequin and shoe incidents, but he must have hobbled out after her.

So what should I do? Follow Sam outside? Get in a *High Noon* shootout with him?

Yeah, right. I may have Grandma's gun in my hand now, but I had no idea how to use it. It wasn't like the only handgun I'd ever shot a long time ago. On it, you pulled back a hammer to cock it, then pulled the trigger. This one didn't even have a hammer.

One of these days I'm going to take shooting lessons. Learn all about guns. Become a sharpshooter. Maybe learn that Krav Maga attack and defense stuff too. Good intentions, should I live to need these skills in the future, but no help at the moment. But I didn't let go of the gun. I stuck it where the guys on TV always stick a gun, under the waistband at the back of their pants. At least, if Grandma got loose, she couldn't grab her gun and start blasting. I headed for the door to the back yard in case Sam came back and caught me there without another mannequin head for ammunition. I'd call 911 and then run around front and find Tasha.

The total blackness of the back yard stopped me short when the door slammed behind me. No light seeped around the heavy drapes in my bedroom. No glow of streetlight filtered through the heavy trees and hedge. No moon or stars shone in the smidgens of cloudy sky between trees. Okay, that was good. Sam couldn't see me back here. I'd just call

911—

A shot. From where? Going where? Was Sam shooting at Tasha out on the street?

I scrambled toward where I thought the gate in the hedge was located. Beware the purple cow! It was back here somewhere. I missed it but crashed headlong into a living, moving body.

"I-I have a gun." I tried to sound menacing. I stuck the cell phone out in front of me in gun mode. But it's hard to sound menacing when you're stammering. And your cell phone is a little short on bullets.

"Ivy, it's me! Tasha. Don't shoot!" Tasha whispered frantically.

Unnecessary advice, since all I had in hand was the cell phone. The gun was still rolling around inside my sweat pants. And I didn't know how to shoot it anyway.

"Where's Sam?" I whispered back.

"Looking for me. I was trying to get to Magnolia's, but I-I was afraid I couldn't make it. So I ran back here to hide from him."

"I know you're back there." Sam's voice roared from the far side of the hedge. Hopefully he didn't know about the gate. Two shots followed. Random shots, but you can be just as dead from a random shot as a deliberately aimed one. Sam seemed to have forgotten Grandma's warning about gunshots being heard by neighbors. She might not like that. Although she'd no doubt approve his aggressive display of family loyalty. Another shot pinged on something metallic in the yard.

"Get behind a tree," I whispered to Tasha. "I've got my phone. I'll call 911."

But I instantly realized I couldn't do that. I'd long ago found that as an LOL I am mostly invisible to much of the younger world, and Tasha and I were both nicely invisible here in the dark of the back yard. But as soon as I flipped the phone open and pushed the power button, that light from the screen, faint though it was, would shine like a thousand watt candle in the dark back yard. And then, no more invisibility. Sam's shots would target us with Lone Ranger accuracy. Okay, I'd put the phone under my shirt to hide its glow and punch in the numbers under cover.

Another shot. Was there such a thing as a 50-bullet clip?

I didn't want to get separated from Tasha, but we had to move. I grabbed her arm. She let out a gasp and so did I. Her arm was wet and sticky.

"You're bleeding!"

"One of the shots hit me. But I'm okay! Just a little . . . woozy."

No wonder she couldn't make it to Magnolia's. I put an arm around her waist to help her along and felt our way with my other hand. I clattered into the wheelbarrow holding a stockpile of parts for Eric's junkyard sculptures. The noise brought another shot. It pinged against the wheelbarrow. I pushed Tasha behind another tree. She sagged against it.

"We need to get you to a doctor!"

"I-I'm okay."

"You can stop acting now," I whispered fiercely.

"You're *not* okay."

Lord, we need your help! My hand shook as I shoved the phone up under my T-shirt. I fumbled it open and ran my finger down to the power button. I fingered the numbers beyond the power button but I'd never paid any real attention to how they were arranged. I punched in three numbers I thought were 911, but nothing happened. I tried again. More nothing.

Change of technique. I snapped the phone shut and then scrunched the T-shirt up over my head. That exposed my not-exactly-svelte midsection, but this was no time to worry about irrelevant details. I opened the phone under cover of the T-shirt. I thought I'd be able to see the numbers, but there's not a lot of room to maneuver inside a T-shirt. The numbers were right in front of my nose. I tried to keep my eyes from crossing as I focused on them. It worked! A 911 person answered.

I whispered the address, but she kept saying, "What? What? I can't hear you. Can you speak louder, please?"

The 911 system probably showed her my number, but the cell phone number had no connection with this address. I repeated the address as loud as I could in a whisper, but two shots blasted the back yard. Something thunked into the tree beside us. I yanked the T-shirt down and shoved Tasha away from the tree. She didn't cry out in pain, but her little gasps told me she was hurting.

The gun in my waistband shifted and slithered down my backside. I groaned. Now I had a weapon, a loaded weapon, *inside* my baggy sweatpants. How come none of those guys on TV ever had this problem?

But I hadn't time to search for the gun now. Behind another tree, I did the T-shirt maneuver and punched in 911again. Same voice answered. I whispered the address. She informed me there was a penalty for misusing 911. I gave up, then had one more idea. Officer DeLora! Stretching the T-shirt to its limit so I could see the contact list, I found her name and punched the call button. She answered.

"This is Ivy—" I whispered frantically.

Another shot. This one sizzled right past my ear.

"I heard something!" Officer Delora yelled. I scrunched the phone up close to my chest to muffle the sound of her voice. "Was that a gunshot?"

"Yes! We need *help!*"

Clomping, creaky noises came from over near the hedge. Sam finding his way through the gate? Another shot, and my shaky fingers dropped the phone. No time to look for it now. Sam wasn't worrying about being quiet and sneaking up on us. He was just shooting. The next blast took out an innocent chunk of tree bark.

"Let's get over behind the shop," I whispered to Tasha. "Lean on me."

We edged in the direction of the shop. At least where I thought the shop might be. Then a noise tinkled above us. A rising crescendo of tinkles.

I groaned again. The wind chimes Erik had strung along the tree branch! I was short enough to go under them but Tasha had clunked right into them. A domino effect as one set of wind chimes collided with another set until they

292

were all in motion. A pleasantly musical sound, but in this situation a deadly arrow of noise pointing directly at us.

Sam was running now, his footsteps hitting the ground like small earthquakes. The wind chimes tinkled merrily, never minding that they were guiding a killer straight to us. An *oof* and curse when Sam sideswiped a tree. I stumbled over something metallic on the ground. Too big to use as a weapon, too small to use as a shield—

A thunk and *boing!*

Silence.

No gunshots, no yells, no thundering footsteps. What was Sam doing now? Sneaking up on us?

We waited long minutes . . . or maybe it was only long seconds. Finally Tasha whispered, "What happened?"

The back door flew open, and an oblong of light flooded out, illuminating tree trunks and wheelbarrow and silhouette of purple cow. I ducked back. Grandma was loose, and looking for us!

I peered around a tree trunk for a better look. No, not Grandma.

"Tammy, where are you?" Eric yelled. Under stress, he'd reverted to her real name. "Are you out here?"

Something moved behind him. This time it *was* Grandma. An on-the-loose Grandma sneaking up on him with that cast-iron frying pan I'd left on the stove after making my grilled cheese sandwich.

"Eric, watch out!" I yelled.

Grandma clobbered him with the frying pan. I'd have gone down like an anchor in a bathtub from the blow, but on wall-of-muscle Eric the hit had about as much effect as a bug on a windshield. He turned and grabbed her, lifting her off her feet as if she were no more than a bug herself. She screeched and dropped the frying pan, and Eric yelled, "Tammy!" again.

Tasha had been on the verge of collapsing, but Eric's voice strengthened her. She stumbled around the purple cow toward him, her gait lopsided with one shoe missing.

I ran toward the doorway behind her . . . and floundered over something beside the purple cow that Tasha had managed to miss. I sprawled head-first on the ground. The gun whacked my backside.

I shook my head to clear the instant fuzziness and then I saw what I'd fallen over.

Sam. That *boing* I'd heard was Sam running headlong into the purple cow.

Was he dead? I fumbled around his beefy neck for a pulse. No, not dead, but out cold.

Beware the purple cow.

Right message on that fortune cookie . . . but, blessedly, a message meant for someone other than me!

I snatched up Sam's gun. So now I had two guns. One in my hand and one flopping around inside my sweat pants. Both as useless to me as a couple of kiwi fruit.

Tasha reached the doorway. Eric still had one arm wrapped around a kicking, squirming Grandma, but he reached for Tasha with the other arm. Then he stopped short.

"You're bleeding!" he gasped.

Oh, no. Grandma and a frying pan couldn't take Eric

out, but a bleeding Tasha could. He'd go down like a sack of turnips when he saw all that blood.

I stood there, momentarily frozen. An Eric apt to faint any moment in front of me. A Sam apt to rise up and attack any moment behind me. A Grandma smack in the middle of everything and screeching her head off. A useless gun trapped inside my sweat pants.

Eric let go of Grandma. She landed on her knees. He bent over. Oh, oh, there he goes—

But he didn't. With Tasha needing him, he conquered his weakness at sight of blood. He gave a mighty shake of shoulders, swooped her up in his arms and yelled, "I'm taking her to the emergency room."

He turned and disappeared into the house. Grandma struggled to her feet. She might be little, but she was dangerous. Bluff time.

"Okay, don't move," I said with as much authority as I could muster as I walked toward her. "I have the gun now." Going back to that good old standard line of TV and mystery novel scenes, I said, "Put your hands up."

I half expected Grandma to ignore the command and tackle me, but she put her hands up. After a tangle with a junk-sculpture chandelier and a lifting by muscular Eric, she was a little worse for wear. A rip decorated her pants leg, and her hair still dripped vegetable-medley sauce. I sidled into the kitchen, hoping I looked like I knew what I was doing with the gun. Although having that second gun slapping around my backside was a bit distracting.

Grandma and I eyed each other.

"You're the real Ivy Malone, aren't you?" she said.

"The one who's been dodging Braxtons for quite some time now," I agreed.

"You killed my son!"

There didn't seem any point in arguing that stubborn position at the moment. "Turn around," I commanded. Her eyes squinted rebelliously, but she did it. "Now open that door right in front of you."

The broom closet. It was already fairly full of brooms and mops and various cleaning supplies, but I shoved her inside with my free hand.

She yelped indignantly. "Hey, you can't—"

Yes, I could. I closed the door, grabbed a kitchen chair and shoved it under the knob.

I wasn't sure how long that would hold her, but hopefully long enough to do something about Sam. I looked frantically around the kitchen for something to tie him up with while he was still unconscious, but the kitchen really wasn't equipped for criminal apprehension.

I looked into the back yard. Sam was struggling to his knees. In another minute he'd be up and after me again. What to do? I could never bluff Sam with the gun.

I spotted Grandma's makeshift weapon on the floor. It hadn't worked for her, but maybe—

I swooped up the heavy frying pan and flew down the steps. Sam was on his knees, shaking his head now. I got around him and—

I stood there, pan raised high overhead. I groaned. I couldn't do this. I couldn't just clobber a man while he was down and groggy. Not even Sam.

Another shake of head, then Sam lifted his eyes and saw me. His grogginess turned murderous. One arm snaked out and grabbed my ankle—

Yes, I could.

I closed my eyes and brought the frying pan down on his head. The blow stung my hands and vibrated up my arms. It did much worse to Sam.

I looked down at him, flat on the ground, out cold again. I thought he'd be out for a while, but just to be safe I ran back inside and yanked on the curtains at the kitchen windows. I tied his hands and feet with the kitchen curtain tiebacks.

Not a good day for Sam. Clobbered on the nose with a mannequin head. Vegetable medley in his hair. Hit with a shoe in that most sensitive area of male anatomy. Bashed with a frying pan. Hands and feet tied with ruffled curtain tiebacks, quite festive looking, although Sam probably wouldn't agree. And his grandma barricaded in a broom closet.

I tallied the score:

LOL : 2

Braxtons: 0

Okay!

Then it was sirens and cop cars screeching to a stop outside the house.

Cops burst through the front door and into the kitchen, Officer DeLora leading the pack.

I was so glad and grateful to see them. *Thank you,*

Lord!

But I prudently took a moment to fumble inside the sweat pants and extract the gun before it went off or the cops decided I was carrying a concealed weapon, whichever came first.

CHAPTER 26

A week later and I was on the road, Madison Street fifty miles behind me. Part of me as exhilarated as a girl on her first roller-coaster ride. Part of me as scared as that same girl walking alone in a dark alley at night.

Back there, Grandma and Sam were in custody. The photo in the newspaper showed him with a bandaged broken nose. Officer DeLora said I might need to return for one or more trials eventually, but it would be someone other than her notifying me. She'd already given notice that she was leaving the police department. With the satisfaction of a "case closed" success, she was happily moving home to Texas to a job cooking in an organic vegetarian restaurant, with plans to open one of her own in the future. "Not everyone is cut out to be a cop," she told me, and then added, "But you already knew that, didn't you?"

Tasha and Eric . . . no, make that Tammy and Eric, because she'd decided to go back to her former name . . . were already moving into my old house. Their house now, of course. They were willing to cancel our deal so I could stay in the house, but I'd kept ears attuned to *Go, Ivy, go,* and turned down the offer. Eric had sold The Purple Cow to a funky natural foods store, and it now sat outside their door with a bell and a flower lei around its neck. Tammy's bullet wound was healing nicely. I told her she had my personal Academy Award for an awesome acting performance impersonating me, plus a fine demonstration of shoe-throwing expertise. She'd just picked up a new acting job. Now, in more padding, frizzy wig and cosmetic pimples, she was going back to high school, because the psychologist wanted a first-hand study on how a nerdy girl was treated by her peers. She was also taking extra advantage of the situation by signing up for high-school computer classes.

I was concerned about granddaughter Beth, so I'd called her mother, identified myself as the assistant of the writer working on the article about the Paso Fino horses, and asked about Beth. Mother said Beth would be living with her indefinitely now, but still working with the horses. Foreman Wayne was running the farm during what she euphemistically called a "transition period." I hope none of this interfered with Beth's hopes to be a vet.

And Lillian Hunnicut? No family had ever been located. Her remains would eventually be buried by the county. I vowed, when I returned to visit Harley and Colin's graves, that I'd take flowers to Lillian too.

Fate of the houses and land owned by Radison Properties was up in the air, but they would probably be sold and the money used to repay investors the Braxtons had swindled in their buy-into-the-company-and-get-a-condo scheme.

Magnolia and Geoff were leaving for Texas in their motorhome in a couple of weeks, Magnolia's faith in family restored. She was eager to meet the newest addition to her genealogical jungle, maybe a fifth cousin three times removed. Or a great-grandma's cousin's half-sister. I was never sure how Magnolia arrived at her classification of relatives, but she was delighted with this one. She'd never had a lady wrestler in the family before. She and Geoff intended to be in Texas in time to root for Tess the Red Tornado in some kind of championship match with the Bombshell Blonde.

Out here on the open road, I jumped between optimism that Mac would greet me with open arms, and pessimism that he'd run and hide in his son's closet when I arrived.

Lord, are you sure about this? I asked as I ate lunch in a little town in Kansas.

No answer thundered or even whispered in my head. Apparently the Lord had said all he intended to on this subject.

I drove on.

***

Heavily forested mountains surrounded Wolf Junction, with a bridge over a whitewater creek at the edge of town and a deer bounding across the road in front of the car. I asked at a gas station in the "downtown" area about Dan MacPherson. Sure, everybody knew Coach MacPherson. His house was right on the far edge of town, several acres surrounding a rustic log house set back from the road. When I pulled into the driveway, I decided the new-looking wing on the left side must be the addition Mac had come to help his son with. I didn't see Mac's motorhome, but it was probably parked out back. If he didn't come up with another proposal, maybe I'd just ask him to marry me!

I went to the door and rang the horseshoe-framed doorbell.

The guy who came to the door was taller than Mac, lean and sandy haired, wearing jeans and a carpenter's apron full of tools.

"Are you Dan MacPherson . . . Mac's son?"

"That's me." Friendly smile, even though he didn't know if I was here offering termite inspection or selling bubble bath. "Can I help you with something?"

"I'm looking for Mac?" It came out a question because, even though Dan's smile was friendly, I was feeling more insecure by the moment.

"Oh, I'm sorry, Dad isn't here now. He left just yesterday."

I tried to hide my dismay. I fumbled for a response and finally said, "The work on the addition to the house is finished?"

"Well, not quite. A contractor had the log exterior done before Dad got here, and we've been working on the interior. The flooring isn't quite done yet. But you know Dad." Dan laughed. "He gets restless being in one place too long. I told him I could finish up here, so he took off."

"Do you know where he went?"

"No, I'm afraid I don't. You know Dad," he repeated. "He keeps in touch, but we never know where he'll be when we hear from him next. He said something about some business he needed to take care of."

"A magazine article?"

"Could be. He mentioned the Oregon coast a couple times. But then he also said something about Arizona."

"I thought he was planning an article about mining and ghost prospectors while he was in Montana."

"He worked on that some while he was here. But he was anxious to take off for somewhere. Are you Ivy?"

"Yes. Ivy Malone."

"I'm really glad to meet you." He gave me a sturdy handshake. Obviously he'd heard of me, but I dodged speculation about what he'd heard. The possibilities were too worrisome. Had Mac somehow sensed I was coming and disappeared into the wide open spaces of U.S. geography?

"Did Dad know you were coming?" Dan asked.

"Well, umm, no. I just . . . happened to be in the area and thought I'd stop in and—" Do what? All I could think of at the moment was, "Return a glove I found after he left."

I doubted Dan bought my explanation about just happening to be in the area, but neither of us seemed to know what to say next. Apparently Mac hadn't confided in his son about our parting of ways, but I figured Dan suspected something wasn't right.

Finally he said, "That's very thoughtful of you. I'm sure Dad wouldn't have left if he'd known you were coming. With the glove."

"Have you heard from him since he left?"

"No, but that's not unusual."

I backed away from the door. "Okay, well, thanks.

Nice meeting you."

"Hey, don't rush off. I know Melanie would like to meet you, but she's doing her clown act for a birthday party today. If you could stay and have dinner with us—?"

I'd rather like to meet a woman who doubled as a clown, but I didn't want to have to talk about my relationship . . . or non-relationship . . . with Mac. "That's very nice of you, but I'd better be on my way."

"Look, why don't you spend the night here? There's plenty of room. Haven't you and Dad been keeping in touch?"

"Not recently."

"We'd really like you to stay. Some friends gave us a buffalo roast, and I'm supposed to put it in the oven—" He glanced at his watch. "Right about now. Ever eaten buffalo? Really good. We'll give Dad a call and find out where he is, and then—"

That suggestion alarmed me. I'd come this far, but I was not going to chase Mac down like some desperate bounty hunter.

"Thanks, but I should be going," I said hastily. Dan looked as if he were trying to think of some stronger persuasion to get me to stay, but I dodged that by saying, "I want to make it to—" Mumble, mumble, because I couldn't remember the name of any nearby town. "—by tonight."

"I'm sure Dad will be sorry he missed you."

I wasn't so sure of that.

"Stop in again if you're ever in the area. And stay longer."

I drove away briskly, as if I had places to go and things to do, although I was really wondering *Now what?*

I got back to what passed for "downtown" and pulled over at the gas station again to look at my map. The red line on it, guideline for my life, ended at Wolf Junction.

Any comments, Lord? This was all your idea, you know.

I didn't particularly want to drive forty-some miles to the next town on the map, a place called Double Wells, but neither did I want to stay in Wolf Junction for the night and risk running into Mac's son again. The guy was so good-hearted I was afraid he might show up with clown reinforcements to persuade me to stay. And/or a plate of buffalo roast.

Actually, now that I took a better look at Wolf Junction, staying the night here didn't seem to be a viable choice anyway. Not a motel in sight. Would Double Wells have one?

I guess I'd find out. If not, I'd sleep in the car. I've done it before. Though I had the Thunderbird back then, and it wasn't loaded with most of my life's possessions and a cat. But I'd manage.

I headed out to the highway. Tomorrow I'd have to decide where Koop and I were going after Double Wells. The world, I reminded myself, did not end at Wolf Junction even if the red line or my map ended there.

I could get along without Mac.

I'd just keep repeating that until it was true.

Hopefully.

***

Double Wells was minimally larger than Wolf Junction. I spotted a combination post office, library, and sheriff's office. And a motel. I asked if they'd accept Koop, and they would, so I registered for the night. By then the sun had gone down, and I went across the street for dinner at the Blue Sky café. They had buffalo on the menu. I'd never tried it, so I ordered a buffalo burger. It seemed like a good time to start getting used to new things in my life.

I took a bit of the tasty burger back to the motel for Koop. My cell phone rang while he was scarfing the meat down as if he had appetite enough for a whole buffalo. I looked at the little screen and recognized the familiar number. I don't know what my reaction might have been, but Koop chose that moment to dig in the Styrofoam container looking for more buffalo and managed to dump the whole container. I leaped, trying to catch it before it hit the carpet, so I was a little breathless when I said, "Hi."

"You okay?" Mac said.

"I'm fine. Koop's fine. Everything's fine."

"Well, I'm glad to hear that. I'm fine too."

I felt like remarking on our scintillating dialogue, but all I said was, "Good."

A little silence until Mac finally said, "Dan called. He said you were there in Wolf Junction, but you didn't stay. Something about a glove?"

"Yes. I, umm, found your glove in the driveway after you left. I thought I'd bring it to you." Not an untruth. I did

306

find his glove. I did have it with me. Though admittedly that left out a few details.

"That's very considerate of you."

"I didn't think to leave it when I was at your son's place, but I can just go back and drop the glove off there. Then you can pick it up when you're here again."

"I really miss that glove," Mac said. "It was my favorite. And I may not get back up that way for a while."

"Maybe I could mail it to you?"

"Well, I'm kind of on the move. Maybe we could meet somewhere? If it wouldn't be too much trouble."

"I guess that depends on where you are."

"I'm in Kansas."

I wondered what he was doing in Kansas, but I decided not to ask.

He gave me a reason anyway. "I was, uh, coming back to see about that glove. It's a great glove. I really miss it," he repeated.

"Where would be a good place to meet?"

"I was just looking at the map. Let's see . . . How about a little town called Abner? Have you ever heard of it? It's over on the west side of Nebraska."

I'd never heard of it, but I said, "I'll find it. But how will we locate each other there, so I can give you the glove?"

"There must be a post office. How about we meet right in front of it? I'm not sure how long it will take me to get there, but if I get there first, I'll wait."

"Okay. If I get there first, I'll wait."

***

I stayed in the motel that night. I didn't quite make it to Abner the next day and spent another night in a motel. About mid-morning the following day I pulled into the small town. The post office was easy enough to find, right next door to the courthouse, with an enormous flag snapping in the breeze. And there was Mac's red Toyota pickup parked out front. I parked a couple spaces behind it.

Mac was sitting on a low concrete wall that circled the courthouse lawn. I got out of my Camry, remembering at the last minute to grab the old glove. It looked even more grubby and greasy than it had when I found it. I held the glove out to him when I walked up to him.

"Here's your glove."

Mac slid off the wall. He was in a blue polo shirt and his familiar khaki shorts, his knobby knees showing. I tried not to think that I'd always found those knobby knees endearing.

"Hey, thanks. I really missed that glove."

The glove had a hole in the thumb, I saw now, but that didn't keep Mac from smoothing it on his hand as if it were a long-lost treasure. He made a fist in it and flexed his fingers. "That was really nice of you to take it all the way to Wolf Junction for me."

"I met your son. And the addition on the house looked—" I grabbed the all-purpose word that seems to get used for everything from a good taco to a rocket roaring into space. "Awesome."

"We weren't quite finished when I left, but I was . . . concerned about that glove. Like I told you, I was headed

308

back to Madison Street to see about the glove."

"Where's your motorhome?"

"Well, I don't have it now. I sold it."

"You *sold* it?"

A lawyer-looking guy in a suit passed us and turned toward the steps to the courthouse. A farmer-type guy in faded denim overalls, with a glum look on his face, was with him. A skinny reddish-brown dog ambled down the sidewalk from the opposite direction.

"This isn't the best place to talk about this. Maybe we could go have a cup of coffee or something?" Mac suggested.

I guess I was feeling stubborn and grumpy. My back still had impressions from what had felt like old corn cobs in the mattress at last night's motel. I folded my arms. "I think anything we have to say can be said right here."

"I suppose so. Well, it's like this. I'm a man. We hate to admit it, but men aren't always right. Sometimes we make mistakes."

"We all make mistakes," I agreed cautiously.

"I made a big one. I found that I didn't want to be on the road without you. I didn't want to be in Montana without you. I don't want to be *anywhere* without you." He poked his thumb through the hole in the glove. "I wasn't coming to Madison Street about this stupid old glove. In fact, it isn't even my glove."

"It isn't?"

"I found out spending my life running around the country, if I had to do it without you, wasn't what I wanted anymore." He looked up and met my eyes. "Ivy, I was coming back to ask you . . . to try to persuade you . . . to marry me. If Madison Street is where you want to be, that's where I want to be too. I won't need a motorhome there. If you'll marry me."

"Mac, that's sweet. I appreciate it—"

"But you don't want to do it?"

"Well, there's a problem. I don't have the house now. I sold it to Eric and Tasha."

"Ivy, you *sold* the house? Why? It was your *home.*"

"I thought it was. But without you, I found out it . . . wasn't. It was just a lonely old house. And I didn't really drive all the way to Montana just to bring you that dirty old glove. I wanted to tell you that if you wanted to be on the road, I did too. I figured, if I had to, maybe I'd ask you to marry me. "

We considered both those statements for a moment. The wandering dog stopped to sniff where dogs always seem to want to sniff.

Finally Mac said, "Let me get this straight. I sold my motorhome so I could be with you on Madison Street. You sold the house on Madison Street so you could be on the road with me."

"Maybe we have a communication problem," I suggested. "Or maybe we're a couple of stubborn old geezers." Caught in a bad melodrama.

"Maybe we are." He grabbed me by the arms. "Or maybe we're just a couple of people in love."

Oh, yes!

"Because I love you, Ivy Malone."

"I love you, Mac MacPherson."

So right there in downtown Abner, with the flag flapping and the dog sniffing, Mac wrapped his arms around me and spun me into a breathless whirl that ended in a great kiss. Then he dropped to one knee in front of me. "Will you marry me?"

No communication problem here. "Yes!"

He jumped up. Another kiss. Although inhibited a bit by the dog sitting on Mac's foot.

"But what will we do?" I asked. "You don't have a motorhome. I don't have a house. We're homeless!"

"We can find another home," Mac said.

"We can get another motorhome and search until we find the perfect place to put down roots together."

Mac considered that. "Somewhere not too big," he said.

"Not too small."

"Not too hot."

"Not too cold."

I thought about past places we'd been, including Madison Street, and what had happened in several of them. "No dead bodies."

"No murders," Mac agreed.

"Will we ever find the just-right place?"

"Don't you always say, The Lord will provide."

"Yes. The Lord will provide."

What will he provide? Good question. With the Lord, you never know what he may have in mind, or what twists and turns he'll take you through to get you there!

What I did know was that he'd already provided. He'd taken the Braxtons out of our lives and brought us to each other. Mac wrapped his arms around me again, and we smiled at each other.

"When did you have in mind for this marrying?"

"The time is *now*," Mac said.

Oh, yes! We might be without a physical place of residence, but I'd never felt more h*ome*.

And a wife is surely entitled to know all the details about a mysterious blue tattoo, isn't she?

The End

If you enjoyed *Go, Ivy, Go!*, I'd very much appreciate a review on the site where you purchased the book.

Visit the author's website at:
https://www.lorenamccourtney.info
Or connect with her on Facebook at:
https://www.facebook.com/lorena.mccourtney

If you'd like to be on the list to receive an announcement when a new book is available, contact the author through the website.

Happy reading!

BOOKS BY LORENA McCOURTNEY

THE IVY MALONE MYSTERIES
Invisible
In Plain Sight
On the Run
Stranded
Go, Ivy, Go!

THE MAC 'N' IVY MYSTERIES
Something Buried, Something Blue
Detour
Desert Dead
That's the Way the Cookie Crumbles

THE ANDI McCONNELL MYSTERIES
Your Chariot Awaits
Here Comes the Ride
For Whom the Limo Rolls

THE JULESBURG MYSTERIES:
Whirlpool
Riptide
Undertow

THE CATE KINKAID FILES MYSTERIES
Dying to Read
Dolled Up to Die
Death Takes a Ride

Lorena McCourtney

BOOKS NOT PART OF A SERIES
Three Secrets (Novella)
Searching for Stardust
Yesterday Lost
Canyon
Betrayed
Midnight Escape
Dear Silver